BETWEEN THE WHITE LINES

MARK SUBLETTE

JUST ME PUBLISHING

Published by Just Me Publishing, LLC.

Library of Congress Control Number: 2015933769
Between the White Lines / Mark Sublette
ISBN 978-0-9861902-0-9
1. Fiction I. Title

Quantity Purchases
Companies, professional groups, clubs, and other organizations may qualify for special terms when ordering quantities of this title. For more information, contact us through www.marksublette.com.

Cover painting: Dennis Ziemienski, *Between the White Lines*
Production and design: Jaime Gould
Author photo: Dan Budnik

Printed in the USA by Bookmasters
Ashland, OH · www.bookmasters.com

AUTHOR'S NOTE

BETWEEN THE WHITE LINES is a book of fiction. There are a few professional golfers referenced to help bring Willy Wilson's character to life. While some historical facts like Jim Furyk attending the University of Arizona and the late, great Billy Casper winning the 1970 Masters are accurate, the situations involving golfers alive or dead are complete fiction, as is Willy Wilson. The last portion of the book is set in 2010 when Augusta National's famous Eisenhower loblolly pine was alive and guarding the 17th fairway.

All the book's characters are fictitious, including art dealers and collectors, except the late Allan Stone, who was an art dealer that represented Wayne Thiebaud, who is briefly mentioned in chapter 23 to help explain price structure for artworks. EARTH KNOWER and TRADITION by Maynard Dixon are actual paintings and considered to be two of his masterpieces. EARTH KNOWER resides in the Oakland Museum of California and is worth the trip to see. Some of the artists mentioned in chapter 23 are real painters who I admire, although paintings attributed to them are fictitious.

Thomas Moran lived from 1837-1926. The work THE LONE CYPRESS at the heart of this novel does not exist and if there is a Moran painting of that title it is not the painting in this book. Dynamite Industries is fictional and any resemblance to any company or individuals associated living or dead is pure coincidence.

Augusta National Golf Club, Pebble Beach Resorts, and Cypress Point Country Club are exceptional golf courses and national treasures to all that love the game of golf. Visiting them was my inspiration for this book. I often play at Loews Ventana Canyon golf course in the Santa Catalina Mountains of Tucson, and highly recommend it. No golf club members, coaches, or players on any of the golf courses mentioned in this book are real.

No book is complete without great cover art and I'm most appreciative of Dennis Ziemienski's artistic vision that brought BETWEEN THE WHITE LINES to life for me.

"There are some things
you learn best in calm,
and some in storm."

Willa Cather
The Song of the Lark
(1915)

CHAPTER 1

PING!

Hail pelted the front door's old broken screen, each plunk representing a lost dollar and the realization there would be no new shoes this spring, a yearly treat in the Hare household. The ice particles tearing the outside mesh announced unwelcome visitors to the family farm during harvest time. Nourishing rain is a godsend for a farmer; frozen water is God's special wrath. For the Hare family and their marginal wheat crop in the mid-1960s, it was the lord's payback. At least that was how Franklin saw it.

Mother Nature was looting the family's meager legacy and nothing short of a miracle could stop her destruction. The Hares' only source of income, the winter wheat crop, would soon be a total loss, the casualty of a colliding cold front and moist Gulf air on the high plains of Oklahoma. April was supposed to be the month of joy, one of the few decent times of the year that Franklin Hare remembered fondly. Most kids have treasured memories of Christmas or summer vacation. Franklin longed for April when the wheat crop came to market and money flowed.

And yet today, April 4th, marked a time of sorrow for Franklin. The number four would afterwards be cursed in his mind, representing pain and loss. Little could the young boy know that like the Japanese who consider four an unlucky number, his own *chi* was being doomed by critical inertia on this blustery day. Afterwards, a predetermined destiny would assume control of his existence, which would reach fruition only years later when once again God's wrath would make its presence felt.

Franklin's world as a child was one of fear and deprivation. He hated anything he could not control, especially Mother Nature's destructive powers. His existence was centered around an alcoholic mother and angry stepfather. His only source of stability was his half-brother Johnny. No pets were tolerated except livestock animals he could love but would soon find turned into the dinner meal.

Outside, Johnny and their stepfather battled to save a portion of the winter crop, the old combine engine whining against the high-pitched ping of ice chips bouncing off the worn-out, rusted orange exterior. It was a lost cause and Franklin knew it. Franklin was fortunate today. His right arm was broken from a "family accident" so he was excused from heavy farm work. His work realm was the kitchen sink and bathrooms until his arm, with its spiral radial-head fracture, healed.

It's rare to be able to pinpoint when your life changes irrevocably, but at age 13, Franklin recognized that moment. He peered out the cracked kitchen window of the 100-year-old dilapidated farmhouse, and watched as the harvester sunk into the mud, almost buried, and hail filled all negative space. He watched as his brother Johnny dug frantically with his earth-encrusted hands to free the harvester's massive rear tires. Franklin marveled at the circus of marble-sized ice pebbles bouncing off his brother's steaming head. The frozen projectiles ricocheted in unexpected directions, each hit causing an involuntary twitch of pain, but their stepfather's anger was Johnny's primary concern, not the hail. If it wasn't for the serious danger his brother was facing, Franklin would have been rolling on the floor at the sight of such a spectacle, but he wasn't laughing.

Time slowed for Franklin. As the front-door screen's pitched battle slowly subsided, his own present dilemma intensified. He stood at the sink, frantically washing the multicolored dishes. Perfection was paramount. The distraction of cleaning the spotless Frankoma dishes helped focus his mind away from the forces of evil that would soon descend on the family dinner table. Franklin feared for Johnny, and for himself.

This test of God's humbling power could be the breaking point for a family on the edge. Franklin could only pray that the storm's fury would continue so he wouldn't have to face his father's rage. Bartholomew Hare, his stepfather, would probably depart his tractor's cab once he realized his crop was doomed, and his next stop would no doubt be the root cellar where he kept his high-grade moonshine, the only quality possession in the household. The night would be a dangerous place in or outside for all the Hare residents, broken arm or not.

As it turned out, farm life in Enid, Oklahoma, would soon be only a memory for the Hare family, and Franklin would never be the same.

CHAPTER 2

THE BOYS' HOME

The devastation to the crop was unmerciful, the entire farm lost, just as Franklin had envisioned. The farm's bankruptcy and the subsequent exit of his stepfather made Franklin's welfare of little importance. His mother became incapacitated from fear mixed with alcohol. Franklin and Johnny stopped going to school and enjoyed unfettered freedom until the state stepped in.

Now, two years later, his right arm had healed with poorer than expected results, not a surprising outcome with parents that didn't bother to follow up with doctors. His arm had been in a cast for three months, two more than necessary. The plaster had smelled rank and hurt precipitously. Franklin had tried to convince his mother to take him to the clinic, but it was a lost cause. Franklin had finally freed himself using a pair of Civil War hand shears left from a previous tenant that had also lost the farm. The fracture healed but his natural range of motion was lost forever. His arm would not straighten fully and never would. The damaged limb was now a constant reminder of his dysfunctional roots. Sports were off Franklin's plate. Even a less demanding sport like golf would be difficult.

Being poor and deserted at a home for unwanted boys meant the chances of playing golf or any sport were nonexistent, anyway. Work was the order of the day. Franklin focused on what he could control: his own destiny and staying alive. He hated his mother for letting the state put them in the Southern Christian Boys Orphanage, he hated his stepfather for being such a poor provider for the family, and most of all he hated himself.

Living in a boys' home in the late sixties and being a freshman in high school was hell to the boy with the damaged wing. His stepfather's beatings were over, but sexual predators were now a real concern. These damaged individuals came in the form of sadistic older boys whose lives were as pathetic as Franklin's and in some case more deviant than his own. Survival required that Franklin develop a sixth sense for trouble, similar to that of his ancestors who had homesteaded the Oklahoma panhandle. These skills included navigating through unwanted sexual encounters. Franklin's one asset in life was that he had notable good looks, which unfortunately also made him a target at 15, with his jet-black hair that never curled even on the most humid Oklahoma days, razor-sharp nose, and chiseled chin.

Being physically brutalized was not on the agenda for Franklin. If Johnny had not run away on his sixteenth birthday, Franklin might have made it through unscathed. Two against one is better odds. But with the early departure of his half-brother, he was vulnerable and needed a plan.

The worst offender at the orphanage was commonly referred to as Nick the Dick. Nick was a sadist, clear and simple. He killed animals for pleasure in his free time, and loved to bully and sexually assault the weaker boys at the orphanage. Nick the Dick's name was appropriate. Not only was he a jerk, he also would force himself sexually on boys who could not protect themselves. Nick had savagely beaten a neighbor who had become too friendly with his mother. Once Nick had gotten out of juvenile detention, she had banished him to the boy's home for good. Nick believed his mother tortured him by purposely driving past the orphanage a couple of times a week in her boyfriend's car, ignoring Nick's presence as if he were dead. The kids who Nick assaulted, prayed he would kill his mom or her boyfriend so he would be taken away to prison where he belonged. Franklin was the main supporter of the "go kill the bitch" camp and any chance Franklin got, he encouraged Nick to get revenge. Franklin's thoughts about murdering a parent who was uncaring did not bother him in the least. If Nick killed his mom and went away, Franklin was safe. Nick's mom was a parent and by definition not a nice person and because she couldn't handle Nick, Nick was now Franklin's problem, thus he hated her. Franklin had grown to hope his own mother and stepfather would die in some horrible fashion, too. He was angry with Johnny but understood him running away and wished Johnny had taken him along.

Franklin decided to help nature take its course. The best way was to watch and listen to everything Nick said and determine his triggers, those weak spots Franklin could manipulate. It required Franklin to endure sexual advances but soon he understood sexuality was power and he enjoyed having the upper hand with such a strong bully. Franklin controlled Nick through sex and if he had his way, Nick's freedom would eventually disappear thanks to him.

Nick had a rhythm to his emotional surges, something that was not lost on Franklin, who was an observant teen. Any interaction with his mom and Nick would decompensate. The breakdown came in many forms: anger, crying, rage, even depression. It was the rage that Franklin wanted to exploit, as this was when Nick was most vulnerable to suggestion and spontaneous fits of terror. Words encouraging Nick's fantasy of hurting his mother were provided in small, fatal doses. "Nick, she's a whore. We both know it. She's going to bring another kid into the world. You can't let her do that. You want the kid to end up here as an unwanted piece of baggage? If you take her out she can't bring any more children into the world," Franklin urged.

Franklin's weekly and then daily prodding to hurt his mother finally resulted in Nick taking action. A plan was hatched. Franklin would cover for Nick, who would sneak away from the boys' home and visit his mother at his old house under the cover of darkness, giving her what she deserved and hoping the cops would blame it on the boyfriend. It was death that Franklin wanted, even though Nick just wanted to "beat her up bad."

The night Nick snuck away, Franklin was not far behind. He wanted to make sure his own torment ended, and in a weird way had grown to hate Nick's mom as if she were his own. It was her actions that caused Franklin to get abused. He wanted to see her pay.

Nick was only 17 but he had a man's strength. He caught his mother just before she went to bed. She was half dressed and the sight of her semi-nude body startled the trailing Franklin. Her exposed breasts were exciting, though his sexual proclivities leaned toward men. Nick, cloaked in a red ski mask, grabbed his terrified mother and threw her up against the wall, knocking down some treasured family photos, Nick's not among them. She screamed, so he covered her mouth. She bit him savagely and he slugged her without remorse. The full force of his oversized hand broke her jaw and he could hear and feel the bones breaking. Franklin, watching the punch land, realized how lucky he had been never to receive Nick's unbridled rage.

Nick's mother was now sobbing and pleading as best she could, her words a jumble of emotion and blood, but the message was clear. She was begging to be spared. The sight of his own mother reduced to a

5

heap touched Nick. He turned to walk away, satisfied he had gotten revenge.

That was when Franklin appeared, holding a shovel in his gloved hand. "What, that's all you got? You punch her and now you're going to let her live? I thought you were a man, not a pussy," Franklin taunted. Franklin knew he was dangerously close to getting stomped into oblivion by the unstable Nick the Dick.

"What the fuck you doing here! You're supposed to cover for me. And who you think you're calling a pussy, you little cocksucker?" Nick exploded.

"That's correct, I suck your *big* dick, but let's face it, you're not a man if you let this bitch live! She's the one who put you in the orphanage. She taunts you. It's payback time, then we can go back to our hellhole we call home. No one will know, 'cause I'm not talking and she won't be either, if you man up."

Franklin's cold eyes and slight smirk revealed a dark side that Nick had never seen before. Then Franklin heaved the shovel over to Nick.

"Finish her!" Franklin commanded.

Nick's mom, who now realized her son who was poised to kill her, began begging, "Don't do it! Love you! We can work it out." Her words were garbled as her unhinged lower mandible made speech difficult.

"Finish her!" Franklin insisted. "I've got your back. She doesn't give a shit about you. If she lives, you'll go to jail and this time it will be the big house!"

Tears causing his red mask to take on a crimson color, Nick was decomposing into a bundle of rage and fear. He seized the shovel and with one massive swing, slammed the metal spade down onto his mother's cranium, splattering blood in all directions and definitively ending her suffering. The next four hits were prompted by Nick's hatred for himself.

The destruction that Franklin witnessed was even more violent than he had imagined. By the time Nick recovered from his emotional seizure and peeled the blood-soaked mask from his head, Franklin was nowhere in sight. He was racing back to the boys' home, where he would directly report that he had seen Nick run off toward town carrying a shovel saying he was going to kill then bury that bitch that bore him. Nick never had a chance, manipulated by a more twisted entity then himself.

The death and subsequent destruction of Nick the Dick gave Franklin a courage he had been lacking. He had seen death at close range and it didn't scare him. In fact, he embraced the power of taking a life without remorse. It was a growing process for the boy who would never regard a human life's worth in the same way.

CHAPTER 3

LEARNING A TRADE

After Nick's departure to McAlester Prison, Franklin's daily world improved. The other kids who were being molested understood Franklin had a role in getting rid of Nick and he was respected for this, no longer a target. For the first time in Franklin's short life, he envisioned an exit strategy from the boys' home and realized soon he would be on his own and would need a job. He hated farming. He had seen at close range how risky it would be as a profession. His schooling was marginal at best. At the orphanage, work was emphasized, not education. Strong backs were the order of the day, not strong minds.

Franklin decided to become a criminal. He had been successful in putting a dangerous bully behind bars. This was easy. The boy with the disfigured arm was obviously not an accomplice, but a hero for turning in the deranged psychopath. This gave Franklin confidence that he could outwit the cops. No longer did he let his sense of right versus wrong serve as his moral compass. Instead, self-absorption became the rule. His life would be centered on his needs and wants, guided by greed to get it all.

Making money through petty crimes was easiest, primarily shoplifting. He enjoyed the act of stealing but wanted more than small payoffs. He decided the best way to develop his criminal acumen was to come up with a set of rules to follow, his own Guide to Thievery:

Rule 1: Steal then move on. Never hit the same place twice.

Rule 2: Steal only things you understand because otherwise getting rid of them is not only difficult but dangerous.

Rule 3: Never trust another thief because they will steal from you, that's why they became a thief.

Rule 4: You may not be able to trust a thief, but it doesn't mean you can't learn from them. Don't try and reinvent the criminal wheel.

Franklin, like his mom, had the alcoholic gene. He learned early in life, however, that drinking and stealing don't mix. At 16, he began working at his first noncriminal job at a local movie theater. Following an afternoon of sipping apple-flavored schnapps, he was caught with his hand in the movie-theater till. It wasn't like this was the first time he'd stolen from the theater's cash register. In small-town movie theaters in the late sixties, everything was paid for in cash. Who really knows how much popcorn and soda are sold on a busy Saturday afternoon? The day he got caught stealing, *The Sound of Music* was making its second run on the high plains of Oklahoma. Enid, Oklahoma, had only one movie theater and a big hit would recycle every five years until every single person in the community had seen it. Franklin couldn't bear to watch the nauseatingly happy Von Trapp children again, their happy lives dictated by dance and music, so he started his schnapps buzz early on, along with the usual filtering of popcorn funds. The act of being drunk while trying to steal led to sloppiness. After the humiliation of being arrested for stealing, he vowed to never be caught again.

"I'll die first or take someone out before I ever get caught again," Franklin whispered to himself as the police dragged him away in handcuffs. Franklin said nothing to the police, his dark, peering eyes staring unblinking under his mop of hair. The sergeant who roughly took him to the little jail near the center of town gave him an unnecessary lecture on drinking and stealing. Franklin already knew that his slow reaction time and sense of feeling invulnerable were consequences of his alcohol consumption. At 16, he decided he wasn't going to ever stop drinking, but he would never again drink on the job, even an illicit one.

The head master of the orphanage was equally displeased as he got a small cut of the salary the theater owner paid Franklin, which was no longer possible. A summer cutting hay was in order for Franklin if he wanted to earn money; no more cushy air-conditioned theater. Determined to never wield another pitchfork, Franklin started looking for another way to earn his getaway funds. Bestowing sexual favors upon older men turned out to be the easiest method. It wasn't that he was necessarily homosexual, or bisexual, it was simply an ends to a means.

Finally the day came when Franklin turned 18. He moved out into an older banker's house, who said it was charity to let the boy stay with him till he got his feet on the ground. In the early seventies, homosexuality was not tolerated in a place like Enid, Oklahoma. The man was Franklin's stepping stone to escaping Oklahoma forever. He would learn what he could about those with money and use it to his benefit. The war in Vietnam was still ongoing, but no worries there. With a serious restriction in his arm's range of motion, Franklin easily got a medical deferment.

Franklin understood his sex appeal was his best asset. He also realized this was a fleeting gift that would not endure. He would need something besides sex to support himself. Stealing and special treatment for sexual favors would not see him through old age.

So Franklin watched, listened, and mimicked those he found interesting, especially those with money. The wealthy always seemed to be smarter with investments, less cavalier with their assets even when they had plenty. Over the next two years, he found the common denominator in these sexually needy men was an appreciation for and interest in collecting art, even in Oklahoma, though not particularly in Enid.

His banker sugar daddy had a penchant for artwork. Franklin accompanied him to Tulsa to buy artwork. It didn't take long for Franklin to realize that good artwork cost significant money, the kind of money one could purchase a car with. The interesting part for Franklin was that wealthy men were not really concerned what a painting cost, but rather whose name was on the canvas, the all-important signature. Franklin realized he could make big money simply by selling a piece of canvas with a certain name. No more petty crime and sex for hire, the art world was his future. At age 20, Franklin found his profession. He would become an art dealer.

Growing up in the sticks of north central Oklahoma hadn't lent itself to learning about art. Dealing art was not considered a career path in the farm belt of Oklahoma, where you learned a trade or worked on a ranch. Franklin's relatives, he assumed, had come up with an additional revenue stream, the idea of stealing land from the Indians, but that was only conjecture. What Franklin knew for sure was that in Enid, conversation revolved around farming and weather. The only time he ever heard art mentioned was in regard to the local undertaker, who could make anybody look good. In an area with plenty of farm accidents, that was a gift. The closest thing to an art museum was the local cemetery with its large, ornate grave stones.

Franklin often wondered how much a nice, carved marble headstone would be worth, but hadn't a clue how to fence one. Understanding more about the business of art required the aspiring art dealer to hitchhike on the weekends to Tulsa to museum shows where he could also meet wealthy men.

Understanding the importance of small talk as an entrée to any world, Franklin began by emulating the conversations he had heard all his life. Weather talk translated to art talk. Social banter like, "No rain for the winter wheat," could be repackaged as, "I'm afraid his health is failing" while referring to an aging artist. Events influenced finances. The main difference was that if the wheat failed, the farmer lost money. If an artist died, the value of his paintings increased. Farmers need rain. Collectors need paintings, preferably from dead artists.

CHAPTER 4

TIME FOR A CHANGE

Franklin Hare, petty thief, left Enid, Oklahoma, and changed his name, legally transforming himself into Ashton B. Charmers, art dealer, initials A.B.C. The new name felt regal, king-like. Now his ancestral origins were no longer land grabbers from Oklahoma displacing Indians, but an important bloodline from England that had ruled over a mythical kingdom, one he would devise over time. He included the B. initial as a subliminal reminder of his past. His father's name had started with a B. There would be no middle name, just the B., a skeleton key to his origins in a place he never wanted to return. Every signature would include the B., a reminder to himself that never again would he be poor or pushed around.

Ashton B. Charmers, CEO of Charmers Fine Art announced his motto on his business cards: "The ABC's of Art Collecting." All he needed to do now was actually learn the ABC's of becoming an art dealer.

Dillinger always said if you want money go where they keep it—the banks. Ashton had decided on California for art, specifically San Francisco. It was a rich, progressive city. He was in his twenties now with continued good looks and enough experience around wealthy men to have a feel for what they would want, even the big-city types. He had started reading about art and was fairly fluent. What he needed now was a better understanding of the art world and more importantly how to make money. His financial education would be completed at art galleries and museum openings frequented by money men.

Ashton's rule two of thievery back in Oklahoma was to have a working knowledge of what he planned to steal. Thus, his first few years living in San Francisco were dedicated to learning about art and sleeping with well-to-do men who would pay the rent. Since Ashton was a mediocre student with respect to book learning, he realized early on he would need to listen to educated people to really grasp his subject in depth. The smarter the person, the more he would pay attention. Granted one never can accumulate more knowledge this way than those one gets the information from, but if one listens to enough people this could be a tremendous education.

His first task: determining who in San Francisco's art-collecting world was a big fish. Verification was accomplished by stealing names from gallery signup sheets and matching them against names on museum donor plaques. This was the late seventies and even though he was a poor reader, slightly dyslexic with a distinct distaste for libraries, Ashton found San Francisco's art scene manageable.

One name appeared on all three of the major San Francisco museum wall plaques, Joseph Penwell III. A man in his mid-forties who had never been married, he was a perfect mark for Ashton. Hopefully he wasn't too fat or ugly, although it really didn't matter as money was the motivator, not the man. Ashton's training needed to be accelerated.

CHAPTER 5

THE MARK

Joseph Penwell III, or J.P. as his close friends called him, was a third-generation Californian who migrated north from L.A. to San Francisco during the summer of love in 1967. He was considered old at 31 for the flower power generation but J.P. didn't care. He embraced the free love movement. He was surprised at how the summer of love was about giving wealth away, yet somehow all the young men still enjoyed J.P.'s money. The age issue seemed to evaporate when his Benjamin Franklins appeared. J.P. enjoyed the sexual freedom and multiple partners that the sixties provided. He had family money so it was generally just a screw-fest every day with drug experimentation thrown in. Drugs didn't really do much for Penwell as time went by, but he had no problems buying them for his many friends as this helped get him laid.

The late sixties turned into the seventies and the summer of love became a disco inferno. Cocaine became the drug of choice and dancing was everything, even for a man pushing 40. J.P. lived life to its fullest. His typical day started at noon with a breakfast of fruit and cereal. Morning, as he referred to noon, could also be awkward as this was the time he generally kicked out the previous night's boy toy. What with the new day, he was already planning for the next encounter. He didn't mind if they slept over but only for one night, one time. When you have money and like sex, variety is the key. San Francisco at this time provided the ultimate buffet of men.

Midday for J.P. was around 5 pm. It consisted of a workout and small lunch, generally soup, salad, and vitamins, after which J.P. would review the day's financials. J.P. studied these for an hour or two every day, making recommendations to his people. This was work, or at least work was how he referred to it. Joseph Penwell was actually quite intelligent and could have been a mover and a shaker in the business world but that wasn't his thing. He came from money and never was told he really needed a job. Sex provided the driving force in his life.

Evening began with a massage, often with a happy ending, and then on to the night's festivities. Dinner was out and varied depending on Penwell's club selection. It was always more than he or his friends could eat and always expensive. Every night included dancing, drinking, drugs for his friends, and of course late-night sex.

This routine, like a pilot's route, was reliable. It might seem exciting to those on the perimeter, but being in the mix eventually became tiring. Sex with countless unnamed, forgettable men started to take its toll on J.P. He needed a change in his life or he might end up as one of those pathetic, old rich men—lost, wealthy souls who never left anything to society other than spending money recklessly and periodically helping to support a rehab facility.

Penwell finally found something he could be passionate about and not lose interest in: art. Collecting art filled a void. It gave him a feeling of accomplishment, a first. To build an important collection required time, energy, knowledge, contacts, and most importantly, a good eye. As it turned out, Penwell had a great eye for artwork. He would tell his admiring lovers, "The eye is something you are born with and can rarely acquire." For the most part, having a great eye for art can be a burden unless money comes with it. It's like being born beautiful but poor. With only looks and nothing to back it up, life can be frustrating. Great pieces of art (or men for that matter) are simply out of your league.

Joseph Penwell III was one of those rare individuals who had the money to back up his discerning eye. This meant he could build an important collection quickly and well. Money was not a limiting factor as it was for most. He actually preferred to pay 10% more than his nearest competitor because it allowed him to get the great stuff. Art dealers live for these types of clients. Good taste and no dickering over price. They always get first crack at the important pieces and are the VIPs of the art world. Penwell knew the position he had acquired and loved the attention. He occasionally missed the wild sex, but the joy of art and the power he felt upon adding an important piece to his collection replaced his nightly romps in the hay with nameless young men. That was of course until Ashton came into his life.

CHAPTER 6

BECOMING AN ART DEALER

Ashton selected his prey, Joseph Penwell III, in the late 1970s and understood his opportunity would come soon. He had to be ready for it. Knowing relatively little about being an art dealer was problematic, but Ashton remembered rule number four: go to a thief who can teach you about your business. A prison visit was in order.

The object of Ashton's mentorship was prisoner B18418 of the California State Prison system at San Quentin, also known as Picasso Louie. Ashton knew he had to be careful and not let Louie know the information he really sought regarded sharpening his skills as a crooked art dealer. It was critical to keep his intentions secret. If Louie found out, Ashton would have to change his name, not something he wanted to do that often. He had heard this con was famous for being quoted in art magazines as one of the bad guys of the art world who had gotten away with it. Ashton figured Louie probably liked the attention if he was mouthing off to magazines, so if Ashton represented himself as a reporter for one of the art trade magazines he might be able to extract more information.

A new business card, a fake press badge, and presto, Ashton became a reporter for *Art+Auction* magazine, known for its inside scoop on the art world. Going into any prison was distasteful for the pretty Ashton. He had always feared this would be his ultimate fate. A boy toy to big men named LeRoy or Manson.

Ashton's first meeting with Picasso Louie was not what he expected. Ashton had a preconceived idea of what all art dealers should look like, but Louie did not fit the mold. He was an overweight, balding man in his late 50s with a very bad comb over. His sloped shoulders gave him the appearance of a man who had a very serious spinal condition, yet it was probably just poor posture with Louie. *A used car salesman*, was Ashton's first impression.

This was the man who had bilked millions of dollars out of unsuspecting art collectors? Who in their right mind would do business with such a pathetic-looking slob? So thought Ashton as he stared across the table at his soon-to-be mentor. The mere sight of this misfit art dealer gave Ashton a hard-on. He knew immediately if a man like this could be a great art dealer, granted one that got caught, then surely he would become an overnight success.

Picasso Louie had been caught switching out an important Picasso, which he had cleaned and conserved for a client, then replaced with a replica. He placed the fraudulent painting in the original Picasso frame, and sold the original for many millions of dollars to an unsuspecting Japanese client he had been grooming for the perfect sale. Louie's Japanese multimillionaire didn't know the first thing about Picasso and failed to research the history or provenance of the painting. He was a man with a big check book who was only head hunting a name painting. Picasso Louie had actually gotten his nickname in recognition of the numerous fake Picassos he had sold. Usually he would change the name on the painting just enough so he could claim it to be a copy and insist anyone with knowledge would recognize it was a Louie replica, thus protecting himself from prosecution.

The Japanese collector was the best kind of prey. He was only after the signature and didn't know anything about art. *Head-hunting* was the term dealers gave to clients who only purchase art because of the name on the canvas. They don't care about the painting, its provenance, or its quality in the spectrum of the artist's repertoire. Purchasing an important name was enough to show taste. Since headhunters don't know dick about art, they figure buying the right name proves they do.

Louie might still be comfortably at home having his requisite evening bottle of French chardonnay if the owner of the fake Picasso didn't get into a financial bind and need to sell the family heirloom. Christie's auction house had the unfortunate job of informing the family their 80-year-old painting was a vintage 1970s copy. They did not take it well. It didn't require long to figure out who orchestrated the switch and Louie went down. The amazing part about the whole thing was Louie only got seven years for a multimillion-dollar crime. Ashton loved this part. It seemed if you didn't use a gun and there were no bodies, the penalty was minor. Hell, he would get that much for selling a couple of bags of coke. Ashton loved the art world.

Ashton easily convinced Louie he was doing an article on the underside of the art world. He wasn't sure of the exact date the article would run, but Louie was part of the cover story and he would

17

get top billing, maybe even the cover itself. Ashton assured him this article would portray Louie as an intelligent, repenting art dealer who just took advantage of excessively rich and lazy collectors, collectors that didn't really matter to the real art world. Louie ate it up.

He launched in with a softball question: "Can one really become a well-known art dealer without having a formal education in art history?"

"Art history helps but it isn't that important," Louie responded. "All you really need to know is one artist, but you have to know everything about that person's work. I picked Picasso because he was the most valuable artist and if I wanted to deal in art, I wanted only the best. I also loved Paris and it gave me a good excuse to travel. Picasso painted in a variety of styles so it was easier to have fakes made when I did that kind of thing. Because of my restoration abilities, I had a front-row seat to dealers wanting paintings manipulated."

"What kind of things would unethical dealers ask you to do?" Ashton inquired.

"Most commonly, to add an artist's name. Often great artists wouldn't sign a piece, say, if it was a study the artist never expected would have much value. Sometimes the artist might use his or her monogram to sign a piece. Dealers would come to me wanting the whole name next to the monogram because they felt it would increase value. Most restorers wouldn't do this, but I was known in the trade as one who would. You would be amazed the number of well-known dealers who used my services."

Ashton prompted, "Like?"

Louie leaned forward. "I had a New York City dealer, big time gallery, bring me in a little Thomas Moran watercolor. It had Moran's monogram, an "M" with a couple of arrows. Now that's a legitimately recognized Moran signature, but this dope decided he needed me to forge the entire name—easier to sell to a headhunter. I remember him saying, 'Hell, we both know this is a Moran, no harm in making it easier to sell.' So I added the name. It's still out there, I'm sure."

18

Ashton pressed on. "What are some of the other ways dealers scam art collectors?"

"OK," Louie replied agreeably. "Say a dealer brings in a client and tells another art dealer he will recommend his client to purchase a particular piece from his gallery, but only if he is cut in on the deal. The client never knows the first dealer is on the take and the guy who is selling the piece isn't about to say anything. He wants to get the deal done and doesn't care if the other guy is screwing his client. After all it's not really his client anyway."

"How much are we talking about scamming off the top?"

"Oh, generally 10%, which doesn't sound like much unless it's a million-dollar deal. Even better, the guy who is scamming is also often getting 10% from his client to get him the best deal and to make sure the painting is right. Not a pretty picture for the client that gets the wrong dealer!" Louie chuckled.

"The dealer could make a tremendous amount, it seems, off a client who would never know," Ashton remarked, playing ignorant.

"Yep, gotta love the art game. It's the Wild West. Must admit, I miss the action."

Ashton upped the stakes: "Has anyone in the art business ever killed to get a piece of art?"

"A question I have never been asked, young man! You know, quite honestly, I don't know of any. The art world, while filled with a lot of white-collar crooks, really is fairly civilized. That's what I liked about what I did. You could steal a million dollars and not get killed for it. In fact, you'd get written up in national magazines like yours, and after prison, blend right back into the art world. There are lots of convicted felons selling high-priced artwork. I would say the kind of person who could kill for art and still be an art dealer would be the worst and best in his field. One could get to the top fast if they didn't get caught. The crooked art dealers I know wouldn't take it that far."
"Interesting observation. My readers will be fascinated." Well, at least Ashton was.

Returning home with his fake reporter's notebook, Ashton took rule four to heart and immediately started practicing what his mentor Louie had unwittingly taught him. You only need to learn about a single artist to be believable. In fact, great knowledge about a specific artist makes it more plausible to others that you are well educated in art, even if you aren't. They will never know you are just bullshitting them. You are an art expert, you have extensive knowledge, or so it seems.

Ashton decided he would focus on the great California artist Maynard Dixon. A major retrospective at the San Francisco Academy of Art entitled "Images of the Native American," was going to be held soon and Ashton knew one Joseph Penwell would attend. Penwell was a board member of the museum and a reported Dixon collector.

So Ashton visited more galleries and museums around San Francisco developing his eye, now aimed towards Maynard Dixon. With Picasso Louie's roadmap to the thieving art world and the luck of having a retrospective in his own city for an artist collected by his mark, Ashton B. Charmers had the tools he needed to become the art dealer of his dreams.

CHAPTER 7

BECOMING A DIXON SPECIALIST

In the early eighties, those in the know realized what a genius
Maynard Dixon truly was even if his price structure hadn't proven
them right, yet. The Oakland Art Museum, which was in Ashton's
backyard, had one of the greatest paintings by Dixon, EARTH
KNOWER, depicting a lone Native American figure in profile
wrapped in a blanket, juxtaposed against cubist cliffs. Dixon's iconic
painting was executed in 1931 while living in New Mexico. Ashton
learned Dixon and his then wife, Dorothea Lange, lived for six
months in Taos in a home rented from the legendary Mabel Dodge
Luhan. The United States was two years into the Depression and
painting sales were nonexistent, so Dixon painted what inspired him
whether it would sell or not. Inspiration became Dixon's muse, not
money, since no one had any. Depictions of clouds, Taos Indians
against cliffs, pueblos, adobe homes with chiles, and Hispanic
blankets thrown over clotheslines would became some of Dixon's
most sought-after imagery.

Ashton saw himself as Dixon's own "earth knower," an individual on
a solitary journey triumphing over all, even the foreboding
mountains of nature. Ashton dreamed of stealing great paintings like
EARTH KNOWER and getting rich, no matter who got in his way. He
would steal a masterpiece as his trophy and resell it someday to his
own Japanese millionaire.

Ashton even visited Dixon's old studio at 728 Montgomery Street.
Walking up the stairs, he tried to imagine himself painting in the
early 1900s. He learned how Dixon had lost all his paintings but
saved his Indian art collection during the great earthquake and fire
of April 18th, 1906. Dixon let all his paintings go up in flames and
instead saved the Indian art he acquired from Lorenzo Hubbell who
owned the Ganado Trading Post in Arizona. Ashton thought it so odd
that anyone would not save their own things first, but Dixon was an
artist used to poverty. Ashton assumed Dixon thought he could
reproduce his own work but not the Indian art. Ashton couldn't
relate to his actions but he could imagine how angry Dixon must
have been when Mother Nature destroyed on a whim all that was of
importance in his life. Ashton's job was to learn the details of the
man, his history and art. To be considered an expert, Ashton had to

know the smallest of details, especially to convince a mark like Joseph Penwell III. There was no room for error.

Successful art dealers knew all the inconsequential minutiae about the artists they sold. Their birth year (for Dixon, 1875) and death date (1946). For good measure, Ashton memorized the precise date, November 13th, 1946, the kind of exacting information that could be devastating when making a point. Dixon was self-trained, rare for a great artist, an extremely important note. Dixon was a native Californian, as was Penwell, who would surely relate to that shared geographic background.

Finally, Ashton believed he was ready for the upcoming museum show opening which he was sure Penwell would be attending. A hardback catalog would accompany the exhibit. Ashton realized there could be valuable information if he managed to get it before the show opened. A date with the museum's bookshop director sealed that deal. The catalog, while beautifully illustrated, held some even more important bits of data: small inserts with the names of painting donors for the show. Ashton's inner thief found this odd and exhilarating. *Why would anyone tell, much less publish, who you were and what town you lived in with a picture of your very valuable painting? Were they just asking for their painting to be stolen?* Ashton couldn't understand pride of ownership, only the opportunity for deceit.

As Ashton made notes on each painting, one in particular made him grin. "Hello there, Mr. Joseph Penwell III of San Francisco, California!" The name was underneath a compelling 30-by-40-inch Dixon masterpiece, TRADITION, depicting Indians crouched in council with looming clouds boiling behind them. A single large Indian figure representing their culture stood in the center.

"Oh, if Mr. Penwell only knew how his arrogance would soon come home to haunt him! I'm afraid this will cost him dearly," Ashton said to the open Dixon catalog as if it were his therapist.

Taking information out of slick catalogs would become Ashton's bread and butter. "Stealing paintings and they give you a road map to their house!" he marveled. Ashton was always amazed at how stupid art collectors were when it came to their artwork, so naïve and sharing. He loved his career path—an unregulated, trusting community, where people will give you their art without requiring any money. A profession his fellow criminals could only dream of.

CHAPTER 8

EXOTIC ROOTS

Eva Cecile De Plain came from a heritage that was like an exotic coffee mixture: African American with a French blend, not uncommon in New Orleans, her childhood home. Her grandfather had been a well-respected jazz musician playing with all the greats, including Count Basie. Her roots in music were natural. Eva embraced them with a passion. As long as Eva could remember, she planned to be a musician, and not just any musician, but a great one. Eva never wanted to be trapped in poverty like her family, but a black superstar, educated, unencumbered, and independent. Not dependent on any man for her living. Music, art, and education became her muses.

It was apparent her grandfather's abilities had been transferred to Eva. From the age of two, she showed musical acumen. Eva's father had died when she was one, a casualty of 1969's Hurricane Camille, and her estranged mother was never a part of her life. Yet she was loved greatly by her grandparents. They were her mentors and she never felt unlucky to have lost her parents so young. Listening to the blues was an everyday event in Eva's world. The blues became her air and jazz her water; necessities of her life.

Eva started playing the piano but quickly moved on to master the violin. Her little fingers were like raindrops on a pool of water, mesmerizing in both speed and complexity. New Orleans at that time was a potpourri of music and musicians.

Eva decided to master the double bass at 12, even though it was almost unmanageable for a skinny, prepubescent girl. The instrument was taller and heavier than she was. She first heard the bass used in recordings by Paul Chambers, a great jazz musician who played in an arco or bow style. Most bass players in the South used a slapping and picking style like Marshall Lytle, the bassist for Bill Haley and His Comets. Lytle was known for his ability to spin and even jump on his instrument. The bass is a unique instrument where showmanship can be as important as the instrument itself, and for Eva this made the bass her instrument of choice.

The bass, she was told, was primarily a man's instrument, a very poor choice for a female musician. This of course made the young Eva even more intent on playing the oversized double bass. *No* was not a word in Eva's vocabulary. She had made up her mind, the bass was her choice. The bass had been around since Hayden's first concerto in 1763 and she would be the best female bassist, and black, to boot.

Eva struggled with the size of the instrument but only when carrying it to an event. Once she was performing, the bass became light and one with her body. The C-bout of the bass mimicked her own curvaceous body and the bass's F-hole openings seemed to caress her thighs as they gently pressed up against them. Eva could pick, slap, and bow equally well. Her range was limitless: jazz, blues, pop, classical. Nothing seemed to change her intensity for the instrument. Eva was the bass and the bass was Eva, one and the same.

Perfection seemed to come immediately to Eva. One would almost say it came easily, if they didn't know how long a road it was.

Eva was accepted to the Manhattan School of Music in New York at 21 with a full scholarship. Her trip from New Orleans in 1989 was her first plane ride and only the second city and state outside of New Orleans, Louisiana, she had ever visited. Nevertheless she flourished in her new surroundings, weekends filled with her other passion, art. She made it her goal to see all styles of art, most of which she had never been exposed to in New Orleans. The most intriguing art Eva experienced was Western art. Eva had never been West. She had grown up with colonial Southern art, the Southern houses with big pillars, hound dogs, and black workers all assimilated in one painting.

Now she could simply walk into any museum and see the West. Eva wondered if the West truly was the way it was portrayed in the paintings, with dramatic images of cowboys fighting Indians and lonely, isolated landscapes, all spectacles of life she could not imagine. Eva found herself most drawn to Western landscapes with huge mountains, expansive skies, and tumultuous oceans. Each weekend, Eva would return to her favorite museums to visit her new friends. As the years passed, she settled on a favorite artist, Thomas Moran. Their connection was not unlike that which she maintained with her bass: an utter commitment.

When a Moran exhibit came to the Metropolitan Museum of Art in 1993, Eva's capacity for love expanded yet again. She decided the most compelling painting she had ever seen was THE LONE CYPRESS, created in 1881 by the deceased Moran. It was here that she met the most serious love of her life, who was still very much alive.

CHAPTER 9

OLD MONEY AND THOMAS MORAN

Eva, now 25, met Bernard J. Rashmusen, who was 36, during the last week of a comprehensive Moran exhibit at the Met. Bernard was from old European blood and not what Eva would normally find attractive. He had a strong chin, thin lips, and fair skin. Eva had always prided herself in her ability to be nonjudgmental when it came to race. She had only dated black men to date, but was one of those rare individuals who were truly colorblind. Her emotional hot button was the compassion a person demonstrated, regardless of color. She melted when she saw it and always would find herself falling for these types of men. True compassion could be exhibited in many ways, and the day Eva met Bernard it came in the form of a museum headset.

She had already memorized all the Morans in the great hall. She had viewed them every weekend for the entire three-month run of the show. This was the final week and Eva felt sad to think it would be soon over, a rare feeling for her as Eva was generally an upbeat person. She had found herself in the museum's great hall every weekend evening just before closing time. The added expense, even with a student discount, severely taxed her limited budget.

Eva's routine was to view the entire show then come back and sit on a long museum bench in front of THE LONE CYPRESS. The painting was only a moderately sized Moran by Moran standards, 30 by 40 inches. It was the smallest of the Morans in the great hall but easily held its own. Moran would work occasionally on huge works five by seven feet, monumental pieces that boggled the mind. This smaller painting captured Eva's heart. It was not about size but the compelling subject matter: a single cypress surviving nature's wrath, precariously perched at the very end of a rocky bluff with no other life forms around. An unforgiving rock offered little obvious sustenance to thrive, yet it did. Massive swirling waters were all around. The tree persevered and managed to flourish, its limbs distorted and bent by the ever present forces of wind and water. It was a tree shaped by the elements, but not defined by them. Eva was that lone cypress tree, a female bassist in a man's world, holding on with every bit of her energy. Bending as she needed, surviving and adapting on the barren island of Manhattan, her rocky outcropping.

Eva had never seen an ocean other than the great Mississippi ambling into the Gulf, so the ocean had always seemed non-threatening. Even the Atlantic had seemed calm as she flew into New York. Moran's ocean was turbulent, defiant, and strong, forces with which Eva identified.

Her first sight of Bernard was as he entered the great hall where several impressive Moran canvases hung, side by side. Like the sun Bernard moved from the east end of the enormous room slowly west, all the while talking to himself as he studied the canvases, never bothering to use the information headset dangling from his craning neck.

Bernard was well acquainted with Thomas Moran, an English painter who ended up in America and became one of the foremost American Western painters. Bernard's great-grandfather, Joshua Rashmusen, had known and respected Moran as an artist and a person. Joshua was of German descent. His family had immigrated to Scotland in the mid-1800s bringing with them a knowledge of beer making that made them wealthy in a country not known for wealth. Joshua Rashmusen was still young, yet understood quality also. Joshua recognized immediately that Moran was a premier artist. He also realized early on that if you want the best examples of art, you had better be friends with the artist or his dealer. Joshua only wanted the best and went to the source: he tracked down Moran in the United States and started a lifelong relationship with the artist.

Bernard slowly reflected on each painting. He even found a reference on one of the walls about Joshua Rashmusen, one of Moran's patrons, and this gave Bernard great joy. Bernard had not done much yet with his life but hoped he would. Success was in his genes.

An elderly lady nearly bumped into Bernard while struggling to read the small print on the museum tags. She obviously could not afford a museum headset, which upset Bernard as he watched her fight to make out the words. He watched as she slowly tried to mouth each word. She was not only missing the content of the writing, but unintentionally ignoring the wonderful paintings she was there to see. As Bernard watched the grey-haired woman with the cane, Eva watched Bernard. Even THE LONE CYPRESS, her favorite painting, couldn't maintain Eva's attention compared with the compelling human interaction she saw unfolding in front of her.

Bernard gently touched the lady's tissue-like skin. As Bernard spoke, Eva could see the compassion on his face and his gentle smile, his touch never leaving her shoulder. The old woman slowly took the proffered headset from Bernard as if she had never experienced an unencumbered gift, especially from a stranger. She had a look of amazement as he showed her how to use the device. Bernard accompanied her back to the entrance of the great room and began retracing her path, revisiting the exhibit. At each painting, Bernard would stop, point, and talk as if he was her personal curator. The old lady's face had a constant grin and she kept covering her crooked teeth as she tried to stop smiling, but couldn't. At one point he started laughing and got more exuberant as he looked at a particularly large Yosemite waterfall scene. By the time Bernard made it back to the center of the room where Eva sat, she knew she was in love with this man. They say love can be instantaneous and in her case it was. She never saw the color of his skin, eyes, height, hair, or even his physical stature. Just his smile and generous emotions as he helped a poor, elderly lady on a late afternoon.

CHAPTER 10

THE ROMANCE

Eva stopped Bernard before he finished his tour of the main exhibit hall, introduced herself, and made sure to give both Bernard and the elderly lady similarly warm greetings. Eva was never one to beat around the bush when she wanted something. She simply said she couldn't help but notice his enthusiasm for Moran and wondered if he would mind her tagging along.

Bernard was dumbstruck by Eva's beauty. It wasn't supermodel beauty, but unique and exotic. Eva was five-foot-three with a figure Rubens would have been proud to paint: generous hips and breasts, her hair straight black with a hint of red when grazed by light. It softly draped her gazelle-like neck, her small, bluish veins discernible barely below the skin. Her beating heart was almost visible too, its rhythm fast and steady. Full red lips with a touch of moisture outlining the edges of her mouth were Eva's most prominent and erotic feature. Bernard couldn't help but notice as she talked that her sensuous lips also seemed to cover perfectly straight, white teeth. Her skin was dark brown, silky, and absent of any blemishes. Eva's eyes were dark green and intense, their color telling of a mixture of exotic blood that Bernard could hardly wait to explore.

When Eva spoke for the first time, Bernard's sexual being was awakened immediately. Her accent was not one he could identify. It seemed Southern but with some foreign quality. The relatively slow cadence of Eva's speech only accentuated her sexuality to Bernard. The timbre was slightly deep. Eva's voice, like the person, was unique. And like his great-grandfather Joshua Rashmusen had once done with a painter years ago, Bernard recognized Eva's rarity immediately.

Their first day together lasted 10 hours, the second, 14 hours, and they were seldom apart after that. Their bonding was like that of two swans, strong and all encompassing. They were overcharged magnets that were never supposed to be apart. Their third day together was their first night as one. Their relationship was a melding of mind and body. Life stories were shared, including dreams, aspirations, strengths, weaknesses, and of course what each wanted in a life partner. Both seemed to understand and accept that they had just found their counterpart for life's journey.

Sex was like they had never been with anyone else. Both wanted to please the other, and the ease with which this was accomplished cemented their bond. Lovemaking started just after dinner. Alcohol, the natural lubricant of love, was never required. Looking into each other's eyes told the story and their intimate intertwining lasted until the early morning. Then the two young lovers finally sank into deep, satisfying sleep.

Bernard and Eva's rhythm of life was one of ease and complete satisfaction. Eva tended to be an early riser. This behavior seemed counterintuitive for a musician, especially one from New Orleans. Eva's grandfather played late-night gigs even into his late seventies. Going to bed at 3 am was the norm and Eva rarely saw him before noon. But for Eva, morning was her time to be one with her bass. The solar warmth of early morning enhanced her ability to bring out the inner soul of her instrument. It was Eva's form of balancing herself for the upcoming day's schedule. She loved the solitude, only the sound of music, the rest of the world asleep. This routine had stayed with Eva into adulthood.

For Bernard, the low plucking of the bass with its perfectly composed rhythms only added to his sleep patterns. A late sleeper by nature, he possessed strong circadian rhythms that were not interrupted by the music. Only the loss of Eva's warm breast leaving his back seemed to waken Bernard. They slept spoon-like from the beginning, simultaneously changing positions to accommodate the other's sleep patterns.

Eva had Bernard and Bernard had Eva; it was that simple. Their social, economic, and racial differences seemed unimportant.

CHAPTER 11

NEW YORK CITY

Living in New York on a limited budget for Eva seemed no different than a woman being a bass player. You dealt with the issues at hand and got on with it. Eva had been living in Manhattan for four years when she met Bernard in 1993 and she had gotten used to the poverty of student life. She never ate out and mainly went to free museum openings, the Moran exhibit being a splurge. Eva was used to waiting in long lines for anything free or nearly free. The Metropolitan Museum of Art, a grand and interesting place, was never missed on a free night. Usually the line to get in required a 45-minutes commitment, winding around the block. This for many would have been reason enough not to go, but for Eva it was part of the joy.

The people she met in line were sometimes more interesting than the art. One person read palms, and another man once had an active business helping people deal with their past lives. His job was to help raise the spirits of individuals who were sad in their current lives. He had quizzed Eva repeatedly about her emotions and how often she was sad. Eva kept explaining nothing made her feel sad; she was just a happy person. He refused to believe she could be so happy and continued to grill her. Eva continued to profess happiness and this seemed to upset the young man named Cosmos. He didn't understand how anyone who had to wait in line just to get a free admission to a museum could really be that happy. What Eva understood was Cosmos was the unhappy person, and dealing with individuals more disturbed than himself was his therapy. The Met line was one of the ways he recruited new business, and she didn't fit his mold. Eva was a happy person who knew who she was and wasn't really concerned with any past lives. This man was actually of comfort to Eva, for she could see how bad a job could be. She had been given a gift, a profession she loved and she would never take it for granted. Life could be fleeting and unpredictable and Eva knew she would always make the most of it, no matter what. She knew the unexpected happens and if that day occurred for her, she never wanted any regrets.

Before meeting Bernard, Eva's food came from the food bank and sometimes the store, but it always came and Eva never complained even if it was less than she needed or not to her taste. If she could practice her bass without her stomach aching she was happy. Eva truly never realized how hard she had to struggle just to stay fed and how limited her housing needs were until she met Bernard, who was of considerable means.

Eva lived in Harlem. She had to carry her bass with her to school. Most New Yorkers were actually pretty helpful no matter what their reputation was. When she needed a hand to lift her instrument, someone was always there to help. Rarely did she find people to be nasty when it came to the large and cumbersome instrument, even in the most cramped public transportation. Instead of being hostile, people were intrigued by the small woman with the big instrument and often asked Eva to play on the subway. If the train's occupants were up for it, she would take her instrument out of its worn, multi-colored cover, and start slapping and picking at the strings. Music would engulf the train like the aroma of fresh, hot bread fills a kitchen. Eva's music would take over the subway car, causing a chain reaction of smiles, shaking heads, and tapping feet. It was obvious Eva was gifted. When playing, she couldn't help the movement of her thighs and head. The way she was able to engulf the double bass seemed impossible yet somehow it happened. If her mood was right, Eva would start singing one of her grandfather's blues songs, her deep, raspy voice melding with the bass's low-pitched tones. Never did Eva try to make money by playing on the train, but she always did. Money came, sometimes in quarters and dimes, but usually dollar bills and sometimes more. Those who had the good fortune of witnessing Eva's God-given talents felt an obligation to give something for the privilege of the private concert they had just witnessed. Her instrument case never went empty. These impromptu concerts allowed Eva to live, eat, and occasionally buy a little something for herself.

Eva never felt the need to accumulate things. Things were just things. The objects that were in Eva's life had a deep meaning, not from a value stance, but from the emotional connection she had with the object. Those rare material goods that Eva actually kept became alive and part of her being.

Her most precious object was an old cane made out of hickory that had belonged to her late grandfather. She remembered him using it.

In his later years, the cane became part of him as he would laboriously go up the steps to his little house. The three steps up to the house could take the old man 30 minutes to negotiate towards the end. The cane was his third leg which allowed him to slowly navigate the steps. This cane had emotional relevance to Eva and that superseded any monetary value.

When Bernard realized Eva lived in such a meager world, it was shocking to him. The poverty seemed omnipresent. He was amazed that Eva didn't seem to regard her situation as somewhat dire. To Eva, it was normal and she considered herself one of the lucky ones. She had seen true poverty in New Orleans and knew life could be very harsh—no food, housing, or social interaction. She had her music and all the things she needed to be able to enjoy and apply her trade.

Bernard suggested moving her to his Upper East Side apartment overlooking the East River. There were white floors and clean, friendly doormen. It was 3,000 square feet, not 250. The bathroom and kitchen were not located in the same room. At Bernard's, one didn't do the dishes in the bathtub. In fact, one didn't do them at all; the maid did. Bernard wanted to improve her situation, but Eva didn't want or need change. Eva had no intention of moving to the Upper East Side.

Bernard told her repeatedly that he had a hard time getting to his job on time, living in Harlem, and he worried about her safety when he was gone. Eva never worried about being hurt. She felt comfortable in Harlem and never saw the bad in people. She did worry about Bernard's fretting. After much convincing, she finally gave in and said she would move, but under two conditions: no maid and no doormen. Their new apartment could be larger than her place and in a safer neighborhood.

Bernard's job was really only as a figurehead. He did feel an obligation to the family's finance and real estate business, so he would come in most days, mill about, then leave for coffee or lunch. His mother, Dorothy Rashmusen, handled the important issues, having taken over the head position 10 years ago after Bernard's father's death. They owned a large building on Madison Avenue with the family office on the top floor. A wide expanse of Central Park was their view. Three secretaries were at Bernard's disposal at any given time but really he needed only one, part time at most.

After Eva came into his life, Bernard's schedule became riding the train with Eva to school, meeting her for lunch which he brought, disguised as if it were homemade, even though it always came from the great delicatessen Zabar's which had served the Rashmusen family for decades and which would put the food in homemade containers and then place them in crumpled paper bags as if they had just come out of the kitchen drawer. Bernard knew Eva wouldn't want him to buy lunch for her, but if he made it then it was fine.

Evening consisted of again meeting Eva at school to help carry the bass home. Occasionally she would let him get a cab, but usually they took the subway and then made the two-block walk home dragging the bass behind in a homemade carrying case made from a discarded kid's wagon, fire-engine red, the word *flyer* barely visible on its badly dented side.

Bernard had a hard time understanding Eva's lack of need for all life's conveniences, but he tried. Eva would tell him, "Bernard, things don't mean anything unless you have an emotional bond to them. Otherwise they are just that, things. The more you expect and need, the harder life actually becomes. Look at me. I'm starting to get ruined. I'm already too used to great lunches that you bring me. If you disappeared it would be much harder for me to adapt to what was left. I can't afford to get used to your lifestyle. I know mine is hard, but if you stick with me you will be a different and I hope, happier person."

It was true. Bernard had already gotten used to life being a little harder. He now drank boiled-down coffee grounds in the morning, instead of a six-dollar skinny venti latte. The increased walking, plus pulling the heavy bass, allowed him to lose the belly fat on his six-foot frame. For the first time in his life, he could see his abdominal muscles. The nightly or bi-nightly sexual marathons didn't hurt his physical condition either.

Bernard had never imagined he would or could live in a 900-square-foot apartment with no art on the walls other than a poster of the Moran show from the Met, but that became their compromise home on the fourth floor of a walk-up on the far Upper East Side. Eva kept commenting that the huge living room was so magnificent she could even hang a large painting in the space, someday.

CHAPTER 12

THREE'S COMPANY

Eva and Bernard had been together 18 months, existing in their own time warp of love. It seemed like somehow they had been together forever. Nothing had changed in the relationship from day one except now Eva had an ever-expanding abdomen. Eva was almost eight months pregnant.

The pregnancy had been uneventful. She had known immediately she was pregnant as her periods had always been as predictable as New Orleans' fall storm schedule, they came and went. So when she missed one, that was it. Eva had started her prenatal vitamins right away and went to an ob/gyn the next week.

Going about her daily life was getting difficult now. She was in her final week of school before graduation. The thought that her professional music career was about to begin and at the same time her first child, a boy, would be born, was exciting beyond belief. Bernard too was thrilled, although his family was less so. His family consisted of only his mother, Dorothy, who first met Eva when she was six months pregnant. The old Rashmusen bloodline was not happy about the royal European blood being diluted any more than it already was, but Bernard was obviously in love and Eva was special, even if in a poverty-ridden way.

Eva and Bernard were not married. For most old-fashioned mothers, that would be considered the wrong way to bring a child into the world. Bernard's mother, while conservative, seemed relieved no economic commitment had happened yet and told Bernard she thought it was very modern of him to just live together and see how it all worked out. In reality, Bernard had tried everything to convince Eva to marry him but she wouldn't. Eva was worried that Bernard's money would affect her and her son, and not in a good way. She liked Bernard's mother, Dorothy, well enough, yet there was a racial and social divide between them that she sensed. She could tell in the way Dorothy avoided introducing her in certain social situations, like she hoped Eva would just disappear someday, a bizarre dream that would be over soon.

Eva felt she needed to wait and see if the baby changed the way Dorothy felt toward her. Time was in her favor. *Just let it play out. Events have a way of coming to the right path even when it's not clear during the present*, Eva's instinct told her.

Bernard had to go to Mexico City on business, a rare event, but this was one of those times. He couldn't stand to be away from Eva for even an hour, much less a week. He begged her to go with him so he wouldn't be alone. Besides, this would give him time to get her out of the apartment so he could get it upgraded before the baby came. Bernard knew Eva would put up an impressive fuss if he tried to do what he wanted, but if it was done while she was gone for two weeks there wouldn't be much she could do, especially if she was nine months pregnant and due to deliver at any moment. A baby's room created from part of the spacious living room and new museum art lights were what he had in mind. Bernard also planned a special present for Eva upon their return, a present even she wouldn't object to since it possessed what she required: emotional connection. It would be a graduation, baby, and hopefully wedding present all in one. A turning point into the relationship, one in which all was shared not only emotionally but financially.

Bernard Rashmusen had everything in place and with lot of begging, Eva finally relented and off to Mexico they went in 1995, flying commercial of course. She insisted.

CHAPTER 13

MEXICO CITY

Eva's first international trip and her second flight on a plane was to Mexico City. How did a poor black girl from New Orleans end up with such a wonderful man with whom she would be having a son? Life was funny, she thought. Eva had always known she would be a musician, but she couldn't have seen this development. How could anyone?

The hotel was one of the better in Mexico City, although not the best. Bernard knew that Eva would never put up with the kind of opulence that came with a five-star hotel, but he did manage to book them on the first floor which had just been completely refurbished from the beams to the furniture, making it suitable by Rashmusen standards. Eva had never stayed in a hotel except one time, a Motel Six with her grandfather when he went to Houston for a jazz gig. She could still remember the excitement of fresh sheets and the Magic Fingers attached to the bed.

Eva remembered the little strip-mall motel as if it were yesterday, all the emotions flooding back as she entered room #18 of the Hotel La Posada. The room was larger than her original apartment in New York. It had one expansive bay window with a great view of a small colonial plaza just a stone's throw away from the heart of Mexico City. The floor was a lovely gray marble, its hand-cut stones fitting snugly together with small Mexican blankets randomly tossed about the surface. The haphazard floor rugs somehow worked, almost like one of her Aunt June's prized crazy quilts, splashes of red and green with Mayan themes. The bed was in a small side room with its own cozy little bathroom containing a converted bathtub/shower. Furniture was all pine, except for a very old sabino wood table with a large blue low-rimmed Mexican flower pot filled with fresh-cut roses and begonias. The smell was a mixture of roses, fragrant lilies from another vase, and a hint of cigarette smoke. She loved it.

Now that she was into her eighth month of pregnancy, it was becoming a challenge. She was laboring to breathe in the high altitude of Mexico City. Her unborn son kept pushing ever upwards on her diaphragm, exacerbating her dyspnea. She could only eat small meals and these had to be bland or she would pay the price.

Eva's legs now had pitting edema, any little pressure on her lower legs resulting in small indentions. Eva found them funny looking even though she understood the implications. She might actually have a problem with her pregnancy and very soon. Eva, like a little kid, would take quarters and press them against her lower legs to see the silly-putty type response left in her skin. She hadn't told Bernard about her leg problem, knowing he would fret the whole time. Eva felt Bernard needed her on this trip. He seemed so lost sometimes.

Eva knew they were having a boy. The ultrasound had confirmed this. She had known the baby's sex for months, but couldn't decide on just the right name. She had considered a great jazz musician's name, or maybe her grandfather's, but for some unknown reason nothing seemed appropriate.

This felt odd and slightly disconcerting as Eva had always been decisive. She decided maybe during pregnancy the swelling affected the mind and it would clear once the baby was born. Eva already knew the things she wanted for her son: the way he should learn, what music and art she wanted to expose him to. The name for some reason just wouldn't materialize. The harder she pressed, the more difficult it became. Eva was a person who could let life happen on its own. Somehow she knew, like everything else in her world, the name would become crystal clear. She just had to be patient and let her boat float down the river of life. And in two days they would be back home in New York. Flying so close to term was a risk, but Eva concentrated on positive thoughts.

Mexico City was as large as New York but that was where the resemblance ended. History and architecture encompassed Eva at all times. The narrow streets with their herringbone designs composed from colonial bricks hundreds of years old were incongruent with the intense traffic. The constant disorganized flow of humanity pounded the slowly decaying streets, gradually leaving only a smooth, treacherous surface.

The city was founded by the Spanish when their prophecy appeared: an eagle with a snake in its mouth sitting on a cactus. Mexico City was built on that very spot, a huge lake basin now filled with choking smog so thick at times one couldn't see buildings a block away. The Mexican people seemed genuine and interesting but the poverty was overwhelming. Eva had never felt more fortunate as when she saw hundreds of orphan children trying to eke out some sort of existence on the streets. On every street these ragtag children with their hands outstretched hoped for any type of kindness. Eva shuddered at the thought of her own child being caught in such a tenuous situation. Each hand she filled was followed by two more, a mob of poverty and despair.

Eva realized how lucky she was to play an instrument for a living, something she would have done for free. Having kind people give her money for making music resulted in ample food and shelter. She wondered if people would notice if sweet music was played here, or if the daily grind of the tremendous Mexican population would just pass by. Music, like art, was an unobtainable luxury for most and like the lost children would probably be ignored, just another noise blending into the city's cacophony.

She made a mental note to never forget her good fortune and never take it for granted. No matter how bad things might get, it had to be better than life for these poor forgotten souls. She had education, talent, a life partner, and soon a wonderful son to share her love. A strong mental image of the city and its people was etched into Eva's mind: *Never forget Mexico's poor.*

CHAPTER 14

SHAKE, RATTLE, AND ROLL

Mexico in the early morning is so beautiful, Eva thought. As usual, she was up before Bernard. She had slept in by her standards, until 6 am, but still the world was calm. She decided to play something classical this morning so that her unborn, unnamed son would have music to enjoy with his usual breakfast of amniotic fluid.

Eva enjoyed standing when she played the bass even at this late uncomfortable part of her pregnancy. Positioning her body next to the window where the breeze blew up and down her legs, Eva luxuriated in the wind's eddies. The sun's rays radiated onto her slightly swollen face. She slowly slapped at the strings of her bass, making the loveliest deep pitch.

The very last thing she remembered before the lights went out was Bernard turning his head toward her to hear the lovely music she was making and smiling at her, his eyes still closed.

A major earthquake is not something one should ever wish to experience. There is nothing in life, except maybe falling through thin ice, that resembles the fear produced by such a sudden and violent force of nature.

Mexico City that day became a war zone. The quake registered 7.9 on the Richter scale. The Richter scale is logarithmic so every increase of one is a magnitude of ten. The quake was like a category five hurricane blasting a city with no warning. The devastation was widespread and complete. A nuclear blast would cause similar destruction. At the epicenter, nothing lives. Just outside the perimeter, there is a chance of survival, maybe. Eva and Bernard unfortunately were near the epicenter. The best hotel in town was dead center.

Eva's first thought as she tried to comprehend what had just happened was, *Is my baby hurt?* She cried out, "Bernard!" No answer. Trying to sit up, she banged her head against a large slab of what must be concrete and steel. Her now-throbbing head with a stream of blood running down her cheek was a minor inconvenience compared to the wincing pain in her left arm, which was trapped

42

beneath the double bass's C-curve. Eva had been holding her left arm at the bridge of her instrument when the hard shake had thrown her to the ground. She had instinctually held on to her prized instrument, clutching it with her left arm as her right grabbed her abdomen to lessen the fall onto the uneven Mexican tile. The bass was now lying on its side parallel to Eva's own body. Her left arm was partially trapped by the corner of the C-curve and the bass's large lower end was trapped between the floor and the concrete ceiling which was only a couple of feet from her head. Somehow the bass along with one solitary piece of steel that had the words DYNAMITE STEEL COMPANY embossed on its side kept the huge mass of concrete from squashing her. She was amazed she could read anything as it was almost pitch black and the dust was so thick she could taste and feel the gritty pieces working their way down her throat. Even though nothing else was recognizable, the large, bold capital letters of the DYNAMITE STEEL COMPANY were undeniable.

"Bernard!" she called again. She couldn't lift her head to see over to the bed, but knew it was unlikely he had survived the hotel's collapse. Her eyes were burning intensely as she blinked wildly, then began crying, which helped her eyes but made her breathing more labored. Eva realized she had to get control of herself and the perilous situation. The sobbing was wasting her energy and more importantly her precious fluids.

She instinctively knew people who survived these types of situations were the ones that kept their heads and did everything right. Eva, almost to term, was determined to give her son the chance he deserved, not to die unborn in a foreign country under a slab of concrete. The thought of her unborn son made her visualize all the homeless children who must have been crushed under the falling buildings. She said a prayer for them and her own son.

Lying supine on her back, breathing was exceptionally difficult. *How badly hurt was she?* Her head was throbbing from her ridiculous panic attack but that wasn't life threatening. The baby was kicking but that was nothing unusual. It was actually incredibly reassuring. Eva's left arm was throbbing with each beat of her heart, but her other extremities seemed okay and she was able to move them even if only in a limited range of motion. Eva was able to bend her knees enough to take some of the pressure off her lower back which had hurt even before being pinned beneath tons of concrete and laying on uneven, hard stones.

"Bernard!" she yelled again, more urgently. "Please be here!" No response. Tears clouded her eyes again as she tried to control her emotions. She remembered the little smile on his face before he was probably crushed to death by the four floors above him. If so, at least she knew the last thought that had crossed his mind was of her. Oddly, she was glad she had come with him to see what was probably the last moment of his life. He was her love, the father of her child if she lived. *Yes, definitely worth it*, she thought as she tried to clear her mind, to avoid panic, to concentrate on breathing slowly and deeply and focusing on surviving. The tears had helped clean her eyes and she felt a sliver of hope.

Where was one of the little Mexican throw rugs when she needed it? Eva had moved them from her practice area so she could feel the bare floor with her feet. The extra friction she achieved by gripping with her toes helped control the large bass which had become cumbersome in her last trimester.

Day 1: Everyone was dying around her. She called out for Bernard repeatedly but no voice answered. She heard dogs whimpering and barking, people moaning, and once she thought she heard a baby crying. These sounds were a cacophony of suffering, expressing the horror of slow death in multiple forms all taking place simultaneously. The only thing Eva could do was listen. She discovered that her right hand could just barely reach over her extended abdomen and pluck the bass strings.

Amazingly, somehow the bass's musical ability still persisted. The tone was slightly changed to Eva's trained ear, but incredibly the bass had saved her life by wedging itself between the steel beam and the concrete slab and it could still make music to calm her. Slowly plucking and slapping at the stings helped Eva block out the sounds of death. The building was in its own death mode. Cracking wood and breaking glass accented Eva's plucking. A rescuer would never have been able to distinguish between the crumbling building noises and the slow slapping, picking, and occasional low singing coming from what was left of room number 18.

Day 2: Eva's arm had stopped hurting and she now felt only a dull numbness. She knew in her heart that this was a horrible sign, but being trapped and alone it seemed a blessing. Eva's first night had been cold and extremely uncomfortable, sleeping only briefly with violent visions of her unborn son. She woke to a hard thud from her abdomen. At first she thought this was it, the baby was in trouble, but soon she realized he had just turned to a new position. How she wished she could turn! Her trapped arm kept her from much vertical movement, but there was almost 12 inches of room between her huge abdomen and the concrete pad. Her legs and right arm were free, but she remained trapped alive in a coffin of concrete and Dynamite steel. Her unchanging pose had required her unborn son to adapt to a more comfortable position. Ironically he was happy and immersed in a pool of nourishing fluid. Her baby's new position, dropped down in her uterus, also eased Eva's own discomfort, even if minimally.

Hunger, a feeling she was familiar with, was now worsening. Eva wondered which would be worse—starving to death or slowly dehydrating with her son dying first, quickly followed by her own demise. Astonishingly, with her right arm she felt something just barely within her grasp. It was the flowers that had been on the 100-year-old sabino table. The blue Mexican flower pot had somehow landed right side up, flowers and most of the water still intact. With a little work, Eva was able to pull the pot close enough to reach the precious fluid inside. Eva stuck her hand in the bowl and it covered her fingers. There probably was about two cups of water and most of the flowers were still comfortably nestled inside the bowl.

Eva ripped off a small portion of her flimsy nightgown and draped it into the pot, soaking up a portion of the precious water. She then worked the water-soaked rag back to her parched, grit-filled mouth. She felt hope briefly at that moment. But who was she kidding? She was trapped in a destroyed building in a devastated city.

At the end of day two, she heard the first sound which she could identify as from outside: a high-pitched squeal that was mechanical. It was fleeting but, again, briefly hopeful. Fear returned and kept Eva up for most of her second straight night.

Day 3: What happens when human bodies decompose all around you at hot spring temperatures is not pleasant. The smell of death pervades all. As dead flesh incubates in a humid, hot environment it reaches necrosis quickly. The breakdown of tissue by anaerobic bacteria produces a methane gas that seems to permeate everything. Eva had tried in vain to keep from defecating for the first two days, but by day three she realized it was futile and the only good thing, besides the abdominal relief, was that the smell of human feces helped blunt the overwhelming smell of death. She felt lucky she was in her night gown and had no underwear on. Her human byproducts passed more easily and were not trapped so close to her body. Eva was using her small water rag to cover her mouth and nose at all times now. The humidity helped her breathe a little easier and reduced the smells and dust to almost bearable.

Eva was glad she knew little about human anatomy as she would have visualized the damage occurring to her trapped and probably dying arm. Her skills for looking at something and memorizing the information were remarkable. The ability to read a passage of music, and then remember the piece, served her well in her career.

She felt the first outside contact on day three, with a small spider. She hadn't felt the spider come up the dead arm but now it was making its way up her neck. A fleeting thought of trying to eat it entered her mind but she probably would rather starve. She wrenched her head sideways to shake the spider off, losing her face cloth and allowing all the smells to flood back in. Eva pitied all those who couldn't move and would have to tolerate the spider and where it might decide to put its web. The thought of rats suddenly entered Eva's mind. She never liked rodents to begin with, but what if one started to chew on the arm without feeling, slowly eating a finger off? Eva shuddered at the thought. She could visualize this as she had seen lots of rats in her life living in two big cities. Eva said a prayer for her life and that of her unborn son. The thought of God and her son all of a sudden seemed to intertwine as one. At that horrible moment, Eva knew why her son's name had not come to her. Somehow God had known this horrific earthquake would happen and that now would be the appropriate time to think of a name for her son, the correct choice. The name came to Eva like a bolt from heaven: Theo, from the Greek, meaning God. To survive this ordeal trapped in the rubble of what used to be a second-floor hotel room, she would need a higher power, God. Only God could pull a nearly term woman trapped under thousands of pounds of rubble to safety.

God must have a plan for me and my now named son, Theo. Theo De Plain. She said it to herself, over and over. Eva slept for 14 hours straight. No more spiders.

Day 4: The hunger was painful. Little Theo was sapping the life source out of Eva. The few extra pounds she had gained during pregnancy had now melted off her. She finally came to the realization that the flowers in her blue bowl were edible and still quite fresh since they had been in water the whole time. Eva had kept them in the bowl even if they sucked up some of the water as their smell reminded her of beauty and helped ward off the stench of death. She slowly worked one of the peonies from the bowl over her breasts and into her mouth. The velvet leaves of the flower had a fine layer of dust over them. They tasted like chalky Rolaids dipped in honey. The flower's aroma was still strong. Eva ate the whole thing—petals, leaves, and stems. The flower's fibrous composition helped tremendously with her abdominal pain. It was her first food in four days. She didn't worry about any more bowel movements. She was already covered in fecal matter and the little nutrients she had gotten from the flower probably wouldn't even make to her lower colon. She would die first. The water was down to the last cup. She would try to ration it and the remaining flowers. Eva started to do the math in her head. Ten days was probably the longest any human had survived trapped without food or water. She figured in about one week the country would have to start blowing up dangerous buildings, those teetering on the brink of disaster. The poor souls who were still somehow alive would soon be statistics of the earthquake's growing death count.

Eva reasoned one week would probably be about her limit. She had little water and basically no food, at eight and three quarters months pregnant. "Yes, one week, that is tops for me and little Theo," Eva muttered to herself in a voice which was now lower than ever. Her only hope was if Bernard's mother had gotten involved somehow. Dorothy knew the hotel and must have people looking. "Bernard, sweet Bernard, he will save me yet," she whispered.

Day 5: Eva had been lying in fecal material for two days and the moist skin around her buttocks was starting to break down. She had seen this in old folks before, decubitus ulcers they called them. Eva lifted her butt up, forcing her extended abdomen to the very top of the concrete mass, allowing a little air to flow underneath and dry out the unimaginable mess below. When she did this, she was forced to breathe through her mouth to decrease the horrible smell. The good thing at least about no food was there were no more bowel movements, and for this she was thankful. She considered breaking the blue bowl and taking the smaller pieces and scooting them under her butt to secure a steady flow of air, which would allow her skin to dry out, but Eva couldn't do it. *That bowl saved my life. The least I can do is leave it in one piece. We both survive intact or neither of us does.* She wondered if she was starting to lose her mind, giving the bowl a human persona, but for some reason it seemed right and Eva listed to her inner voice. Fate had taken over.

Eva continually plucked and slapped at the bass. The only sounds now were the creaking of lumber with the occasional loud muffled boom of some building being leveled on the outside. No more cries of people or dogs or anything alive, just the noises of destruction, her bass, and the occasional low singing of Eva De Plain. A lullaby mixed with the blues. Eva had always heard the phrase *doghouse bass player*. She had asked her grandfather what the old term meant. His response was, "Can't explain it. You just have to live it and you ain't lived it yet." Eva understood the meaning now. Trapped in her own claustrophobic doghouse on the floor, with only music to help dull the pain, Eva truly understood how those blues singers could get emotion out of their voices. They experienced a tragic event and it impacted them, deeply and permanently. Eva heard for the first time her voice intertwined with that of her grandfather's.

The ray of light that pierced the room late on day five was blinding. Eva had been in near complete darkness for five excruciatingly long days. She felt as though God himself was reaching out to her. The ray was a single strand of light like a laser beam, hitting Eva directly on her extended abdomen. She now knew where the term *ray of hope* must have derived from. Eva started to drum and pluck and sing very loudly, her energy renewed. Then as quickly as the ray had appeared, it was gone. Return to darkness.

Was it real? Maybe God was coming to take her and little Theo. Eva slept in fits on night five. If this was a chess match, Eva was entering the end game.

Day 6: "The last of the water and flowers gone today." Her voice trembled as she said it out loud, as if someone would help her. It wouldn't be long before she would die. She felt an urgency to get out. Panic raced through her body. She screamed for help, writhing and kicking. She had been afraid to move too much as she might cause the Dynamite beam and the bass to give way and end her and her son's life. But sometimes you have to take a chance when you're down to your last few moves, or it's checkmate.

Were there any water droplets left in the blue bowl? Eva maneuvered the flower bowl closer, turned it upside down with her one free arm, scooted it past her right breast and pushed it up against the strings of her bass. She wiggled her trapped body till the bowl was perched on her lowered chin, then jutted her lower jaw out as far as possible, allowing her to grasp the bowl's rim with her lower teeth and pull it securely into her mouth. With a great snap of her neck the upside down bowl landed squarely over her head, covering it completely. A few remaining drops of water slowly dripped down the sides, just missing her mouth. Eva's swollen dry tongue jutted back and forth like some grotesque metronome out of control, hopelessly trying to secure the last drops of water.

"What can I do, so that someone can hear me? I must make noise!" Eva said, talking to the bowl as if it were her best friend. "You and I have to get out of here. I have a son to raise and you have flowers to hold. We must work as a team. I'll do my best to save you, as you did for me, but I need you now. Be strong and we will get out together!"

She realized with the bowl on her head, she could bang it against the steel girder. She would then pluck as hard as she could at the bass strings and hit the beam in perfect cadence. "My last concert as a bassist," she said out loud, then corrected herself, "Our last concert." The bowl was her partner. Her head wound reopened and swelled with each collision against the beam, the bowl's inner surface now staining with red droplets of blood. Drips of blood dropped onto her dust-covered checks intermixed with tears as she persisted.

Then the unimaginable happened. The beam banged back. She stopped all movement and waited for her ears to stop ringing. She could hardly believe it, but she had felt and heard it. A vibration, a noise not made by her. "Help! Help!" she shouted. Someone had heard her. Eva yelled at the top of her lungs. The air was stale and had the taste of death, the heat was incredible, and the putrid air hurt her lungs which had not been fully inflated in almost a week, yet she kept yelling. It was now or never, and she knew it had to be now. No response.

Day 7: The abdominal pains started slowly but the intensity increased with each wave of uterine muscle tissue contraction. Eva was in labor, crushed underneath a building, trapped with a gangrenous arm, covered in feces, and unable to move more than a dozen inches. Could she even pass the child out if she wanted? She had no idea if there was any wreckage that would block the delivery. Being poor and growing up in the South, Eva did know about birthing babies. She knew it all, especially what would happen if someone didn't cut the baby's cord, or deliver her placenta. All the scenarios were horrific. The baby would die if the cord was not cut, Theo's blood draining back into the now useless placenta. She couldn't imagine how she could get her teeth close enough to do it herself.

Eva was no longer yelling, she was now screaming. Her screams were fierce. She used every contraction to her benefit. If the contractions hurt, she let it out in a bloodcurdling shriek. She wanted someone to know that time was of the essence. Theo was coming and he didn't care that his mother was trapped under a thousand pounds of concrete. It was his birthday.

CHAPTER 15

THE RESCUE

Sunlight blasted through the uncovered window pane next to Eva's head, ushering the first smell of unfettered air with it. She screamed louder. The bowl was still on her head but the light filtered into the bowl's inside surface and for the first time she saw an old water ring, the calcium layer she had tasted in the last few gulps of water. The saltiness had tasted so good.

Suddenly, there were footsteps, then voices in Spanish, screams surrounding her. She recognized the word *Jesus*, and *God* and what sounded like *miracle*. Light engulfed everything. The sound of moving rocks and grating metal was everywhere.

Then Eva heard the most horrible sound she would never forget: that of her bass being crushed. The instrument of her childhood, the one constant in her life. There was the crunch of cracking wood, then strings popping, one by one. A high-pitched pinging noise the bass had never made and then a swish as the last metal string let go.

The blue bowl suddenly came off her head and a set of dark, peering eyes over a handkerchiefed face stared back. A voice in broken English urged, "Must go, pronto, the building she given way."

With one great pull from the man and his helpers, Eva was freed. The bass gave out and seconds later the space she had so uncomfortably resided in for the last week was gone. A great swoosh, crash, and the bass was reduced to kindling in seconds. Eva could see the blue bowl tossed to the side of the wreckage, a fresh chip in its rim, yet remarkably still intact. The huge concrete pad of her living tomb was completely covered with debris, hiding all but the very end of her bass. A fresh plume of dust rose above the rubble. The scene was a frenetic parade of paramedics, military, and the curious destitute.

Eva had survived and Theo didn't wait. With the sudden yank by her Mexican rescuers, a huge gush of water came rushing out between Eva's legs as her amniotic sac broke. The men in red-and-white handkerchiefs seemed perplexed as this small black woman erupted with an explosion of water where none should be.

"*Dios mío, Dios mío,*" the chanting erupted. Surrounded by death and destruction, a new life emerged. It was a miracle. The blue ceramic bowl was used once more as the search and rescue team filled the bowl with fresh water to clean newborn baby Theo. The last thing Eva remembered saying before she passed out was, "Save the blue bowl! I promised."

CHAPTER 16

THE HEADLINES

Eva's new baby boy was born next to his dead father's crushed body amid the remains of the Hotel La Posada, mother and baby afterwards rushed to the hospital. That Eva was alive was a miracle in itself, but to be pulled out in the nick of time to give immediate birth to a baby seemed like it must have been divine intervention, even to Eva.

Eva's left arm was amputated an hour after her escape. The surgeon removed it at the shoulder. The bass had clamped down on her radial artery and caused the arm to die and become gangrenous. Her musical career was over as she had known it. She was a one-armed bass player. No more did gender matter; the arm loss trumped that. What was worse, Eva would never be able to put her arms around Theo.

The baby was a healthy six-pound male whose birth certificate read Theo Bernard De Plain. Place of birth: the rubble of a once lovely hotel.

For one day in 1995 the world's newspapers proclaimed, "Miracle baby born after seven days under rubble." The press ate the whole event up. Cameras, reporters, people offering her book deals, and companies wanting endorsements. She was in shock and horrified by the spectacle. She had lost the love of her life, her arm, and her profession in one week. If ever there was a reason for severe postpartum depression, this had to be it. Now they, whomever they were, wanted a book deal. The thought of capitalizing on Bernard's death and her survival made Eva as sick as the smell of the still uncovered decomposing bodies in Mexico City. *Never will I make money or even talk of this event again. Never. I must start over, beginning now,* she told herself.

She struggled to sit up in bed with her small, brown baby suckling her right breast, the same breast that had helped position the bowl onto her head to save their lives. Next to the bed were numerous flower arrangements, including a cluster of peonies and roses. She smiled at the ironic imagery, gently picking off a single petal and carefully placing it in her mouth, pondering all that had happened during the last seven days.

At the far end of Eva's hospital room sat a blue bowl with a small, fresh chip on the rim. Taped to the bowl was a note written in Spanish. Translated it read, "Your gift from God to always keep you and all those around you safe."

On seeing the bowl Eva immediately rang for the nurse, whose English was very good. Eva asked for the bowl to be brought closer and inquired who had brought it? The nurse had no explanation. It had been there when she arrived. Eva told the nurse under no circumstance was the bowl to ever leave her room, and when she finally checked out, the bowl was to physically accompany her. The slightly damaged Mexican blue bowl had saved her life. She would never forget it. She had the nurse set some red roses and yellow peonies in the bowl, fill it with water, and place it on the table by her bed. The bowl was part of her and it would always have a prominent place in her life.

Dorothy Rashmusen, Bernard's mother, flew to Mexico City to see Eva on day three of her hospital stay. Dorothy had idolized her son who had been her only living relative. Bernard's loss had obviously affected her deeply. She now looked much older than her actual age of 65. Her hair was in a tight bun at the top of her pale head. The sharp tip of her nose was red and raw. It was obvious she had been crying a great deal. Her blue-grey eyes were swollen and partially shut. A significant aftershock jolted the room but Dorothy never looked up. She just sat next to Eva's bed, staring at the floor without speaking a word. When she finally did speak, she got right to the point: "Eva, did you see Bernard when the earthquake hit?"

Eva explained about Bernard's smile, which seemed to make Dorothy breathe easier. Knowing her son's final moments had been joyful relieved her pain. She was gratified he apparently didn't suffer and his last thought was of Eva and his unborn son. Dorothy was also happy that part of her beloved only child persevered. Theo Bernard De Plain was now her only living relative.

Bernard's crushed body had been found in the same place that Eva had last seen it, on the queen-sized bed, underneath 10 tons of rock, comprising floors two through four. Eva was only one of three people in the hotel to survive its collapse, all on the renovated floor.

Eva had known Bernard came from a moneyed background, but she had always tried to ignore his past. There was no ignoring the obvious now when Dorothy arranged for herself, Eva, and Theo to be flown home in a large, private plane as soon as they were given medical clearance. No words were spoken by either Dorothy or Eva on the trip. There was only the deep breathing sound of the sleeping, healthy newborn during the four-hour and 18-minute flight from Mexico City to New York. The plane swooped down smoothly carrying its still-quiet passengers: Eva, Theo, Dorothy, the remains of Bernard, and one slightly damaged blue Mexican flower bowl.

CHAPTER 17

PENWELL FALLS IN LOVE

Ashton B. Charmers had one predominant goal in September 1981: to meet Joseph Penwell III during the retrospective of the early California artist Maynard Dixon at the San Francisco Academy of Art. The ticket price for opening night was an unbearable $250 and one had to join the damn museum. Ashton hoped his new profession was a good choice as it was turning out to cost more just to get his foot in the door than he used to make in a good month of scamming little old ladies.

A small black-and-white photo of Penwell which Ashton had clipped out from a museum bulletin of donors was Ashton's guiding force. The event was packed and Ashton was thinking of maybe appropriating a jacket at the coat check before he departed in order to help defer the cost of his admission. Being well dressed had become an obsession for Ashton, having had nothing but worn-out clothes in Oklahoma. Even though he couldn't afford the best off the rack, he found that in San Francisco there was always a way to acquire something of quality. Tonight the coat room was looking ever more alluring: at least he would come away with a nice-looking jacket or two.

All the men looked like the crumpled photo Ashton had been carrying around in his billfold for the last two weeks. Finding Penwell seemed to be a lost cause. "I have to find a nondescript, middle-aged, well-dressed man at a huge museum opening in San Francisco," Ashton sighed, realizing that at 27 he was the only one remotely young at the gathering.

Then fate intervened. The Dixon exhibit contained a large group of Native American subjects ranging from small landscapes filled with Indians to larger figurative pieces. One of the two Dixons that Ashton had already seen in person before the night's opening, EARTH KNOWER, loaned from the Oakland Art Museum, was directly in front of him.

Ashton was shocked that he could become so enthralled by the painting. He actually had a guttural response to Dixon's Indian portrait. The artist had captured the essence of humanity, something even he could appreciate. Being from Oklahoma, a land whose desolation could be palatable, Ashton understood the loneliness and isolation that exuded from Dixon's painting, created a half-century earlier. Ashton the art admirer and potential coat thief was mesmerized by Dixon's composition. It was during this rare moment of reflection—similar to that of watching his brother being pelted in the head by hail and knowing his life was about to change—that Ashton once again felt something deep in his gut. However this time it was a positive feeling.

As the art gods would have it, it was at this very moment that Penwell noticed Ashton. In a twist of fate, Penwell found Ashton, not the other way around. The young, semi-hot Ashton, dark hair slicked back and intensely staring at the painting, captured Penwell. Both portrait and viewer made for a compelling sight.

"Amazing how Dixon understood composition so completely. Looks like you get him," Penwell commented, admiring Ashton's smooth skin and hair.

Ashton was shocked his mark had found him. It took him a couple of seconds to register that the man in the crumpled photo was talking to him, and not only talking but sizing him up appreciatively. Ashton snapped back into stalking mode.

"Yes, yes, you're right. Dixon was a master. I'm especially mesmerized by this 1931 painting EARTH KNOWER. I've seen it before in Oakland. It's a shame they weren't able to get the preliminary study to go along with the piece. My understanding is it's also right here in northern California." Ashton had been practicing this speech for weeks, trying to get the words to sound spontaneous. He had planned to bring his prey to this very painting once he had located him. It was to be his way of communicating what a great art dealer he was. The speech had come out well. He was particularly pleased about the word "preliminary" as it was an art word he had never used in conversation other than before his bathroom mirror. The sudden appearance of Penwell worked in Ashton's favor, as he believed he sounded completely sincere.

"Wow, you really know your Dixons! I don't think we have met before. I'm Joseph Penwell."

Ashton thought to himself, *Don't forget "the third." That's what got me here. The third. Gotta mean generational wealth.* Then he smiled, extending his hand which Penwell quickly grasped. "Ashton B. Charmers. I'm rather new to San Francisco. It's nice to meet someone who loves Dixon as much as I do. I think of myself as somewhat of a Dixon-phile. This show is sorely overdue. As an art dealer, I'm shocked that Dixon's prices are so undervalued. It has to be only a matter of time before the market catches on." He was reciting what a couple of well-heeled San Francisco dealers had said to him. Ashton loved calling himself an art dealer. It sounded real. He felt like he was an art dealer.

"Yes, you are so right, but don't be telling all your clients that. I'm trying to get a couple more major pieces before the rest of the art world figures it out," replied the obviously smitten Penwell.

"More major pieces! So you have one, do you?" Ashton acted impressed.

"Yes, it's here in the show. One I'm very proud of that's fairly important."

Ashton of course knew this already. "There are a couple of pieces in private collections that I think are exceptional. Like TRADITIONS, Dixon's 1922 masterpiece. That painting gives me the chills, which usually is hard to do, if you know what I mean." Ashton knew it was a risk to mix in sexual innuendo so quickly, but if he'd gauged Penwell's body language correctly, he thought the hint would set him off.

"Really!" Penwell replied with his right eyebrow twitching ever so slightly. "Well then this should really make you excited: that's my painting and you're welcome to come visit it at my house once the exhibit runs its course!"

Vindicated by the not-so-subtle invitation, Ashton leaned forward and touched Penwell's hand. "I would like that very much." With that, the two bonded and walked side by side for the rest of the evening, Penwell stopping every so often to introduce Ashton to the art world VIPs. They then left together for Penwell's home on Montgomery Street, an early preview of sorts. It was just a few blocks from where Dixon's old studio used to be.

CHAPTER 18

MAKING MONEY

Penwell fell hard for Ashton, the kind of infatuation that hurts if you're left alone. It was surprising for a man used to having the upper hand.

Ashton knew he had his victim right where he wanted him. He quickly solidified his new position as significant other. He spent plenty of time in bed with Penwell, knowing this was his strong suit. The more he could control Penwell's sexual desire, the easier it would be to gain trust.

Money came from all directions once Ashton had the confidence of his middle-aged lover. Every day was spent looking at art, working out, having sex, eating at the best restaurants, and of course searching for new pieces to add to Penwell's growing collection.

Ashton was gifted with a gold-card introduction to every art dealer in the city. He was now referred to as Penwell's art advisor and close friend. This was Penwell's code to let any potential suitors know Ashton was his, so stay away. A few envious friends still made passes at the dark-haired new boyfriend. They figured with Penwell's great taste, Ashton must be special. Of course Ashton understood this innately and stuck close to his human ATM, no matter how tempting it might be to wander.

He concentrated on sharing Penwell's priorities. He searched for the artists Penwell discussed over dinner, those he was looking to acquire, and then did a preemptive strike. Ashton called all the worthwhile dealers, let them know he was looking for a particular artist's work, then arranged his own finder's fee ahead of time. Any dealer offering Penwell a painting would be expected to give ABC a secret consulting fee of 10 percent of the cost of the painting.

An additional consulting fee was doled out by Penwell to Ashton for negotiating the best deal on his behalf from the dealer or person who owned the painting. As far as Penwell was concerned, this was a miniscule price to pay for a loving companion and occasionally he figured it actually saved him money. Penwell's reasoning was he might even do much better in the long run as he despised negotiating for a break on the price and all the art dealers knew this flaw, thus rarely giving him much in the way of a discount. Penwell also expected that for his fee, Ashton would check out the painting's condition along with any restoration or provenance concerns. Ashton didn't really understand what this entailed but he would grill the dealers when looking at a piece for Penwell. He would recite verbatim to Penwell what the dealer had said, then listen and watch intently for Penwell's reaction.

If a painting had restoration around the edges where the frame had bumped the canvas, Penwell might say, "Well I don't think a little in-painting should kill the deal." Ashton would parrot, "Exactly what I thought. It is after all minimal and a great piece." If there was an old tear in a significant area of the painting, Penwell would fret, "I am not sure about that tear, it's in the face and it's so prominent. I just think it might bother me and affect the value later on." Ashton would easily manipulate this to, "My feelings exactly. I know you love the painting but as your art consultant I don't know in good faith if I could have you buy this piece. The repair is in the face for god's sake. It's not like it's in-painting."

In this way Penwell made all the decisions about whether to buy or not based on Ashton's advice, advice he had given Ashton himself.

To further secure his consulting job, Ashton celebrated every purchase with a night of Penwell fun. Ashton wondered if each art purchase was prompted by a sort of Pavlov's dog reaction, Penwell knowing a guaranteed treat would be forthcoming from the new artwork they acquired.

Charmers increasingly learned how important restoration was. He slowly picked up on the terms and what the financial implications were. He began asking dealers, "Do you know who did the restoration on this piece?" Once he had that knowledge, it was easy enough to call the restorer and let them know he was working for Mr. Joseph Penwell III, after which they would amazingly give up confidential information about paintings they had worked on. Penwell was a powerful force and if he blackballed somebody, many of their restoration jobs would dry up.

Most importantly, Ashton found out that restorers could be a great resource for artwork. He would show up unexpectedly as an excuse to check on a painting for Penwell, and then snoop around the studio looking for anything great. A little prying and the restorer might unintentionally share the owner's name of said painting on the table for cleaning. If a dealer owned the piece, Ashton would contact them and let them know he was looking for a specific artist. If it also just happened to be the same painting getting cleaned and being prepared for sale, so much the better. Ashton was however surprised to find the restorers didn't really bribe well. He would offer a little "finder's fee" for helping him obtain something out of a private collection, but it did no good. *Irritatingly honest, not like art dealers.* Charmers made a note of this fact, one that would be useful in the future.

The art world, Ashton decided, was like being a cop. There was a brotherhood. Dealers rarely squealed on each other. The only dealers he would badmouth to Penwell were those who didn't give him what he considered to be an appropriate cash kickback, which of course Penwell knew nothing about. Ashton's customary remuneration was five to ten percent, but sometimes he squeezed out more if he believed that the dealer he was doing business with really wanted to move the painting along. Ashton assured he would be buying many more paintings for substantial amounts in the future. He was amazed how the art dealers never ratted him out. If they had, Penwell would have dumped him, great sex or not. Dealers would rather pay Ashton his bribe than potentially lose the sale. For the first time in his life, Ashton had found a job that fit his abilities and colleagues with whom he could work harmoniously.

CHAPTER 19

THE MAKING OF A KINGPIN

Tommy Thompson was raised on the outskirts of Oklahoma City in a hardscrabble neighborhood. T.T., as his friends called him, was born in 1945 into a lower middleclass family with two hardworking parents. His mother was a stay-at-home mom who made clothes and churned goat cheese for extra money. Joe Thompson, T.T.'s dad, ran the local Woolworth's store in Elk City.

Growing up in Oklahoma was safe but boring for a boy who had large expectations for his life. Tommy had never met anyone famous or rich. He knew very few people who had even gone to college, but somehow he knew he would rise to the wealthiest ranks. T.T. had a natural gift for numbers. He probably would have never left Oklahoma but his father had always encouraged Tommy to shoot for the stars. Joe Thompson repeatedly told T.T., "Don't limit yourself by staying in Oklahoma. Go to California. That's where you will find your destiny and make your fortune."

Joe Thompson had tried to move to California in the early 1930s following the great migration of Okies escaping the Dust Bowl. The birth of Tommy's older brother had kept Joe from completing his journey to the Golden State. It was a dream destroyed, haunting Joe for the rest of his life. He believed if he had made it to California he wouldn't have been stuck working in a dead-end job at Woolworth's.

T.T.'s grades in school were always A's, except in art class. He found art an area too subjective and frankly boring for his analytical mind. T.T. didn't worry about a couple of B's on his transcripts. Tommy told his father, "Who really cares about a B in art, Pops? It's not like I plan on ever becoming an artist. I could care less about art history." Joe couldn't disagree with his son's reasoning, but worried because the school counselor had scolded Tommy for ruining what could have been a 4.0 average.

Joe wanted to make sure that T.T. got a proper education. "Son, you will never have to be at the call of others. Your dreams can be your own, not predetermined by someone else's interpretation of your abilities," he insisted. Joe's advice to his son stopped suddenly. After working every day of his life, Joe died at 58 of a massive heart attack on T.T.'s 18th birthday. He died on the job at the Elk City Woolworth's. He was struggling with a heavy box filled with ceramic bowls from Mexico. He collapsed on the spot.

T.T. got his acceptance letter to OU, the only school he had applied to, the same week in 1963 as his father's death. T.T. could only imagine how excited his father would have been, knowing his youngest son would not have to toil away his life away in a job with little hope of advancement as he had. With the death of his father, T.T. vowed he would not let his father's words go unheeded. He would succeed and own that very Woolworth's someday and put a plaque up with his father's name.

The four years at OU were some of T.T.'s most cherished. The football team, a tradition at the University of Oklahoma, won three national championships during T.T.'s four years there. Amazingly, T.T didn't see a single game. He was too busy studying. Not that he didn't like football, he just liked learning and was too preoccupied to take three hours out of his day for fun. Tommy's innate ability with numbers and his love of geology drove him to succeed.

The only sport T.T. allowed himself time to play was golf. There was something that clicked with golf and the budding entrepreneur. It was a game of ethics. You called penalties on yourself and no one checked you. Tommy would hit the links in the late afternoon when he could play fast. The quicker, the better. Nine holes in one hour. That was all the time Tommy could spare from school. The golf courses he went to in Oklahoma City were not country club quality. The only ones he could afford were on the outskirts of town, run by individuals who loved golf more than they had sense. Paying five dollars to hit a ball onto buffalo-grass fairways with scraggly elm trees and small, bumpy greens was T.T.'s kind of fun. They were poor man's golf courses, situated on the worst land, unsuitable for agriculture or grazing. Playing golf in Oklahoma in the summer toughened T.T. for life. The air was thick with humidity. A 105-degree day with a 30 mile-per-hour wind was a typical summer afternoon. If he didn't finish before dusk, he would be surrounded by mosquitoes and no-see-ums and spend the next week tending bites. Whatever lush areas he did see around the mainly barren course were filled with poison ivy, just begging him to come in and look for his lost ball. So much for Oklahoma golf.

In a harsh environment, only the tough survive and flourish, learning to adapt when things don't go as planned. Be prepared and stay focused. You must have enough water (or capital) in a hot environment. These were the life lessons Tommy took away from golf on Oklahoma's high plains.

T.T. was able to do some of his best creative thinking during his afternoon games. It was while playing one of his fast rounds of golf that he came up with the concept of shale oil and natural gas. He saw small hills of shale oozing an oily-like substance and often smelled methane gas. Occasionally he would hit a ball over to one of the outcroppings of fossilized shale and find himself picking through the layers of fragile rocks, rubbing two stones together and carefully examining the residue between his fingers, smelling the oil scent: money and power.

Oil had always been an important part of Oklahoma's history and growing up working summer jobs in the oil fields gave Tommy a unique understanding of the limitations of the business. He realized early on if he could increase the productivity, money would follow. So T.T. spent his days underneath the OU stadium in his small laboratory, working on complex algorithms to remove oil and natural gas from the shale reservoirs of the Great Plains basin. When the Sooners were playing for the Big Eight title, T.T. was deep in thought planning his life in Oklahoma oil and gas. It was really quite simple, he thought. *The world runs on oil, there is a limited supply, and the world is growing fast. Simple supply and demand.* He would always hold golf in a very special place in his heart for his awakening.

T.T.'s biggest decision came after his graduation from OU He was admitted to both Stanford and the Wharton School. Both had exemplary business programs. It was a huge accomplishment for a young man from such common beginnings. Tommy graduated in 1967, the year of San Francisco's Summer of Love. Coming from a small cow town, a conservative and inhibited environment, Stanford sounded more inviting. His father had told him go to California and T.T. never looked back.

CHAPTER 20

CALIFORNIA LAND

Tommy Thompson entered Stanford with some of the best and brightest minds that would become America's most influential business leaders. He realized the people he met would become his lifelong friends and business associates, replacing his Oklahoma childhood friends who didn't understand his drive to succeed. His high school classmates were happy to work, live, and die within a hundred miles of where they grew up. The Stanford group was driven and very aware of the future. The class of '68 would become legendary for the number of leaders in the field of business it produced. These class connections were crucial for T.T.'s future accomplishments.

With a degree from Oklahoma in mechanical engineering and an MBA from Stanford, T.T.'s first job was helping an old California family, if there was such a thing, manage their money. The patriarch, Elias "Lucky" Baldwin, whose Ophir Mining Company was at the northern end of the Comstock Lode in the Virgin Range in Nevada in 1859, became wealthy overnight and his descendants still managed to retain much of his extraordinary fortune. A Stanford classmate who had watched T.T. breeze through all his classes recognized T.T.'s unique intellect and made the initial introduction. T.T. actually secured his first job before he even graduated from Stanford: managing the Baldwin family fortune.

T.T.'s greatest gift was his ability to see years into the future. He didn't think in terms of months, but years. He looked at five- and 10-year increments, which is rare for a man in his twenties. Crunching numbers came innately to the tall Oklahoman. He observed social events and used his logic to turn this into money. His first big play was buying up land on the California mid-coast. T.T. knew land was a limited resource and would be increasingly valuable in the very near future, 10 years at most. He figured the Vietnam War wouldn't last forever and Nixon, who was likely to take over as president in 1969, was a smart man who understood business. Businessmen realize you can't wage war too long before it starts to hurt the economy. T.T. figured Nixon must also see the future. It was so obvious. Land was like oil, a limited resource.

In the summer of '68, Tommy presented his plan to put the Baldwins' capital to work ahead of the curve. He predicted the young men would come back home from the war, start families, build homes, and where better than California? Everybody loves California with its great weather. This would be where the boom would start.

T.T. was very convincing in his presentation to the Baldwin family and obviously smart. His calculations of profit returns, if correct, were huge. He encouraged investing in very large land purchases even though real estate was flat at best for the moment. Unfortunately, the ever present wild card, Mother Nature, threw a curve ball at him. The worst flooding in a decade occurred in January of '69, causing $30 million in land damages. Nine days of torrential rains with 12 deaths was an extremely adverse beginning for a young man who expected to be extremely wealthy someday soon.

The Baldwin family called a board of directors meeting to discuss their land purchases and the disastrous consequences. Five of the dead had actually occurred on the Baldwins' recently purchased land north of Santa Barbara. A hillside overlooking the ocean gave way, burying three families in coastal earth. Included was the CEO of a large movie studio. His family would sue for lost wages and this would amount to at least an additional $4 million in damages. The topic at hand was what to do with the brilliant young Mr. Thompson. His short tenure had probably cost the family close to $10 million in capital, a less than auspicious beginning.

The final vote came down to gut feeling. The majority of the family members truly liked and believed in the good-natured Tommy. One of the heirs reminded the family their original wealth had come from Lucky Baldwin's great silver find and land purchases. Maybe T.T. was correct in his thinking. If they believed in Thompson's analysis of land profits, which were calculated excluding mineral rights, the family would have to believe in the assessment and stand behind the young gun.

One way to find out how committed a person is to an idea is to make them financially liable for the investment. The Baldwin family decided to ask T.T. to be personally liable for his land purchases. They would keep him on and give him a share of the land as his pay, but he also would be responsible for any liabilities and subsequent losses that might result, no matter how large.

66

T.T. agreed but with one caveat. He wanted a five-acre lot next to the Cypress Point Club golf course on the Monterey Peninsula specifically deeded to him as his portion of the deal. He would be responsible for buying the lot at the current market price, which was now significantly depressed due to the widespread floods. He would also be equally responsible for any further lawsuits that might occur due to landslides and if land values went down he was on the hook for that as well.

The Baldwins agreed to keep T.T. on board and give him his five acres. The land he wanted was hard to build on. The wooded lot consisted of mainly cypress trees and large rock outcroppings, though it did have an incredible view of the 16th hole of Cypress Point Golf Course. T.T. thought, *How could land which is overlooking the greatest hole of golf, surrounded by sculpted cypress trees, not be extremely valuable someday?*

The CEO's family who lost their breadwinner happened to be very reasonable people. T.T. explained that the Baldwin family had just purchased the land that had given way and the responsibility might actually lie with the original landowners who did not disclose any topographical weakness. They would probably have to sue both parties, which would take years of litigation. T.T. proposed that since this was hallowed ground, so to speak, to the family now, he would give the family the 10 acres that fell on top of their house for free as well as cover any costs that weren't covered by insurance to fix their badly damaged home. He explained his vision of the future and what land values would become. He suggested if they could hold onto the land for 20 years they would be rich beyond their wildest dreams, as large lots overlooking the ocean would become extremely valuable soon. If they would just keep the land, they would do better than if they filed a lawsuit.

He was so sure that the family would benefit this way, T.T. agreed to put into writing that after five years, if the family wanted out of the deal, he would purchase the 10 acres for $5 million regardless of current value. If the family added additional upgrades to the house, he would also purchase their new home in five years at whatever the cost to build the structure was or the current home value, whichever was greater. The family agreed. No lawsuits were filed and T.T. was off to make his fortune.

T.T. knew at the present time all he owned were the rights to five acres next to Cypress Point and a job that was tenuous at best. He had five years to make at least $5 million to cover the bet, so to speak, and much more if they built up their home. T.T.'s total net worth was $50K at the time. Work took on a whole new meaning.

His first step was to try and recover the potential cost of rebuilding the damaged CEO's house. He contacted the old owners of the land and explained the libelous situation now brewing. He didn't want to sue the ex-owners but thought they had not been forthcoming in the disclosure they had given the Baldwin family regarding the land. Since the Baldwins had a team of mainly idle lawyers, he felt obligated to use the family resources to renegotiate their land purchase. After very little negotiation, he secured more than enough in compensation to pay for rebuilding the CEO's family home with money to spare.

The land purchases finally started to pay big dividends in the early 1970s, which allowed T.T. to progress from managing other people's money to managing his own. With his investment in the land deal he was able to walk away with nearly $5 million in cash and the Cypress property. His commitment to the CEO's family to repurchase their land still had two more years before they would call his hand, so T.T. went to work to double down his earnings.

T.T. decided it was time to revisit his past: oil. Removing oil deposits out of shale was still not cost effective as oil was only three dollars a barrel, but it was obvious that demand for oil would only expand in the United States. The war was winding down and people were spending on themselves, most of which required oil or its distillates. Commuters, with a penchant for heavy, fast, fuel-inefficient cars and work trucks, would lead to increased oil consumption and money for T.T. He just needed to partner in an oil company and wait for the profits to start building.

If you're from Oklahoma you go back to your roots in the Sooner state, knowing there's lots of oil there. T.T. reunited with boyhood friends and contacted each one who potentially had mineral rights or knew how to get them. The entire year of 1972 was spent rounding up these mineral rights with the plan to drill for oil. T.T.'s goal was to spend the entire $5 million he had made and double or even triple it before he had to buy the Santa Barbara land. He had discovered that if you had one acre of land with numerous owners you could still drill for oil, so ideally he would find a couple of neighbors with enough land to make an acre, form an LLC, drill the well, and hopefully split up the profits. T.T. would take his share for putting the deal together, he would buy any land that had to be purchased, and he would help to arrange for drilling and long-term care. This same strategy had been executed in West Texas in the rich and long-lasting Permian Basin oil wells by Pleas E. Smith, whose court cases T.T. had stumbled on. Smith was a school principal-turned-entrepreneur who became very wealthy by putting dry land farmers together and taking just a small percentage of each oil well. Bigger oil companies had sued to stop the process but the courts upheld the deal. Turns out you don't need much of a percentage of something if the holdings are substantial enough. With oil at three bucks a barrel, T.T. reasoned that he would invest in a small percentage of a whole bunch of his neighbors' land. This was right up his alley. T.T. could talk the talk and knew his neighbors.

By early 1973, T.T. was in full gear with numerous producing oil wells. Some he owned outright. In others, he was a minority partner. Many of his wells were in initial production. The year 1973 turned out to be a very good year to be in the oil business. On October 6th, 1973, Syria and Egypt attacked Israel in what became known as the Yom Kippur War and on October 17th, the Arab oil-producing nations placed an embargo on the United States and other countries that had helped Israel. Oil prices doubled overnight and gasoline prices tripled. Oil shortages occurred and the United States was in its first oil mess. T.T. couldn't have been happier. The United States had to take oil seriously for the first time. The Strategic Petroleum Reserve was instituted. Oil was rationed and Daylight Savings Time began, all to save energy.

T.T.'s wealth exploded overnight. He wasted no time taking advantage of the situation. He knew people would panic and pay more than they should for all things related to oil. So he sold part of his oil ownership to those who would pay more than it would be worth in 10 years. He sold as much oil as he could and also future oil sales at high prices to lock in the profits. Because of T.T.'s ability to see the future, he knew this first shortage would ultimately pass because it was purely driven by OPEC and emotions, not actual oil demand. The world had to have a huge increase in demand to maintain these prices and that was another 30 years off. He understood there would be plenty of opportunities to repurchase the same oil wells he had just sold at better prices in the near future. T.T. simply had to wait until the world became complacent again with regards to its diminishing resource, oil. Most of the world's countries subsidized their oil costs. Until oil was priced around $80 a barrel, not seven dollars, these high valuations for oil and gas would not persevere. He understood the current scare would allow him to make a shitload of money in a short time. The real oil problems were still decades away. T.T.'s oil company was fairly small by oil standards, DYNAMITE INDUSTRIES, inspired by his initials T. and T. The oil embargo lasted through March of '74 and then oil prices dropped to more normal levels. T.T. would be ready for the next oil crisis. He just had to read *The New York Times* and *Washington Post* to know when to buy. The trick of course was to buy five years in advance of the shortage. No problem for the man who saw the future and the future was oil.

CHAPTER 21

BILLIONAIRES CLUB

In 1974, Tommy Thompson wrote a check to the deceased CEO's family for their property north of Santa Barbara. Even though he assured them they would have a far greater return on their land if they could just wait until Santa Barbara exploded, which it surely would, they didn't listen. No matter. T.T. was flush with cash, his ship coming in on oil purchases. Writing the check for $5 million for the coastal land was no problem due to his oil windfall. He also agreed to purchase the $600,000 home they had rebuilt. He overpaid for the package and gave them another million. T.T. actually felt bad for the family. He understood the money would represent the majority of all the wealth this family would ever have, due to the untimely death of their breadwinner. It reaffirmed T.T.'s belief that those who have the capital to wait will always have the upper hand in business.

He wrote the check, held onto the land for 10 more years, and sold it for $25 million. Tommy Thompson was one of those men that always had a golden touch, never had a mortgage, and was a billionaire by the age of 43 in 1988. His home base was near Carmel, California.

When you are in your prime and don't have to work ever again, you get bored. To keep life interesting, wealthy people handle things differently. For some it's more money, more work, more money. The only way to judge one's worth is by financial holdings. For others it's charity work, finding a cause to believe in and throwing money and talent toward that goal.

The super-rich are often very unhappy, especially when wealth comes early. It seems hard to imagine how one could be unfulfilled when there are no worries about mortgages, food, clothing, or even gasoline prices. How bad could it be? The pressures on the super-wealthy are in many ways like those on movie stars. People seek you out who have a weird need to be close to the epicenter of power. Everyone assumes the super-rich must have extraordinary intelligence to have become so successful. While often the case, this is not always true.

The billionaires club has its own groupies, whether wanted or not. Finding true friends becomes difficult. Often, billionaires only feel comfortable with other super-rich individuals or childhood friends or the occasional relative who treats them normally. Finding true friends who understand them as a person, not as a freak of nature, are rare, leaving most in the billionaires club with few friends and often without spouses.

Tommy Thompson fell into the typical billionaire's mode. His childhood friends became wealthy through their gas leases, but isolation became a fact of life. The feeling of being alone at the top was one of the most depressing aspects of wealth.

T.T. assumed the typical traits of the super wealthy. Outer appearance seemed of less importance now. Dress usually consisted of an old golf shirt or tee shirt and a baseball cap. Haircuts occurred but only after Tommy's true friends, not the groupies, started to make fun of his unkempt appearance. Because there was no longer a need to show up at any kind of work, business attire and grooming became habits of the past. T.T. always had a golf hat covering most of his early gray hair. In fact, it seemed odd to see him with no hat as his hair developed a permanent twist where the inner rim made contact with his head. The caps themselves were often unusual, adorned with logos of unknown companies or restaurants, like "Bloom's Gallery." The hats were gifts that had meaning only to T.T. and would confuse those who sought to put greater relevance on the brands worn by such a powerful man. "That must be an exceptional restaurant. Maybe he owns it? It has to be great," people would speculate, assuming an extreme endorsement by a great thinker. The fact was, it was just T.T.'s quirky personality. He liked the guy who gave him the cap, nothing more, nothing less. The only cap that actually promoted something of T.T.'s was one embossed in red stitching against a charcoal background: DYNAMITE INDUSTRIES. He didn't wear it to brag, but because he was proud of his company and its many divisions, especially his highly regarded steel production branch.

Clothes were never by designers or fancy. He preferred an assortment of shirts, many from the golf clubs he belonged to or had visited. It wasn't about bragging, just ease of purchase or gifts. No business shirts except for the occasional board meeting and never a tie except for dinner at the Augusta clubhouse, where it was mandatory. Pants were almost always shorts, because as a billionaire one only lives in temperate climates. Like birds, the super-rich follow the weather in their Gulf Streams. Many end up in California, which has the largest number of billionaires per million population. The taxes are high but the weather is great year round.

T.T. kept his life busy by focusing on three areas of interest: golf, sex, and work; not always in that order but usually. Trying to keep boredom away was the goal.

His routine rarely changed. He woke up at 4 am to read the business papers, determine what had happened in Europe and Asia, and prepare to see what New York would bring. He checked the oil and steel prices. He called the office to see what was happening in the commodities market and steel industry. Lunch was made by a personal chef, usually nothing fancy but always of quality and low fat. Living to a ripe, old age was a goal and T.T. planned to accomplish it through exercise and good diet. Dying at 58 like his father was not part of the plan. By 1 pm, Tommy calculated the total for the day's take or the rare loss, and considered his work day over. A good day could profit him $5 million, a great day, $50 million. The money didn't seem real for the country boy from Oklahoma. These were just numbers, a way to count and be counted.

If he thought about the fact that his daily income surpassed most people's entire lifetime's wealth it would be utterly depressing. Just numbers, not real money, was how T.T. tried to deal with his ever-growing empire. Great wealth became a burden. He kept all his personal phone numbers secret or solicitations for donations would be overwhelming. T.T., like most billionaires, had a trust set up and preferred to give big chunks of money as large capital infusions which made a difference rather than small gifts which didn't seem to affect many people.

CHAPTER 22

HOME

T.T. had two homes besides his house near Carmel: an Oklahoma residence for taxes, and a vacation house in Aspen, Colorado, for skiing and profile. These were small and nothing more than hotel-like abodes that didn't really reflect the essence of the man. By the early 1990s, the time had come to build a real home and it was to be placed on the land looking over the 16th hole of Cypress Point, the same property he traded for in that early business deal.

He named his California dream home the 16TH Ranch. He wanted the ranch feeling he remembered growing up in Oklahoma, envisioning a low-profile home that would be mid-century modern and built into a hillside. It would be similar in some ways to the old berm homes Okies were known for, but in a Richard Neutra-meets-Walker Evans kind of way. Instead of a farmer's house with sod and grass on the roof, it would be designed by the best architect he could find who also embraced the Neutra sensibility. Unlike the poor farmers of Oklahoma, T.T. was concerned with security, which was a significant issue for the man with the golden touch, as it is with all high earners. Tommy's huge house would have only two doors to limit access and of course the latest in technology. The area was gated with a security guard to take care of his needs. T.T. was lucky his name was common, Thompson, not Hearst or Rockefeller. Thompson was plain and unknown and he wanted to keep it that way. He encouraged his friends to call him T.T. That way, if he was referred to as Tommy, he knew it was a stranger approaching. T.T. went to extremes to keep his name out of the limelight and did few interviews. The more you were known, the more problems. He had a friend who had been kidnapped and nearly killed. *He was too well known. Always keep a low profile and it will keep you away from real trouble.*

T.T. hired Narz Wieslander, the Norwegian wunderkind, to build the house. At 40, Narz had collected an impressive résumé of public buildings, mostly in Europe. The 16TH Ranch was his first major American residential project. T.T. selected him because he was still young enough to accept direction, a critical consideration for a man who was accustomed to getting his way. T.T. had a vision for his home. It was important that the architect didn't lose sight of this.

The whole project almost didn't get off the ground, courtesy of the Department of Fish and Wildlife, which shut it down before it began. Apparently T.T.'s land had the unfortunate distinction of housing a population of small, endangered insects known as midges. These midges had been found on the Thompson land during a California impact study just weeks before he was scheduled to break ground. T.T. protested to the state land commissioner, pointing out that a major golf course directly next to his land was in existence and how could that property have been built without endangering the midges? It was explained that in 1928 when Cypress Point was built, there were no environmental impact studies required. It was thought then that this species only existed at the national seashore of Point Lobos.

One thing T.T. understood was a mess could often be controlled or even fixed if you hired the world's expert to work on your behalf. All the roads in this odd field of midges led to Dr. James Martin Wolfgang, interestingly an Oklahoma graduate like himself. Professor Wolfgang was working in Portales, New Mexico, at Eastern New Mexico University. Doc W., as his students called him, was not one to leave his laboratory for anyone, including a billionaire. He would agree to investigate T.T.'s problem only if T.T. would fund his nonprofit foundation dedicated to his lifelong passion, the investigation of new species of chironomids, or nonbiting midges.

T.T. eagerly agreed, $100,000 was placed in trust for the New World Chironomid Foundation, and T.T. sent his jet for the professor the next day. Doc W. set up a comprehensive system of traps and carefully identified all of the midges in and around the Thompson land. The only midges discovered were of the common species and of no relevance to the world of endangered insects. It turns out, the unique gnat population had simply blown in while swarming over adjacent Point Lobos, just a visitor to the property during the initial impact study.

Now Narz could get down to business. Sixty percent of the home was built into the side of the rocky hill, with the remainder peeking out like lichen gripping a stone. The roof was covered in tall grass and three old cypress trees. The only way to tell it was a roof was the three massive rock fireplaces above the berm. These were camouflaged as small huérfanos instead of manmade structures.

Great windows of bulletproof glass looked out onto the ocean. Each pane was individually fabricated in Germany at a cost of $75,000, but money was not an issue, just safety. The 400-square-foot deck was made of Dynamite steel and copper. It snaked its way around the semicircular-shaped exterior.

T.T. took great care and spared no expense to save all the cypress trees on his lot. The few specimens that stood squarely in the footprint of the house were carefully transplanted to new, safe locations. Each tree cost $50,000 to move. The trees were what made the ranch special. Even a single lost cypress would be considered a failure on his part. T.T. personally watched each tree's removal and replanting. No trees died on his watch. The 16TH Ranch was snuggled into its old-growth forest as if it had always been there. He understood Mother Nature could be unforgiving. His tornado years on the high plains of Oklahoma had shown him this firsthand. He tried to be in balance with his natural surroundings, and hoped those surroundings would likewise care for him.

The Thompson house was built primarily made of steel. More steel was used in the construction of the house than Narz considered necessary, but T.T. realized of all the perils that could cause an untimely death, a major tumbler while he was sleeping was the most likely. If it occurred, it wouldn't be due to a structural problem with the 16TH Ranch.

T.T.'s steel company had been purchased during a distress sale, his favorite way to buy. An out-of-date Youngstown steel factory had floundered for nearly a decade. Competition overseas had become too great. He realized the steel company could still compete in a world market but would need to specialize if it was expected to succeed.

Focusing on making his steel the highest-grade strength any steel company had to offer, but at a competitive price, T.T. knew he had the capital to make a great product. He would lose money until the brand was established, then he would take the market share. Once again, his superior capitalization would give him the upper hand. Who wouldn't buy better grade steel if it was as cost effective as the shitty stuff coming out of China? The tag line for Dynamite was: *Even dynamite can't hurt our steel.* All of T.T.'s homes utilized liberal amounts of Dynamite steel. T.T. used his uncanny ability to see into the future once more, predicting that once the steel was in place it would only be a matter of time before some natural disaster would occur and hopefully his buildings would still be in standing. Among the markets he built in commercially was Mexico City. Many substantial buildings were retrofitted using Dynamite steel, with its impressive large logo embossed on every beam. For now, when it came to constructing his own home, using too much steel was impossible, and only one kind was allowed, Dynamite steel.

CHAPTER 23

ARTWORK FOR THE 16TH RANCH

After three years of construction on the 16TH Ranch, T.T.'s Cypress Point home was completed in 1996. With the house finally finished and all the common species of midges safely buried under 10 tons of concrete and steel, T.T. decided to decorate his home and realized he didn't know jack about art. He now wished he had paid more attention during his high school art classes. He hated being uninformed about any subject, especially one that involved putting hard-earned capital at risk. Currently his art holdings were limited to a golf hat with a gallery name embossed on the front, a gift from one of his golfing buddies.

What T.T. did know, as Doc W. had proven, was that there was always an expert he could consult. He had an acquaintance he knew from a board relationship in San Francisco, so he gave one Joseph Penwell a call.

Penwell was flattered when T.T. asked if he might be able to help him with art acquisitions for his new home. Of course, Penwell was well aware of Thompson's ranking in the financial world. Penwell was wealthy, but Tommy was a freak of nature, one of the richest men in the world. Spending time with the rich and powerful was something Penwell relished. He loved the art world but also loved collecting rich and famous people in his inner circle. So Penwell invited T.T. up on the weekend for a private viewing of his extensive art collection and to give him some ideas on what he thought important when starting a collection.

Penwell lived in a nondescript building on Montgomery Street. Its plainness was limited only to the exterior. Inside, the energy thrived. Numerous gallery walls with well-thought-out lighting and minimal furniture punctuated the enormous foyer where Penwell's impressive collection of pop art began. The lineup started with an early Lichtenstein from the sixties, a large painting with a fist hitting a man's face and the red letters "POW" inscribed. There was a Warhol of the yellow Marilyn variety, and also a huge 72-by-140-inch canvas by Billy Schenck depicting a cowgirl naked from the waist up roping a calf.

Upstairs was a modernist floor, then an impressionist floor, an Early California painting floor, and even a throwback to Victorian times, an Indian room. This incongruent room was filled with California baskets and Navajo rugs along with a few simple-looking Hopi kachinas interspersed. Penwell explained in the 1880s to 1900 it was not uncommon for wealthy collectors to dedicate a single room like this to Indian arts and crafts. Native populations were being obliterated and it was assumed the majority of Indians in America would be exterminated by the 1920s, thus it was important to collect their artifacts. These arts and crafts had become extremely collectible and were now recognized as fine art. Indian casinos were building their own museums and displaying great examples of work from their tribes. Values had skyrocketed. Most of the big casino collections were from tribes in California. It happened that Penwell loved early California baskets and had acquired a large collection of these before prices had escalated, including numerous examples by the master weaver Dat So La Lee. Penwell pointed out, "Not all art escalates in value, of course. The world of art can be brutal. Everyone I know has some scars if they're a serious collector."

T.T. instinctively understood the best art always appreciated more than the rest even if he overpaid. As a savvy businessman he understood going in that he was an easy mark in this field and figured a man like Penwell, who had dedicated his life to collecting art and was a big benefactor to the art world, must know the ins and outs of such an unregulated and imperfect market. Because T.T. understood market force he realized that there was no definitive way of gauging art values. These niche markets are rare in business, but when they occur the margins can be great, which of course is a deterrent if you don't know what you're buying. In an imperfect market such as this, there are generally no leaders in the field. There were some large companies that sold art—Sotheby's, Christie's, and to a lesser extent, Bonhams—but with respect to the overall art field, they were only a small component. Art dealers generated the majority of art sales in the United States, which was in the billions. In fact the black market alone was a $6 billion industry. Big money and no real regulation was not a business model Tommy Thompson was used to but one he found interesting.

What made something worth 10 times more than a similar sized painting often came down to taste, year made, and various unexplainable elements a very left-brained analytical person like Tommy Thompson could never wrap his mind around. He fully understood his shortcomings when it came to art evaluation and this was where Penwell came into the equation, to guide him and help him avoid the art scammers who understood it would be easy to take a client like him to the cleaners. For T.T. it really didn't matter if he overpaid for a piece, but he didn't want to buy a fake or a poor example.

As if he was discussing business with his board, T.T. launched into the no-nonsense rationale for his newfound interest. "What I want are a few good paintings I can enjoy which hopefully will be a decent investment. I know what I like and don't, but don't know what's good. I have a few key places I want to fill at my new home and my decorator will do the rest. I am willing to wait for the right piece and cost is not that important. I'm only interested in quality, which is where I'm hoping you can come in?"

Penwell was excited to have the opportunity to guide someone of Thompson's wealth, as obvious from his high-pitched response. "T.T., I live for art! How about we start by strolling through my art galleries and you tell me what turns you on?"

It didn't take long for the man from Oklahoma to know that modern art was not on his art menu. A small drip painting by Jackson Pollock and a bigger piece by Willem de Kooning looked like oil spills he used to see under his '57 Chevy. It seemed absurd that someone would pay millions of dollars for what he viewed as dirty pieces of cardboard.

A slightly peeved Joseph Penwell realized this was typical of a beginner. With the correct encouragement, T.T. nonetheless might become a big donor to one of his favorite museums and it was important he was guided in a proper fashion. Penwell hoped he could groom the billionaire to help when it came time for museum acquisitions, which would help solidify Penwell's own position in San Francisco's social hierarchy.

Finally two paintings caught T.T.'s attention. They were two large Yosemite landscapes of Half Dome, one by Wayne Thiebaud and the other by Gregory Kondos. Penwell explained these two artists had worked together, had similar pop-art styles utilizing heavy pigment, and both were extremely good artists.

The price difference was what T.T. found most interesting. "The piece on the right by Kondos, which is the same size, looks to my untrained eye to be very similar to the Thiebaud. You say they were both done at the same time on the same trip, yet one painting is worth 50 times more than the other? I don't get it."

"Alright," replied Penwell. "Let me explain. Kondos, who in my opinion is equally as talented as Thiebaud, did not get the same exposure. Allan Stone, a great art dealer in New York, represented Thiebaud for decades. Thiebaud did these seminal works of cakes, pies, hot dogs, and lollipops, which are now highly collectible. You saw one on my first floor, remember? It was three slices of multicolored pies?"

"Sorry, doesn't ring a bell."

This irritated Penwell as it was one of his more important pieces and he had discussed it at length, explaining the pop art genre versus realism, but he ignored T.T.'s response. "It was a seminal work of Thiebaud's and had once been in Allan Stone's gallery. That gallery was an important venue for art, especially in the sixties. The exposure Thiebaud received is one of the big reasons these two artists are now so differently priced. In fact, it is my understanding that Kondos even helped box and ship the Thiebaud painting you saw downstairs to New York! Ironic, isn't it?"

T.T. didn't seem to grasp that irony.

Undeterred, Penwell went on to explain that Thiebaud's Yosemite pieces were not nearly as valuable as his early pastry pieces and probably never would be because they were not what Thiebaud was best known for. Yes, the Yosemite painting was larger and very compelling but it was not a row of key-lime pie slices, which is what the fans wanted.

T.T. was frustrated. "I know I got a B in art class in high school, but how could a small painting of pies be worth so much more than a magnificent scene of Yosemite, one of the great wonders of the world? I don't get it. I like the landscapes. I would much rather have them than paintings of cakes or cookies or whatever kind of pastry he is known for, and for that matter, I like the Kondos just as much as the Thiebaud, which apparently is not nearly as valuable?"

Penwell was encouraged that any progress was being made with this neophyte. "OK, now you're acting like a collector, figuring out what you like and don't. So from an investment perspective, the rise in value of the Kondos may actually be greater once the world figures out the relationship between these two great artists." Penwell, with a dry laugh, added, "It's funny how time and the death of an artist help move the process along."

"Dead is better?" queried T.T.

"Yes," assured Penwell. "In this business, death is always a good thing for prices." Penwell, not liking his own words, even though true, quickly changed the subject. "T.T., if you like landscapes, let's move on to my early American and California wing."

In a dark room on the top floor where dozens of paintings were lined up on a salmon-colored wall, Penwell continued, "These are what I would consider to be the best of the American traditional landscape artists. Most are traditional in their imagery, though Thomas Benton and Maynard Dixon may be stretching it a bit as many consider them quasi-modernist."

This didn't mean dick to T.T., but he nodded his head respectfully. Then all the art babel he had been listening to suddenly clicked for T.T., a man who knew his own mind. "That one, I like that! I understand it and I like the romance of it." He pointed to a large, horizontal painting that was 50 inches by 80 inches, entitled GREEN RIVER VALLEY WYOMING, 1872, one of the greatest works by Thomas Moran.

"Good taste, my friend. That's an outstanding and extremely important painting, in fact one of the most expensive in the house. Well in excesses of $1 million if you went out and tried to find one. Moran was one of our greatest and earliest painters of the West. He is primarily known for his Yellowstone and Grand Canyon pieces. He even did a few down by where you live, near Cypress Point."

"Now we're talking! I would like to get two of those, as large as possible and preferably of Cypress Point," T.T. blurted out as if he was at McDonald's.

Penwell laughed. He couldn't help himself. Totally unprofessional of him, he knew, but T.T. just standing there saying, "I'll take two please," and, "Oh by the way, I want them to be big, the rarest, and the best please," showed how little he understood the art market. The billionaire making such a ridiculously ignorant request amused the man who fought to get every one of the paintings on his fish-colored wall. Collecting masterpieces required education, diligence, connections, and of course, great patience. Money was a secondary requirement.

T.T. rarely felt embarrassed, but he did now. "Obviously this is harder to do than I just made it sound."

Penwell allowed, "I'm sorry, that was rude of me. It's just the process by which one acquires a major Moran of such rarity can take years of searching, great art connections, and plenty of luck. It would be like me wanting to drill two or three wells somewhere in Oklahoma and expecting to make a fortune. I'm sure it isn't that easy."

"You're right about that. It takes years and luck to hit a mother lode, even in a state like Oklahoma. Unless you're working with me," T.T. winked at Penwell, letting him know he understood his giggle was warranted. T.T. realized he might be a billionaire and own important companies but the art world was not his domain. He would always be a B student, and not on the top of anyone's collecting list. "So, Joseph, if you could help guide me into finding a nice painting by what's his name here...."

"His name is Thomas Moran and call me J.P., all my close friends do," said Penwell, trying to say "I'm sorry" in his own way without sounding condescending.

"J.P., if you could help me get a Thomas Moran for my home, I would greatly appreciate it. Obviously I can afford one and when I decide I want something, I generally make it happen. If you could guide me in the right direction I would be grateful."

Penwell loved hearing this. Just what he hoped for: a grateful billionaire. "Not a problem, it will be my pleasure. I know all the people that are in the know, including a very close friend of mine who is quite good at coming up with leads on expensive paintings."

"Great," T.T. wrapped up, mission accomplished. "Please give him my personal contact information. Also, could you discreetly inform this individual of my concern for privacy when it comes to my personal data. I'll have my secretary fax over the details. What your friend's name so I can put it into her list of people who have access to me?"

"Ashton B. Charmers. He has helped me acquire quite a few nice works."

CHAPTER 24

LIFE IN AUGUSTA

Nat Wilson was a sanitation worker who had been employed for 15 years in waste management for the city of Augusta, Georgia, by 1970. Nat was a tall, strong man with a good back and a strong sense of right and wrong. He never complained about his work and idolized Martin Luther King, Jr. When King was murdered in Memphis helping sanitation workers on strike for better wages, Nat took it so hard that he used up a week of sick leave. It was the only time he had ever missed a day of work. Nat had a broad face with a dark complexion. He was proud of his African heritage but still referred to himself as a Negro. Nat's sister, who was the only one to have ever left Augusta, much less Georgia, and resided in Salt Lake City, Utah, had traced their roots all the way back to Kenya. Though no one had ever actually seen proof of this claim, she assured him it was fact.

Deloris, Nat's wife, who had married him when she was 18, worked as a cook at a little chicken shack. She had the distinction of possessing the best fried-chicken recipe in town, thanks to the Wilson family. Her fried chicken was almost as big an attraction as the annual Masters Golf Tournament in April, and even though she was eight months pregnant in April 1970, she wasn't slowing down.

Everyone, including the VIP golfers, made the pilgrimage to devour Deloris' fried chicken. Quite a spectacle, hundreds of middle-aged, generally wealthy, white men pulling up in their big vehicles, then ducking into the little joint to laugh and enjoy their chicken as the only waitress rushed from tiny table to table. Beer flowed, as did the talk of golf. April meant golf and only golf.

For most that live in Augusta, The Masters is like crabbing in Alaska, a short season but if you know what you are doing it can make your year. The poor in Augusta don't play golf, in fact most have never set foot on a golf course. They are well aware that Augusta National Golf Club is a major attraction, just not one you play at as a local. Maybe you occasionally make it into Augusta Country Club, the other club in town.

Augusta National, which has hosted The Masters since 1934, is one of the majors in golf. There are four major tournaments in golf: The

Masters, which is always held in Augusta; the U.S. Open and the PGA, which both change venues every year; and the British Open, which is held in England and changes venues, though not as often as the U.S. Open and the PGA. Of the big four, the biggest is The Masters. It also provides an enormous boost to the income of all Augusta citizens, poor and wealthy.

Augusta National opened in 1932 when Bobby Jones built the course with the famed Scottish architect Alister MacKenzie. Originally it was intended as a course for the people of Augusta but it didn't turn out that way. It turned out to be a course for the business elite. Even with all its social stratifications, it is considered to be the greatest golf club on earth and playing it is golf nirvana. All who come here, including the ultra-elite, feel they are part of something rare and exclusive at the meticulously maintained and beautifully designed course. To be a golfer and have the opportunity to play Augusta is similar to a mountaineer climbing Everest. It's extremely hard to do and once you have, you will cherish the moment forever. The problem is access.

The local Augusta residents understand and somehow respect this elitism. Respect for the course and what it brings to the town crosses all economic barriers, whether black or white. If you're from Augusta, you're happy when April arrives. Master's time in Augusta is akin to Christmas but much, much bigger. The entire town's survival depends on this event, especially that of Augusta's poor. It's trickledown economics in its most basic form. Rich, mainly white men show up and spend as if it was the last day on earth. Every person who makes the pilgrimage acquires some merchandise, usually a few hundred dollars' worth. In 1970, the Augusta pros still ran the merchandising stores. The money would be stacked so high the local sheriff and his deputies would have to stand guard at night as the daily stacks of $100 bills were counted.

During Masters week, the town puts everything on hold. All schools close. Principals and teachers moonlight as hosts, bus drivers, or in the concession stands. For many, their one-week earnings exceed months of pay at their usual jobs.

Ticket scalping is legal except for a few hundred feet in front of the actual event. Everyone needs tickets. The police have to contend with crowd control; no time to worry about scalpers. A ticket with a face value of $50 can bring $1,500. There are cottage industries set up all around town to handle the extreme demand for Masters tickets and everyone makes money on their resale. If you want to find out where to buy a reasonable scalped ticket, just ask one of the off-duty cops. They will not only direct you to their favorite place, but may add, "Just let them know I sent you. They'll take care of you."

The first three days of the tournament consist of practice. These are the only days you can bring a camera and get very close to the players, as long as you stand outside the white lines. The players are on the inside of the lines, while the rest of the world peers in.

The lines are nothing more than thin, white ropes stretching the length of all the fairways, outlining the players' restricted area. A child could easily knock over these thin barriers, but it is understood that the lines are never to be crossed. The only way to breach the white lines of exclusivity is to know a player or a member. They're the only people that can access a coveted Masters badge for a friend. Regular Masters tickets, extremely hard to come by in themselves, don't allow the holder to penetrate the white lines. Only the badge holders can cross over those lines. The white lines represent the inner sanctum of golf's most holy ground.

Masters badges are color-coded. Each color represents a different level of access. A red badge can get you inside the white lines to the club for eating, buying merchandise, and bathrooms. The most sought after is the blue badge, which enables access with the players to their lockers.

Very few people get blue badges and they are strictly monitored. Augusta National officials ensure proper access by color and name. The guest and sponsor names are both printed on the badge. Badges of color are rarely scalped as the punishment for this to the member would be severe. The rich, important, and famous obtain badges through connections, never scalping. They are the lucky few, other than the invited players, that get to enjoy the privileged land between the white lines.

The locals line up at the club's entry fence like grizzly bears at the base of a huge waterfall, waiting for the salmon (in this case: the golf lovers) to make their annual run. The locals sell plastic ticket holders, water, sodas, programs, souvenirs, and of course, Masters tickets when they can get them. Each Augusta native, like an old bear, has their favorite area they stake out, year after year, and you don't want to mess with a bear and his territory.

Masters week translates to hard work for young and old alike, although rarely does a native Augustan use one of the valuable tickets to go and watch the tournament. If you're an Augustan and you score a ticket, you sell it to obtain clothes money for next fall.

"No pregnancy is going to stop me from getting that Masters tip money," Deloris insisted when her husband Nat begged her to only work half shifts this year. Nat helped his older brother Ed, who was a caddie at Augusta, work the trash detail during the 1970 Masters. A large storm blew in during the first practice round and all fled, but not the Wilson brothers. They had work to finish. They kept hauling trash cans, oblivious to the pounding rain and clap of thunder overhead. The great golfer William Earl "Billy" Casper witnessed this from inside the club house, looking out on the 10th tee. During the next day's practice round, Casper spoke to Nat when he noticed the same black man struggling with two full trash cans. "Now that's a real man's work," Casper commented. "Thanks for helping the course look so nice for us. We sure do appreciate all you do."

Nat was stunned that one of golf's finest ambassadors from the other side of the ropes not only noticed him but thanked him. It made him feel special, a real part of the Master's tradition.

As it turned out, the tournament that year was a particularly good one with a play-off by Casper. Besides their personal connection, Nat loved the fact that Casper had lots of kids, many adopted, and also that Casper was like him in stature—portly—which made the great golfer seem more like a real person than some superstar athlete.

Casper won the tournament that year. Deloris worked through the entire Masters, including a 12-hour shift just three days before she went into labor. She gave birth four days after the final day of the 1970 Masters. As Nat saw it, God had given him a sign through Casper. So Nat's last son was named after a white Mormon man from Salt Lake City: Willy Casper Wilson. Deloris liked Willy better than Billy, and insisted that it was close enough and God would be fine with the literary license. Like so many things to come for Willy Wilson, it was meant to be.

CHAPTER 25

LEARNING THE GAME

Willy Casper Wilson was a scrawny kid with a full, frizzy head of hair. His skin was dark like his father's. When he smiled, which was constantly, all his teeth showed. Willy's front two teeth had a wide gap between them, which seemed to dominate his face but in a positive way. Willy liked sports from the get-go. He could kick a ball while running at age three, hit a baseball at four, and at five he had his first experience with golf when Nat gave him a set of clubs he had found on his sanitation route. Not a bad set either. Amazing that someone would just throw them out like some used newspapers, not worth the trouble to give away.

"Rich white folks do dumb stuff like that. Trash a perfectly good set of golf clubs, rather than give them to Negros like me that might want to take up the game," Nat commented to his trash truck, nicknamed Nellie, as he carefully removed the clubs from a pile of rotting vegetables that engulfed the nearly perfect golf bag. He and Nellie had a long relationship. She was an older model of truck with the number four emblazoned on her back and front. Nat treated her as if she was part of the family. Talking to her was daily therapy. He stowed the clubs under his cab where they would not be seen. Nat didn't want anybody saying he stole them. "Never know, Nellie. Some folks might say we took 'em from this garage. Best keep them out of view."

The set was made by a company called Burner and even had a completely full side pocket of balls. In the bag was an old Augusta National ticket buried deep in the pocket. The tag, still in new condition, was stuck to the side, invisible until all the old golf balls were fished out. Nat knew the tag was worth money to people who liked golf and he thought he would wait until the next tournament and sell it on the side of the road next to the entrance. Once again Nat felt this was a sign from God. So Nat Wilson pinned the old ticket on young Willy's bedroom wall and gave him his first set of slightly used and very old Burner golf clubs.

Nat told his son, "Now you only have 18 balls and that's going to have to last you as long as the clubs, so you had better be careful with each one. We aren't rich folk like the Augusta golf crowd. Golf balls are something you take very serious. Only hit a ball if you know where it's going to go, ever!"

Willy knew his dad was not one to mince words and even at five, he knew Nat's word was law. If Willy wanted to play golf, he'd better learn how to do it and not lose any balls. Willy took a pen and with Deloris' help numbered them all, one through 18. To play with the adult clubs, Willy had to stand on an old wooden soap box to give him enough height to make contact with the ball. He was a natural at golf. The rhythm of the swing was somehow ingrained in his being. He hit his balls over and over, until one by one the balls started to wear out, the numbers re-stenciled on numerous times. The slow demise of the balls' outer coverings was due to their continuously hitting his family's wooden backyard fence.

By the time Willy was seven, he had mastered hitting with every club in his bag. His uncle would come over and work with the boy on his swing, providing golf lessons and teaching him how the game was played. Years working at Augusta National caddying had given Ed Wilson an insight equal to if not better than that of any golf professional. He first explained to Willy that golf was a game of rules, honor, and sportsmanship. "It's the only sport where you call penalties on yourself," Ed explained. "Those with the best score on each hole get to go first on the next hole and if your ball is farther away from the hole than your opponent's ball, you hit first." He also explained, even though it was highly unlikely young Willy would ever hit an errant golf shot during his long golf career, if by some chance he did, he should yell, "Fore!" so anyone in the direction of the ball could drop to the ground and take cover before the ball smashed into their face. It was especially important as not many black folks played golf and hitting someone without yelling, "Fore!" might lead to the police being called. Willy paid attention and focused on ball control.

Each club's specific use was described, along with why it was critical. Ed noted that clubs known as woods are used for long shots. Woods have larger heads and shafts than irons, and with them it is harder to control the direction of the ball. A driver is a type of wood used to start the hole. It's the hardest to control but it hits the ball the longest distance. Woods with a smaller head, but still larger than an iron, are used for long shots, generally two hundred yards or longer.

Every golf bag holds seven different clubs called irons. Each has a number on the club which represents its loft. The smaller the iron's number, the flatter the face of the club and the less loft the ball has once it's hit. A five iron goes much farther than a nine iron. In a good golfer's hands, a ball hit with a five iron can travel 185 to 200 yards. Its trajectory is fast and low. A great golfer can also use a five iron for a short chip shot they need to keep low, for instance if the ball is under a low-hanging branch. A little half swing and the golf ball hit with a five iron will only go only a hundred yards or less, avoiding the branch.

Willy learned each hole has a rating based on how many shots it should take to get the ball into the cup. Scoring *par* means the player got the ball into the cup using the exact number of strokes at which the hole was rated. A birdie is getting one less then par. Two less is an eagle (hard to do). One over par is a bogey, two over par a double bogey, and so forth. For most 18-hole golf courses, if you could get par on each hole you would score a 71 or 72 and this would be a terrific score. Breaking 100 for most golfers is good. Pros try to get anywhere in the mid to high 60s. The record is 59 in a PGA tournament.

Ed realized letting his young nephew only use adult clubs was a difficult way to learn the game of golf, but he figured growing up in America and being black also required one to overcome obstacles, most of them bigger than oversized golf clubs. Ed and Nat both thought this was a good test for little Willy. Young black boys had to grow up fast in Augusta. If they didn't get used to hardship they usually didn't make it through life.

Ed Wilson was Nat's older brother by two years. Like his younger brother, Ed had a great work ethic and even a stronger back. His years as a caddie had instilled in him a stellar sense of morals. Ed understood right from wrong. He could easily handle two full golf bags for 36 holes and not be out of breath, even smoking two packs of unfiltered Camel cigarettes a day. He'd been a caddie almost all his life at Augusta. He knew the game backwards and forwards. Ed had never played a round of golf in his life, but knew a great swing from a good one. Even though he only had a sixth-grade education, he'd memorized every rule. His ability to assess the greens and then explain what he saw to his clients was legendary. His clients included the powerful and wealthy. He had even caddied for two Presidents, including Eisenhower. President Eisenhower loved the game of golf and played as often as possible. He also loved Augusta, except for one tree. A large and strategically placed hundred-year-old Loblolly Pine guarded the left side of number 17. This tree caused so much havoc for the President that he campaigned for its removal. In Augusta, not even President of the United States has authority. Request denied, the tree stayed and forever after was known as the Eisenhower tree, a story Ed shared with each new person he caddied for.

Ed loved his job and was an expert caddie. He made a very good living by Augusta standards and had great social standing in his community. Ed had never caddied in his 20 years for a woman or a black man. He didn't know if black folks even played golf but if they did, it seemed like one example was going to be little Willy. Ed would brag constantly about his nephew to his fellow black caddies saying, "My boy Willy is a one of kind, a natural swing and he don't have shit for clubs. He's the real deal and I know, I've seen them all."

Like his brother Nat, Ed believed Willy was destined for greatness and it was their responsibility to give him as much help as possible. This is why Ed would come over after work three times a week to coach Willy's swing and talk to him about what he understood about golf from the white folks he watched playing it. Ed explained to the young boy about scoring, a difficult concept for any seven year old, but by the age of 10, Willy would be able to tell you everything about each hole on Augusta National even though he had never stepped foot on the property.

Ed felt there were only two types of players: ones that cheat and ones that don't. Most cheated. Even a President was known to "improve upon the truth" with a lie. Ed advised Willy, "If you want to be good and you're black, you better not cheat. Ain't no room for cheaters if yer black and play golf. You got to be better. You got to know all the rules and never, ever cheat."

So Willy worked on his game and the rules. At age 12, he finally grew into his adult set of Burner golf clubs. He still had all 18 of his original golf balls but one through 17 were worn down to the hard rubber. He had always saved his number 18 golf ball, which was still brand new. He wanted to use it for a special time and place.

92

CHAPTER 26

THE FIRST GOLF COURSE

Ed Wilson hoped to get Willy onto Augusta National as his "junior" caddy with a little luck from the famous "Tonight Show" host Johnny Carson. Carson had already featured a young black kid showing his amazing talent in golf. One of Augusta National's members, a rare Augusta native named Billy Bob Braxton, had seen the show. He used Ed as his regular caddie. Billy Bob remarked to his weekly playing partner, "Can you believe a colored kid could be so good at that young age? My God I bet I see him here at Augusta someday. We may never have any black members but that kid I'm telling you will play and win Augusta someday. He's one of a kind. He even had a name of a champion, Tiger Woods. That name I will remember."

This was the opening Ed had been waiting for. He never talked to his clients unless they talked to him first, and he then tried to limit it to "yes sir" or "no sir" if possible. Ed had caddied for Billy Bob once or twice a week for 15 years and never once started up a conversation with him. But before Ed knew it, Nat had blurted out, "My nephew Willy is better than that Johnny Carson kid and he lives right here in Augusta."

Billy Bob was taken aback by the fact that Ed had spoken to him as if he were his golf partner. Ed had caddied for him at least a hundred times and never said a single word to him unless it was related to the game he was playing. Billy Bob was for once at a loss for words. "Ed, what was that you said? You have a nephew that's better than that Negro kid on TV?"

"Yes sir, he's better, and I can prove it. Anytime you all want to see him hit a ball, just let me know. I'll set it up and you can let Mr. Carson know, too."

Billy Bob started laughing, and with a deep booming voice still filled with laughter, he offered, "You bring that boy of yours by tomorrow before we go out. If he's as good as you say, I'll let him walk the course with us and take a shot or two!"

Ed was as dumbfounded as Billy Bob probably was. First, that he had spoken out, and second, that his nephew would get to play a shot at

93

Augusta National. Ed had walked the course for 20 years and not once swung a club on the course except to kill a cottonmouth snake along Rae's Creek. A black boy playing Augusta National? "Yes sir, all right then. You will see he's better than that Lion Woods kid," Ed quickly sealed the deal.

"I believe it was Tiger."

"Tiger, Lion, it don't matter what kind of cat, my Willy's the name you want to remember. He was named after the great Billy Casper and can play golf just as good."

Billy Bob was impressed that Ed's nephew had the good sense to be named after a famous Masters winner. "That Billy Casper was a good golfer for a Mormon boy. I remember 1970. Won me a nice little bet. I'm looking forward to meeting your nephew, this Casper Jr."

Ed Wilson only worked one 18-hole turn that day. He usually did two, but left early to get his young apprentice ready. First he had to get him decent golf clothes. He knew Billy Bob would expect he would be well dressed. Ed figured he was expecting someone like Billy Casper, not the garbage man's kid, so he wanted Willy to be prepared mentally as well as golf-wise. Besides, Augusta had strict clothing requirements, rules Ed was well aware of.

Ed went home and retrieved his stash of found Titleist balls, all with Augusta logos on them. He would usually sell these but for this special occasion he would give them to Willy so if he got the chance to hit, he would get to use a decent ball.

Willy had never used new balls to hit with. For that matter, he had never hit a ball much outside his own back yard. He would go down to the old baseball field occasionally to use his driver. Mostly, he would hit 17 balls, then go out to find them all, line them up and hit them back to his starting point, and then repeat the pattern. When you have to look for balls, you make sure you hit each one straight and the same so you don't spend half your time chasing it down. In the last year, Willy's golf balls had lost their elasticity, so they stopped traveling as far. Willy found by accelerating his swing's follow through he could get the balls to fly almost as far as they had in the past.

Now, Ed told Willy, "You need to mark all these new balls with your own special mark so you can find them. You don't want someone else saying that's their ball. It needs to be special so you will know."

Willy thought for a long while, and then took Ed's old magic marker and carefully marked each golf ball with the number four, after his dad's garbage truck. Without her supporting the household, he would have never gotten the opportunity to play. "OK, I've got a bunch of new balls and I don't plan on losing any. Nobody's going to steal any of these. I have never had balls like these and I'll put up a good fight if somebody says they're theirs."

Ed chuckled, "Boy, I've been caddying for a long time and that there number four is a good mark. Not one person I have caddied for has used that number. That's now your mark. Those new golf balls of yours should surely be safe."

Willy entered the gates of Augusta National for the first time in 1982, age 12 and in complete awe. He had seen it only on TV and driving past in his family's car. It seemed perfect to him. No leaves or sticks anywhere, just Augusta's green and white colors as far as the eye could see. The azaleas were almost all bloomed out but he noticed the occasional patch of color. The dogwood trees still had large flowers. He felt like he was observing it all on the family television, even if his television was only an old black and white set, one of his dad's other finds.

After entering through the caddies' entrance, Ed and Willy checked in with the head boss. Ed's boss was an old, very proper Southerner who had worked at Augusta National it seemed since its beginning in 1932. He took a long, hard look at the tall, skinny black boy with a new plaid golf shirt and kinky black hair that was spilling out of a much-worn Masters cap, before he uttered a single word. He knew to expect the boy as Mr. Braxton had explained the circumstances, but still, this was highly unusual. Not the Augusta way.

"I hope, Ed, that this isn't going to be a problem for Mr. Braxton or you down the road. Taking a black boy out on our course is unheard of, you know that." The caddie boss then sternly added, "You had better put your nephew here in a white caddie's outfit. Otherwise it might end up looking very bad, a black boy acting as if he is one of our clients."

Ed thought about it for a long moment. He realized his job and all he had worked for his entire life was on the line. Then in a firm, slow-paced voice, he replied, "Sir, I know you are a very smart and generous man and are only thinking about my welfare and I do so appreciate it as I have known you nearly as long as my wife, Tilly. But I think we will go ahead and try it like this and hope nothing bad happens. I do thank you so very much for all your concern."

With that, Ed, in his usual white Augusta caddie's uniform, and Willy, in his new golf shirt, turned their backs on Ed's flabbergasted boss and walked out to the driving range to meet Billy Bob Braxton and make Augusta history.

CHAPTER 27

BLACK IS IN AT AUGUSTA

"Not a very big fella, are you there, Willy," observed Billy Bob Braxton. "Not like your namesake, Billy Casper, that's for sure."

Willy eagerly replied, "Mr. Braxton, I appreciate the opportunity to see Augusta National first hand! You know I was born just four days after William Early Billy Casper won the 1970 Augusta National and I have been in love with golf and Augusta as long as I can remember being alive."

Braxton loved the kid from the start. "Seems we got a kid who understands how special our little piece of heaven is. I'm finished warming up, so we can go over and tee off on number one if you're ready there, Willy. Your uncle says you're as good as that Tiger Woods kid. Hope it's true. It would be a real shame if he was just blowing smoke and was nothing more than some proud uncle."

Willy gulped, standing up as tall as his thin frame would allow. "I've heard of Tiger. He's in California but I'm a Georgian so I got to be better, don't you think?"

Billy Bob let out a deep guttural laugh. "You're right. How could someone from California be better than a native Augustan. Let's go tee up. You got your clubs?"

Willy had his old, now much-worn Burner clubs with an old Augusta National ticket proudly taped to the outside of the golf bag. It had to be the worst set of clubs to ever be played at Augusta National.

"Young Casper, I'll give you the honors. Do you have your balls marked? Don't want to get ours confused, though I'd expect mine will be quite a ways out in front of yours," Billy Bob chuckled, as he expected to out-drive the kid by a mile.

"Yes, sir. All ready to go." With that, Willy teed up his new ball with the freshly printed number four in a bold red color. Willy took his first and only practice swing of the morning and then proceeded to hit the ball 275 yards down the middle past the far right side sand trap. Willy watched intently as the ball flew straight with just a hint of a draw. He almost ran after it as he had a thousand times before, then remembered today he didn't need to. He did watch exactly where it landed. He had never lost a ball and didn't plan to today, especially with the first new ball he had ever hit and one with an expensive Augusta logo on it.

"Oh my God," a stunned Billy Bob exclaimed. "That was unbelievable. Ed, you were not shitting me. Young Casper here can hit the ball. I guess we'll have no trouble determining my ball because it will be the one 50 yards behind my newest golfing buddy. Willy, have you played a lot of golf?"

"You mean 18 holes of golf on a course?"

"Yes, of course."

"Today's the first time I've been on a golf course, but I've been hitting golf balls for seven years, more or less."

Braxton's mouth fell so far open his whole tongue was visible. "Son, it is only right that your very first golf shot should come on Augusta National, number one! You're going to give Woods a run for his money someday. Ed, grab that boy's clubs. I have some more questions for him, if you don't mind."

Ed followed them, amazed. His nephew was walking step for step with one of the biggest good old boys in the state of Georgia as they played golf, chatted away, and Billy referred to the black boy as his golfing buddy. Billy Bob Braxton had never asked Ed a question that wasn't golf related in the 15 years he had caddied for him. Hell, Ed thought to himself: "If this can happen, what's next, a black President? Not in my lifetime, but this sure is something. Yes sir, it sure is."

Willy Wilson shot his first round of golf at Augusta National at the age of 12 from the blue tees. He carded an 82 for his first official score. Ed read every green dead-on for Willy and no balls were lost.

CHAPTER 28

A MINI CELEBRITY

The next day's paper had a complete story about a 12-year-old black boy whose first game of golf resulted in a score of 82 on Augusta National. In golfing country in 1982, this was big news. It even made the Atlanta papers.

The 82 was impressive but it was more newsworthy for the fact that a poor black kid had somehow managed to get onto Augusta National to play his first round. Some in the city thought it was outrageous but most were proud of their native son and embraced Willy as a semi-celebrity.

Braxton, a man who still up to that point occasionally called black people Negroes, made it a point to let everyone know he had been the one to find young Willy Casper, as he called him. Billy Bob added Willy to his golf match once a week with Ed on the bag and started to share with Willy the ins and outs of golf at the Augusta level. These regular golf outings became somewhat of a minor spectacle, with many of the members following the group around just to watch young Willy hit the ball. Billy Bob ate it up. Slowly, Billy Bob's attitude towards race changed. He started to see color a little differently as the matches went on and he got his white butt beat by a scrawny black kid on a regular basis. Billy Bob even started to talk to Ed like a person and not the hired help.

Willy liked this white man and wondered if they all were like him since he really hadn't met any white people other than at his mom's restaurant. Willy loved golf and the notion of being a professional golfer. He also liked the fact that he would probably be the first person in his family to go to college on a golf scholarship, of all things. And so it came to pass.

At 18, Willy was named the number-one golfer in Georgia. It was 1988 and he was offered numerous scholarships to great programs including those at Georgia State and the University of Georgia. He was tempted to stay close to home because he loved Augusta and Augusta National. Billy Bob wanted Willy to go to his alma mater in South Carolina just over the border from Georgia, and was even willing to help pay for trips back to Augusta National to play golf every so often.

Willy's final decision was a shocker for his family but not Willy. During a tournament he met high-school golf champion Jim Furyk from Pennsylvania. Furyk had come to Augusta on a golf trip. Willy liked him so much he thought, "I'm going where this white dude with the funky swing is going." They were less than a month apart in age and both extremely driven when it came to golf. They had visions of a national college championship. So the University of Arizona it was, in some place called Tucson. Real hot but no humidity, Willy was told.

When Willy left for the U of A he had the distinction of being the first black person to play over 100 rounds of golf at Augusta National by the age of 18. A poor black kid whose dad worked on the sanitation line, he had his home club, Augusta National, embroidered on his brand new golf bag, courtesy of one Augusta National member, Mr. Billy Bob Braxton.

CHAPTER 29

THE U OF A

Willy had never flown before he went west to find his fortune and fame. He was amazed how everything looked so small, even golf courses, while flying far above. He had his face plastered to the window for the entire three-and-a-half hour trip. Getting off the plane and walking down the un-air-conditioned runway, Willy was hit with a hot blast of air directly in the face. So hot, he worried, "Shit, that plane could be on fire."

Thirty minutes later, as he walked out of the airport with his new university golf coach, Willy discovered it was just typical late August weather of 108 degrees. "No fire, but damn sure felt like it," he told his Uncle Ed later on the phone.

The first weeks of school were exciting, scary, and more than Willy could imagine. The college had a beautiful red-brick campus built over a hundred years ago. The trees were nothing like in Georgia. Many were small and frankly, scrubby looking, interspersed amid huge palm trees like he had seen in the movies. Cacti were most interesting to Willy, especially the saguaro cacti with numerous huge arms that grew to heights of 40 feet. Willy told his Uncle Ed, "There's cactus out here big as our old oak that sits in front of the clubhouse at Augusta National. I'm not kidding."

Willy learned the hard way about the Tucson desert his first day on the course. Ventana Canyon Golf and Racquet Club, a new resort and semiprivate tract in the foothills of the Catalina Mountains, was the U of A's home course. The Tom Fazio-designed course was so foreign looking to Willy, it was hard to believe this was now his home course. Ventana was a classic desert golf course for target golf. You have to be accurate. You're in the desert and you don't want to be hitting out from a cluster of cacti.

The second hole on Ventana's mountain course is a straight forward short par four, 360 yards. Willy hit a great tee shot leaving it on the far right side with a lovely approach to the back of the green's pin position. A ball that close to the edge of the course can become an issue if you haven't learned to respect the hostile desert environment. Willy learned respect on number two. He crouched low to look at his approach, concentrating on the next shot. As he backed up, his skinny black butt came in direct contact with a Sonoran Desert jumping cholla. The name comes from the fact that the first time you are stuck, you swear the cactus jumped out and grabbed you.

"Ouch," screamed Willy as numerous sharp, hook-like spines stuck deep into his right glutes. This would have been bad enough, but Willy's immediate reaction was to reach back and grab at his butt that had the large arm of the broken cholla dangling out of it. Wildly grasping at the cactus, his hand also became entangled with the spines, so now buttocks, cholla, and hand were all entangled as one painful unit shrieking for help. Willy had been hurt golfing before. He'd been stung by a bee, gotten poison ivy, even had a tree branch fall onto his head, but nothing came close to the pain of this ass-cholla-hand debacle.

Getting unstuck required a seasoned golf coach who kept a metal fork handy for just such emergencies. Gently placing the prongs between Willy's butt and the cholla spines, the coach gave one quick yank. Phase one: cholla removed from Willy's butt. Phase two: using the same fork, the broken cholla was extracted from Willy's hand as Willy writhed on the ground. Last phase: all the remaining cholla spines were expertly removed, one by one, leaving five small, bleeding holes in Willy's palm.

"So, we call that a cholla and we see a lot of these lovely plants on our golf outings. I highly recommend you learn to recognize the plant and give it a wide berth. We play fast golf here at the U of A, and pulling chollas out of your ass will slow us down," his coach instructed.

Willy sheepishly nodded in agreement, then very carefully backed up with plenty of head turning to make sure not to collide with any more cacti. Willy cleaned his now bloodied club, re-gripped, and proceeded to birdie the hole. Forever after the hole would be known to the team as "Willy's butthole, number two."

Hole number three was the course's signature hole, a beautiful short par three with an isolated green in between a crack in the mountain. The tee box and pin somehow wedged in between a canyon of cactus, mesquite trees, and rocks. To get to the tee box the golfer has to climb a steep hill surrounded by cholla and prickly pear. Reaching the green requires a high floating shot, 100 yards over the canyon terrain to an elevated green. As Willy walked his way up the hill toward the green he heard a strange noise, a sound he vaguely remembered from some TV program. A rattling noise. Willy stopped short in his tracks when he saw what was making the sound: a large snake with a diamond-shaped head poised above its tightly coiled body and a black-and-white striped tail with eight large rattles, all of which were vibrating violently. Willy's right leg was less than two feet from the snake's body. Willy's butt, still twitching from the cholla's recent painful sting, suddenly gave way under a giant muscle twitch of fear and pain. He fell down, tumbled backwards, then scrambled back down the path away from the snake screaming, "Rattlesnake!"

Harlan Jones, a local boy from Tucson who was the poorest player on the star-lined U of A golf team but was hell of a nice guy, came running up the hill to Willy's side. "So you got to see one of our little darlings, did you, Willy?"

"Big rattlesnake, rattling," Willy said, his breath laboring in the 102-degree heat.

Harlan calmly removed a three iron from Willy's bag, walked uphill towards the snake, and slowly picked up the snake and moved it off the golf path. "There you go, fella. You're scaring my friend Willy. Go find yourself a nice, fat pack rat."

"Come on, boys, we've got 15 holes of golf to finish. Enough of this playing around," yelled the irate coach. "You boys have plenty of time later to go hunting for snakes."

Willy slowly strode up the hill again, looking right, then left, scanning for cacti, snakes, and any other dangerous thing the desert had to offer. He had already decided his lifelong streak of not losing a golf ball had just come to an abrupt end. If any of his balls marked four rolled into that hell of a desert they would stay there. The rattlesnakes could have them.

At the U of A, Willy's social life was different than it had been back in Augusta. There was a very small population of black females, which made dating difficult. Willy had never gone out with a white girl and he wasn't sure if he just wasn't attracted to them or if it was a social thing. So Willy decided he would focus on golf and study for the next four years. If any good-looking black girls happened to show up, then great, but he'd come for golf and an education. Dating was on the back burner.

The first year at the U of A went like a well-written script. Willy was the freshmen Big Ten player of the year. He set the course record at Ventana and never got stuck by a cactus again.

The pain started in Willy's back just before he returned to Augusta for the summer. It was like a toothache, dull but constant. It hurt during golf, sleep, and just sitting. He figured he'd twisted it somehow and didn't bother to go to the team doctor.

Being an athletic 19-year-old who had never been injured, he found the unrelenting pain to be a foreign concept. He lived with it, thinking rest would fix everything.

Back in Augusta, Willy began his summer job as a teaching pro at Augusta Country Club, a lovely private course with many of the same characteristics as Augusta National. There were great old trees, manicured fairways and greens, and a wonderful old colonial clubhouse full of vintage photographs and silver trophies.

Teaching was painful but doable. Golfing was not. By July fourth weekend, the back pain had gotten too great to bear and Willy went to his boyhood doctor. The x-rays revealed a small amount of bone loss, a very unexpected finding in a 19-year-old. The family practice doctor had only seen this once before in his 30 years of practice, in a bone cancer patient who was quite elderly. A chest X-ray was ordered, showing small bilateral plural effusions, in layman's terms, water on the lungs.

Willy's boyhood doctor, Dr. Marks, became extremely concerned his patient might have bone cancer and it looked like it had also metastasized into his lungs. Dr. Marks had known Willy his entire life and had done all his sports physicals, including his entrance physical for the U of A. Numerous additional tests were ordered. Willy was thankful he had gotten student health insurance as his medical costs were skyrocketing.

104

After two weeks of tests and no definitive answer, Dr. Marks was stumped. Willy was in pain but had not lost much weight. He looked healthy. If it wasn't bone cancer, what could it be? He sent Willy to an oncologist, who ordered a bone scan and what turned out to be Willy's most painful experience since the cholla stick, a bone marrow aspiration. To perform an aspiration requires taking a long, thin hole punch and slowly grinding it into the pelvic bone to obtain a plug. If the person who is performing the procedure isn't strong enough, you will hear them start to grunt as they try to push the long straw through very hard but sensitive human bone tissue. The pressure is immense and it takes time to push the metal rod through to the deep bone marrow, yet somehow for Willy it was probably slightly less painful than the unexpected jumping cholla. The bone marrow biopsy came back negative for cancer but did show an exceptionally high eosinophil count. Eosinophils are associated with diseases of inflammation like rheumatoid arthritis, and allergies, not symptoms Willy was having.

Finally a smart Atlanta doctor who was asked to consult called the U of A's team physician. The team doctor, Dr. Pearson, was a young black osteopathic doctor. He had only seen Willy Wilson once and that was for his initial athletic physical required of all scholarship students. The physical was unremarkable and Willy never sought medical treatment while at the U of A. Dr. Pearson listened intently as the Atlanta doctor summed up Willy's medical findings. He asked for all the symptoms and findings and then declared, "Willy has valley fever and it sounds pretty severe. You better treat him right away. Blacks, and I can speak to this first hand, have a high tendency for dissemination. We don't know why but it does occur and I have seen it before. The disease, which is fungal, can destroy the integrity of the bone if you don't act fast, and this kid is a world-class golfer."

The doctor in Atlanta was stunned. "What the hell is valley fever? What valley?"

Dr. Pearson explained valley fever occurred primarily in the Sonoran Desert and was caused by a fungus known as Coccidioidomycosis. In most individuals that move to the southwestern states of Arizona, California, and New Mexico, getting the disease causes only mild flu-like symptoms. But in the few unlucky ones, valley fever can make them very sick and even cause death. Black people, Willy found out, are more susceptible to the disease. Willy was sure he had never seen that statistic in the Arizona school prospectus. "No wonder there were no black chicks in Tucson. The damn fever has killed them all off," he said jokingly to his Atlanta doctor. After three weeks more of diagnostic testing, the diagnosis the Arizona team physician had made in five minutes over the phone was conclusively confirmed. Willy was relieved it was a treatable disease and not bone cancer.

Treatment for valley fever is with an "azol" family drug, an antifungal. In severe cases, multiple drug therapy is required. Willy had a severe case. The fungus had taken up residence in his lower spine. Willy was going to have to undergo a long treatment, which would include more tests, many potentially dangerous drugs, and no golf for at least six months.

He had no choice but to withdraw from the U of A for medical reasons, hoping that after a year of treatment and back rest he might be able to return. His summer job at Augusta Country Club was graciously extended into a permanent position as head pro. Looking on the bright side, there were a lot more good-looking black women in Augusta than in Tucson. Willy preferred to look on the positive side of any situation, even one that might end his hopes of a college education and becoming a pro golfer.

CHAPTER 30

EVA COMES HOME

Dorothy Rashmusen had her town car meet what was now her only family at Kennedy International Airport. The thought of Bernard never being a part of her living family ever again was heartbreaking. She hoped Eva and the baby would stay with her in her home on Long Island tonight, but Eva insisted on going home.

Jackson Peabody, the Rashmusen driver, had worked for the family for twenty plus years. Dorothy normally liked to drive herself as it made her feel more normal, so most of Jackson's time was spent polishing the Lincoln town car and reading murder mysteries. Tonight Dorothy was in no condition to drive. The spotless sedan drove Eva and baby Theo back to their home on the far Upper East Side. Their apartment was on the fourth floor with no elevator. That meant four long flights of stairs with only a thin handrail for support —details that Eva and Bernard had formerly overlooked with youthful nonchalance.

Carefully placing little Theo in the baby sling that the hospital had so thoughtfully provided, Eva began the journey upward. Eva was the one who had suggested the apartment on the fourth floor with no elevator. She took the rickety old metal steps slowly, followed by Dorothy, then Jackson with the luggage Dorothy had provided Eva. To steady herself, Eva had to walk at half her normal pace. Before the earthquake, she would sometimes run up the steps, using the sound of her footsteps as a rhythm to a wild beat in her head. Even carrying her old bass with her, Eva had been able to navigate the floors faster than she could now, missing a limb. She felt much older than her 27 years. *How's a one-armed musician to make a living?* She trudged up the stairs for the first time as a handicapped person.

When Eva finally arrived at apartment 418, she stood stunned as she looked at the number. Theo's birthday was also 4.18. And room 18 was where Bernard had been crushed and she had lost her left arm. Eva had never thought about the apartment number until that very moment. She was not a superstitious individual. Even growing up in New Orleans and seeing voodoo performed at her friends' houses didn't faze her. But something stuck in her mind now. "My little Theo, I would have to think 18 will be a special number for you," she murmured to her baby, realizing Dorothy was probably wondering if her almost daughter-in-law must still be traumatized from the earthquake. Maybe she was.

Eva handed the baby over to Bernard's mother, sling and all, while she fumbled with the house key the apartment super had lent her. One hand was a struggle. The stairs had taken their toll on both women. This was Dorothy's first visit to her late son's home, previously refusing to visit somewhere that required four flights of stairs. Eva got the key in the lock and opened the door, pushing it with her foot and then grabbing it with her one arm. She knew in her heart she would eventually be able to master most household tasks with a single arm, except for playing her beloved bass.

The room was dark. Eva stumbled, looking for the light switch. When the lights came on, she was in shock. The entire place had been remodeled while she had been in Mexico. The room for the first time was well illuminated. In the center of the freshly painted wall in the living room was one very large painting. Unbelievably, it was the magnificent Thomas Moran landscape she had loved and visited so many times at the Met. The very same Moran under which she and Bernard had found each other.

A single, large cypress tree battled against nature's most severe elements. The lone cypress precariously perched on the end of an open rock outcropping surrounded by danger yet managing to thrive. Never had the painting seemed more apropos than at this moment. Eva was that tree with one of her branches missing, trying to steady herself and survive against all odds, no matter what was thrown at her. THE LONE CYPRESS had mesmerized her when it was at the Met and now it held even more meaning. "I don't understand," Eva said, stepping closer to the painting. "What is this painting doing here?"

Under the painting was a note taped to the frame. Written in Bernard's hand, it read, "I hope you will accept this Moran as a token of my love. Will you please marry me? Love, Bernard."

Dorothy was as stunned as Eva. The painting, which had been on loan to the Met, had been a gift from Bernard's grandfather to his father, then from his father to Bernard. Now it was on Eva's wall with a note from Bernard. The painting was worth close to one million dollars and it clearly was meant as a gift to Eva, however, a posthumous gift, to be exact. The lawyers would have to untangle the official ownership issues.

Eva sighed, "Oh, Bernard, I would gladly marry you, my love! I'm sorry you never saw your son. He's as strong and handsome as you!" She burst into tears, which was something Eva never did. She sobbed harder than she had in her entire life. True pain, loss, and joy all hit her at once. Not even under the rubble of the Hotel La Posada, trapped and alone, had Eva cried this hard. This was the cry of a pivotal moment in one's life, a final realization of a permanent change.

Dorothy didn't know what to do or say. Being conservative by nature, it was difficult to observe such pure, raw emotion. She felt like crying for the loss of Bernard and one of the prized family heirlooms, yet understood she needed to keep her emotions in check. Her only grandson needed his family. Dorothy looked at the lovely Eva, with her only arm buried in her bruised and healing face, and explained, "That painting has been in our family for generations. It was borrowed by the Met for the retrospective." Then she extended little Theo. "Eva, your son needs you."

Eva realized she had to be strong for Theo. She reached out with the one arm and gently cradled Theo close to her swollen right breast. She raised a milk-filled breast from underneath her dress and positioned little Theo closer to her. Theo reflexively awoke and started suckling. They sat down in front of the Moran on a bench Bernard must have had replicated from those at the Metropolitan Museum of Art. Eva stared into the magnificent vista of Moran's Pacific coast, which seemed so far away from her isolated Manhattan flat.

Dorothy took in the ironic scenario with all its implications: her son's last note, the family's magnificent Thomas Moran, the low-end apartment with a one-armed black woman breast-feeding Dorothy's only grandson as she sat in front of the painting as if it were still hanging at the Met. Dorothy wondered, "Who could have ever dreamed this up? Only in some farfetched dime store novel, and not a very good one at that. Yet the reality was in front of her and undeniable. How can life be this strange and unpredictable?" Her lip slightly curved up in a dry smile.

Dorothy knew she could bring the ownership of the Moran into question. If Bernard had no will, it was technically still the family's painting. Bernard's note was not a will, not legally anyway. Yet Eva was family now. Theo was Eva's and Bernard's son, that was clear. The infant boy had her son's nose and close-set eyes and he was obviously half white. Dorothy's wealth was fairly great and quite frankly one million dollars wouldn't make any difference. Then again, the painting was from 1881 and that's a long time to be in one family. She knew it had to be addressed, but not now. Later.

CHAPTER 31

ONE ARM IS BETTER THAN NONE

Eva's first worry was how to be self-sufficient in the apartment with only one arm and a newborn. Her second worry was money. She had managed to put away $20,000 in savings, a remarkable feat for anyone in their twenties, much less a single, black female who made a living mostly as a bass musician in the subways. Her bass, she discovered, was not covered under her flimsy insurance policy because it had been destroyed by a natural disaster. If the bass had been covered, it wouldn't have been worth much anyhow as old as it was, but there could be a time fairly soon when even a little money could be critical.

Eva was angry with herself for having let Bernard pay for everything. True, his generosity had allowed her to save practically all her money, but it also had made her soft. She never wanted to be weak or need help from anyone. Eva's own mother had used the state government often to help fill in during hard times and Eva had vowed not to do this, yet here she was. She wondered if being reduced to state help was a black thing or a circumstance encountered by all poor people, including her if she didn't find some kind of work soon. Work for a black, one-armed female who recently gave birth to a child, with a music degree as her education? *Sure, the offers will be flowing in.*

On the plus side, she had finished a degree at the prestigious Manhattan School of Music. Yet in her current state she couldn't play or teach. Nor did she have much of a social connection to her community. Her life had been Bernard. Now he was gone. And she had a newborn she could barely care for with one arm, much less carry up and down those wobbly stairs along with groceries.

Maybe Dorothy would fill in somehow? Dorothy's only son was dead. Perhaps little Theo could fill a void for both of them? But Eva was the type of person who innately could tell things about people. It wasn't something she tried to do. It just was. This ability had helped her on the subway. She sensed when someone would connect with her music and those individuals she got a warm feeling from would likewise intensify her playing, which always led to more tips. Dorothy's dismay upon seeing the Moran on Eva's wall had been apparent to Eva even in her deteriorated emotional state. Eva knew the Moran was something Bernard wanted for her, but she didn't feel completely right about taking such an important painting from the family. The one thing she would never want was something bad to happen to such a remarkable masterpiece.

She was fortunate that Bernard had pre-paid six months of rent on their apartment and she still had three more months rent-free. But after that it became dicey. Bernard's was the signature on the lease. The landlord probably wouldn't renew the lease to a black, unemployed, one-armed musician. Just too much of a risk. And she'd be better off without all those stairs.

Where to live and how to make a new life? It seemed that NYC had too much baggage. Eva had always counted on music to provide her with steady money and a way to support herself, but now her situation was different. She had never thought of losing this musical gift of hers. Youth has a way of blinding you from danger. She also knew if she could survive for one week under a collapsed hotel in mind-boggling heat and pregnant, she could survive this situation. The earthquake, as traumatizing as it had been, had made Eva a stronger person. Obstacles were challenges to be overcome, not blockades to keep you from your goals. Her goal was to have a happy, productive life and provide for her son.

Eva's left arm still felt as if it was there in her mind. The doctors called this condition phantom limb syndrome. The brain synaptic cords were still in place, but the appendage was gone. It's a weird feeling to have a sense of something yet have nothing. It was like losing Bernard. She often had fleeting thoughts, "Oh, Bernard would love to see this," then realized how stupid the thought was. He was dead, gone, his skin already decomposing, yet he was there in her thoughts. Maybe when her false arm feelings abated, so would those of Bernard? She knew time was a factor but hated the thought of not being able to conjure up his face whenever Eva wanted. She could almost live without the arm easier.

She was lucky in one way: she had lost her left arm, not her dominant right. She felt a true appreciation to have lost the weaker arm.

Dealing with the consequences of only one arm was akin to learning a new musical instrument. It was incredibly frustrating at first. The simplest task became a test of will, beginning with going up and down those stairs. Because her arm was amputated high up, there was no good anchor for a prosthetic. Eva hoped technology would catch up, but that would also require money.

Dorothy had generously paid for her Mexico City hospital stay and was sending weekly deliveries of groceries despite Eva's protests, but Eva needed to be able to fend for herself.

The book and movie deals that she had been offered after surviving the earthquake were starting to look like a last ditch resource she might be forced to consider, though the thought of it sickened her. The Dynamite Steel Company even sent a PR guy to her apartment to offer an arrangement as some sort of spokesperson. Eva was polite but begged off for now, hoping it didn't come to that. The earthquake memories were still fresh in her mind and her nights were often plagued with images of being trapped under concrete. To make a living off her tragedy didn't sit well with Eva's sense of self or her ethics about what was right and wrong. How would she sell the story of the death of her two loves, Bernard and music?

The best solution was to move on with her life and she would begin by dressing herself and Theo, instead of waiting for the neighbor she'd hired to come over every morning to help her give the baby a bath and lend a hand, literally.

I hate socks! How in the world can I put them on with only one hand? Pull here, then there, 10 minutes for socks! Is this my life now in slow motion? God, are you testing me? Looking upward at her living room ceiling for an answer, incredibly one came. At that monument she noticed for the first time a faint bulge in a cream-colored ceiling tile, obviously a new wet spot. As Eva calculated the cost to repair the ceiling, a single drop of water formed from the middle of the bulge. It fell, landing in the blue flower bowl with a ping. Seeing the droplet triggered memories of her ordeal but for the first time they didn't cause her heart to race. A slight smile even lifted her lips, for Eva believed some higher force was making it clear to her there are worse things in life than having only one arm to pull up a sock.

Upon the realization of how fortunate she was to have Theo and to be alive, her face lit up. She just needed to follow her heart. It was time for an exit strategy and it wouldn't include Dynamite Steel. She would be all right. She had found her inner strength again. Socks would get put on, ceiling tiles fixed, and she and Theo would move on with their lives, here or elsewhere.

CHAPTER 32

LEAVING NEW YORK CITY

If she left New York, where would she go? What was left of Eva's family was no longer in New Orleans, her mother and father being deceased. Eva hadn't seen her mother since she was four but knew from Aunt June that her mom had developed diabetes and had gotten a foot infection that had turned septic and killed her in less than a week. Eva found this ironic. She had survived being buried alive under thousands of tons of debris for a week, no further damage than her lost arm. But her mother's problems with drug and alcohol addiction, plus her unsuccessful attempts to control her eating and sugar levels, had led to her eventually dying of a common staph infection. Life was unpredictable and often unfair, but that was life and Eva understood it better than most.

Aunt June Osborn, her mother's older sister, had lived in Augusta, Georgia, as long as Eva could remember. It was the third-largest city in Georgia with almost 200,000 people. Eva knew little about this part of the South. Atlanta was a metropolitan city that seemed like it would be more to her liking, since it was probably more similar to New Orleans. However, Augusta was cheaper and her savings were seeping away. Her Aunt June was a good-hearted woman who had reached out to Eva immediately upon her return to NYC after her Mexico City tragedy. Aunt June convincingly told Eva she had plenty of room, she loved babies, and after all she was family. Eva had been home now for over a month and her relationship with her almost-other-relative, Dorothy, wasn't really progressing: it mostly consisted of stilted phone conversations.

So after weeks of contemplating it, Eva decided Augusta was the next stop. She figured she could go to the local university and within a couple of years earn another degree, one that she could make a living with. Getting though the diaper years would be a bitch for a one-armed, single parent without help. Aunt June could provide that help and wouldn't mind. In fact she seemed to relish the idea. Her Aunt June was her closet relative and she could count on her to be there when she really needed her, which was now. Eva made up her mind with a final convincing argument: *How bad can Augusta be? I remember seeing that Masters Tournament on television and it looked gorgeous there. The real old South.*

Eva was not naïve. She knew to expect the old Southern crackers with their hatred of all people of color. You always found a few of these bigots in any of the deep South's cities. Eva somehow always ignored this type of behavior and treated everyone the same, even the racists. Theo might have a harder time growing up in the South but this probably wouldn't occur till middle school and by that time she would be ready to move on. For now she would keep her son's family history to herself, although with Theo's straight hair, narrow Anglo-looking nose, green eyes, and light brown complexion it wouldn't take long for people to figure it out. She knew bigotry crossed all racial lines, black and white.

CHAPTER 33

GOOD BYE, MORAN

The whole time Eva was painstakingly packing with her one arm, she wondered what to do with the Moran. She knew it was an important painting and had to be extremely valuable but she just did not feel right keeping it. She should probably give it back to Dorothy. Her main hesitation was for Theo's sake. *Maybe I'll let Dorothy know I would like the piece to be left to Theo for his future, if she so deems it, as his father Bernard would approve?*

The painting looked magnificent on the largest living room wall, three well-placed art lights illuminating the large canvas showing as well as it had in the Metropolitan Museum. Eva sat on a packed box, oblivious to the museum bench next to her. For over an hour, Eva gazed at the painting. She finally decided to discuss it with Dorothy when she came by this evening. Dorothy wasn't even aware that Eva and Theo were moving. That had been a topic too difficult to broach on the phone.

Bernard's Moran had been a steadying influence for the two months since Eva had gotten back from Mexico City. Now, she tried to memorize every aspect of the piece as it was probably the last time she would ever see the painting. When you really study something intently with all your energy and concentration, little things emerge that you never noticed before.

The frame was cracked in two opposite corners, the red gesso base peering out from underneath the now missing gold leaf, which had flaked off due to the passage of time. Moran's clouds seem to caress the cypress tree perched on the craggy outcropping. The foam of the water was so adeptly painted that one could almost smell the ocean air as the water crashed against the rocks. Eva closed her eyes and tried to visualize the scent and sounds the waves would have made as Moran had experienced them over a hundred years ago.

The signature, which was something she never had paid attention to, was camouflaged in the far right foreground. One had to look carefully to see it. A red "M" monogram with two arrows blended into the letter next to his Moran signature. The painting's date, 1881, was in very small script and almost invisible in the rocky foreground.

Noticing the Moran's date for the first time sent a shiver down Eva's spine... 1881, eighteen and its mirror image. Again! Eighteen had been the hotel room, 418 the apartment she now lived in, and Theo was born on April 18th. Eva had always felt things happen for a reason. Her shiver was one of excitement, not fear. This was meant to be. Somehow there was a connection. The Moran was meant to be tied to Theo and her. Was she wrong to give up this painting?

When Dorothy entered Eva's home, she was shocked to see Eva surrounded by chest-high boxes marked "glass," "pots," "shoes," and "baby." It was obvious Eva was moving and her departure was imminent. Eva looked ready to leave, except for the Moran. The large painting with its hand-carved frame and slightly broken corners was still on the wall where Bernard had arranged for it to be carefully placed. Nothing else was left unpacked, except the bench and the Moran.

"What's going on, Eva? Where are you going? You may need my help, especially with the baby," Dorothy said, seating herself on the bench.

"I'm leaving New York. The past is just too present here. I need to earn a living somehow and I have to get my and Theo's life back to normal. I just can't see it happening here. It's just too painful," Eva got to the point. Then, after a drawn-out pause, "I need to talk to you about your Moran."

Dorothy was struck by how Eva used the term "your Moran." Was she going to give it back? It was still on the wall, it was "your Moran," maybe the problem of clarifying the ownership was over. *She must know that it's terrifically valuable*, Dorothy thought.

Eva explained, "I don't know if it is right that I take this. I know Bernard gave it to me, but now that he's gone, I don't know that I should keep such a valuable painting."

She does know its value, yet she's giving it up? Dorothy thought.

"So if you would," Eva continued, "I was hoping you could arrange to take the piece with you. I would like you to consider—when Theo is old enough—leaving him the painting since it is a family piece and he is your grandson."

"Eva, if you think that is best, I will keep it for Theo," Dorothy quickly agreed. Now that she had possession of the painting again, she could be agreeable.

The two made small talk for the next few minutes and then Eva asked Dorothy to help her take the painting off the wall. They lifted the painting from its special gold hook. Looking one last time at the cypress tree, Eva handed off her part of the frame to Dorothy, tears running down her cheeks. Eva turned away from the painting, trying not look at it ever again.

"Eva, have you seen the back?"

"What back?" Eva reluctantly turned toward Dorothy, exposing the tears dripping down her face.

"The painting. There is writing on the back and it's to you, my dear!"

On the back, in Bernard's hand, directly below the title Moran had assigned the painting in 1881, was a dedication: "Eva's Moran, for now and forever. With all my love, Bernard." The signature was in indelible ink. Bernard had wanted the inscription to be part of the painting's history forever and it would be.

"Eva, this is your painting! Bernard wanted it to always be yours and so do I," Dorothy decided. She had to respect her son's wishes. "I'll have an art handler I use come over and get it packed and shipped for you. Where do you want it sent?"

"Have them send it to me in care of Ms. June Osborn, 404 East Elm Street, Augusta, Georgia, 30919."

It was the last time Dorothy Rashmusen would ever see Bernard's handwriting, Eva, or her grandson Theo. Two weeks after changing her estate to show that the Thomas Moran painting titled THE LONE CYPRESS was no longer an asset, but instead was classified as a gift to one Eva De Plain, Dorothy was killed in a head-on collision a mile away from her home. It was a hit and run at the intersection of 18th Street and Oak. Her driver was at home reading a book, Dorothy having insisted on driving herself.

Unfortunately, Dorothy had never changed her will, just the estate portion dealing with her painting collection. The bulk of the will was scheduled for revision in a week. Dorothy had decided it would read Theo De Plain was the sole heir to her estate. No one knew that except for Dorothy, so that information died with her. Instead, all the Rashmusen art collection, excluding one very important Thomas Moran, went to the Historical Society in Long Island, a sizeable donation. Her home, her Madison Avenue office, and her money, in case she outlived her son Bernard, all went to an endowment to help the homeless of New York City.

CHAPTER 34

AUGUSTA IS NO NYC

Eva had visited her Aunt June twice as a teenager. She didn't remember Augusta being so poor and disenfranchised, with burned-out cars and crappy, discarded refrigerators lining the fronts of the homes. It was late 1995 now. Maybe the city had hit upon hard times.

Aunt June's home was in a fairly safe neighborhood by Augusta standards—not much drug dealing and no drive-bys—although very poor by most other standards, including Eva's. She once again regretted having let herself get used to the good life with Bernard. "Going backwards is harder than going forward," she told herself. It would take a while to get used to not having things. She planned to use her remaining savings judiciously. The first thing was to get some kind of training. Eva was smart but she was a right-brained creative person. Not the office worker type. She needed her own tempo, whether work or play. Augusta College was close by and she wanted to find her niche, but the syllabus was depressing. She was not about to go to business school. Science was out. English was possible.

Then she looked at the Medical College of Georgia. It offered one of the only medical illustration courses in the nation. The course was only 21 months in duration and then she could be earning money. She would learn how to create detailed drawings to be used for medical books and surgical equipment, something a one-armed person could do and be creative. In 21 months, Theo would likely start walking and she could be working from home if she was any good at her new profession. Eva liked to draw and she had a right arm that worked beautifully. As a child, Eva's grandmother had even told her repeatedly that she was going to be an artist. Her grandmother could see what the future might hold. Supposedly foreshadowing was a gift that ran in the family, although except for Theo's name coming to Eva she had never experienced that part of the De Plain legacy.

She enrolled. Medical illustration involved copying the human body. Eva had seen dead bodies in her short life and it had never bothered her. Even when she was trapped and it looked like she would die, the thought of her body being found didn't repulse her. In fact, she had considered trying to write a note donating her and Theo's bodies to science so some good would come from their deaths, as pregnant corpses were probably rare.

All the creative juices she had channeled toward playing the bass were transferred to illustration. She found drawing human cadavers was oddly freeing. The smells of death did bring back memories of her week underground. Death, whether pickled human or crushed and rotting human, is the same, a distinctive odor not easily forgotten. The occasional flashback bothered Eva but she was a strong woman.

It took months, but Eva eventually found her own little two-bedroom house, a place she could call home. She had bonded with Aunt June in that short time. She saw in her what her own mother could have been, but Eva was an adult and needed her own space.

The great thing about "the other side" of Augusta was that houses were cheap and people would carry a loan. The thought of going to a bank to secure a loan made her laugh out loud.

"I have $10,000 in savings, not including my million-dollar painting, my major asset. Yes, I'm interesting in purchasing this $50,000 dollar fixer-upper. Mm-hmmm, that's right. I have a million-dollar painting, an authentic Thomas Moran, which I own free and clear. You may have seen it if you visited the recent Moran show at the Met in New York."

The thought of seeing her bank loan officer's face when she explained her assets was ludicrous. Visualizing the woman's reaction to this highly unlikely story made Eva want to see the real response, but she knew no one should know such a valuable painting would be sitting in a fixer-upper home in Augusta, not even Aunt June. It was her secret and only hers.

So Eva kept her Moran safe in Dorothy's art box until she got her own place. She loved Aunt June but knew she wouldn't understand about the Moran. She could hear Aunt June's voice insisting, "You have to sell that painting. You and Theo need the money. What are you thinking, girl?" It would be a heated discussion of money versus things, and in June's eyes, a thing could never outweigh living better. Eva knew selling the painting would be the smart move financially but it was never about the money for her. The painting was an emotional connection to Bernard's soul. No amount of money would ever cleave that from her heart.

Finally ensconced in her own home, Eva rose early to hang her Moran for the first time. She wanted to see the piece as the sun's rays first peeked through the tattered yellow kitchen shades. Removing the Moran from Dorothy's professionally packed art box was a thrill. Seeing THE LONE CYPRESS emerge provoked tears, which bounced onto the gold frame as she viewed it for the first time in nearly nine months, the same amount of time she carried Theo during her pregnancy. Images of Bernard helping the old lady at the Met show flashed through her mind, followed by coming home from her tragedy and seeing it hanging, so lovingly arranged there by her departed Bernard. After 20 minutes of studying it with deep sadness and love, it was time to hang the piece, not an easy task for a one-armed person.

Eva set the painting on the kitchen floor, leaning its massive frame against a five-dollar garage-sale chair. The size of the Moran was overpowering for the wall she had chosen, but the natural light was perfect. Eva had seen the painting in two different lighting environments: the Metropolitan Museum and her New York apartment under the perfect lighting Bernard had arranged. But neither site was nearly as compelling as Eva's kitchen wall in her little Augusta home, the morning light shining in from the opposite window. Eva stacked two plastic garage-sale chairs on top of each other. Then standing on one leg she lifted the painting up and balanced it on her left leg until she could slide the left edge of the painting's frame onto the chairs. Once the painting was resting on the plastic chairs, she crouched under the artwork and used her upper back and arm to balance the Moran. Then she blindly stood up on her tiptoes until the wire finally caught the painting hanger which she had nailed into the wall. The painting was hung on the same special art hook Bernard had used when he had it placed professionally in their New York flat. It was obviously made just for that purpose, as Eva had never seen any nails like these. Razor-sharp ends cut through the old house's sheetrock as if they were magic. The kitchen faced east and the morning light hit the Moran full force shortly after Eva hung the piece.

"Well, my love," she told Bernard as she looked at the Moran as it was illuminated by the natural sunlight, "thank you so much for your lovely gift. It will always be in my mind, as will you. Nothing but my death could ever take my LONE CYPRESS from my possession."

Eva felt more at ease when she could find her rhythm in life. It became a ritual for her to wake before the sun came up, brew a cheap blend of coffee in her 1950s kettle, then wait for the light to slowly spread across the kitchen. The first rays would graze the ornate frame, followed by streams of light that would burst onto the magnificent Moran's canvas. Eva would open the yellow window shades to allow the most illumination possible. It was her time to discuss with Bernard what was new in her and Theo's world. Sometimes the conversation was spoken out loud but more often than not, simply thought. She felt the painting was her medium to her Bernard. The private spectacle of light that enveloped the painting each morning was unchanging, except for on cloudy days. Eva believed that Moran must have painted it at sunrise too, experiencing the moment like she did. Eva had wedged the museum-replica settee into the kitchen, positioning it across from the mismatched plastic kitchen chairs. The painting was hanging above her cherished blue Mexican flower bowl at the far edge of a blue linoleum table. The low ceiling didn't allow the painting breathing room, its elaborate gilded frame nearly touching the edge of the bowl's rim, but this decorating faux pas didn't bother Eva. She felt the cohesiveness of the painting and the bowl. It was as if they were a part of her being.

Eva decided to sketch the painting in its entirety every morning as she conversed with Bernard. As her illustration skills improved, the images became more detailed. She would do a week's work, choose the best three, and throw out the rest. It became a cathartic therapy of reevaluation for her, comparing each week's trio of best drawings with the prior week's, then saving only the top three. Studying the water lapping over the rocks brought her back to the present and helped her focus. It was her safe place. As time went on, she relied on it more often.

Aunt June watched Theo at her home during Eva's school hours, then Eva would pick up food, usually chicken at Kenny's, and retrieve little Theo.

Meanwhile, she learned the art of medical illustration. Her artistic aptitude, which she had suppressed to play the bass, was quite exceptional. Maybe the Moran had been speaking to her subconsciously to follow the path of an artist all along. She was approaching 28. She could be an artist much longer than she was a musician, unless something else unexpected changed her life course.

CHAPTER 35

AN ART DEALER'S BIG DEAL

Joseph Penwell and Ashton B. Charmers were on the outs as a couple. Time has a way of making sex seem dull and routine. This was the case for most couples, and Penwell and Ashton were no exception. Ashton was fine with this. He had gotten what he wanted: connections and the legitimizing of his role as an important art dealer. He only needed a few more good contacts before he moved on to New York City, the pinnacle of the art world. The night Penwell told him about one Tommy Thompson, CEO of Dynamite Industries, Ashton performed like it was first love again and for Ashton it felt like it was. Major money would be coming his way.

Penwell explained that Thompson was naïve about art but had the money to buy, billions in fact. Thompson was only interested in the big names and wanted to start with a Moran. Penwell made sure that Ashton understood that if he found anything of significance by Moran, he was to give Penwell first right of refusal unless by some chance he actually was able to turn up a California ocean scene. These were so rare that Penwell had no problems being magnanimous. "No way is Ashton finding such a painting. He might find a great Grand Canyon though, and if so I've got first dibs," he thought as his mind returned to the present and Ashton's enthusiastic bedtime chores.

Introductions were made the next day by phone in a three-way conference call.

Penwell explained, "T.T., I've told Ashton what you are looking for and he knows if he finds a large California piece from your neck of the woods, you can have first right of refusal."

Ashton chimed in, "Yes, you get the next one I come up with. It may take a while. They are quite rare, as I'm sure you know."

T.T. acknowledged, "I understand. So Ashton, what do you think a large Moran will cost? Any ideas?"

Ashton had learned early in his art-dealer career not to quote a price; this will screw you every time. If it's too high, you can scare them off. If you get a great deal, you might leave too much on the table. With Penwell on the three-way call, he wanted to be as general as possible. "T.T., all I can say is that I would expect it to be in the seven figures." Ashton knew Penwell had told T.T. this, but he suspected T.T. wanted to hear the response for himself.

"That will not be an issue. But what about a time frame?" queried T.T.

Again, Ashton knew not to commit to any time frame. This is where Ashton did what the best con men do. He changed his accent back to his Oklahoma roots just the slightest bit. He knew all of Tommy Thompson's history, including their common background growing up in Oklahoma. And one thing old Franklin Hare, aka Ashton B. Charmers had always known, was how to make those small linguistic adjustments. He had perfected it talking winter wheat in Enid to the farmers he would eventually steal from. The key was subtlety, so T.T. would feel more at ease and not realize it.

"I'm going to get right on it, Mr. Thompson. You will need to have some patience with me, but I will find you a piece." Ashton put an emphasis on *piece* with just a little longer "e" than normal.

"I'll be patient, Ashton. I know you will make me happy. I can hear it in your voice. Joseph, I hope this doesn't interfere with your own painting hunt?" T.T. said sincerely.

Penwell replied, "Not a problem, T.T. Just remember, when you get tired of the Moran my Ashton will find you, I would love to see it in one of my favorite museums here in the Bay. Don't be giving it to one of those Oklahoma museums."

T.T. chuckled, "Generally when I like something, I hang on to it. You know I still have the land I got as profit from my first business deal."

Penwell agreed, "All right, no promises, but keep it in mind. Maybe you will have beginner's luck with your painting and get one quickly."

T.T. wrapped up, "Hope so! Ashton, call me when you find something."

"Yes, Mr. Thompson. I hope we will talk soon."

127

"Call me T.T., all my friends do."

"Yes, T.T."

CHAPTER 36

FINDING THE PREY

Finding an important coastal California painting by Moran turned out to be much more difficult than Ashton had anticipated. He was still fairly inexperienced as an art dealer. It takes decades to really understand the business and its connections, and know where the paintings are buried.

No dealers had anything, or at least if they did they weren't talking. Ashton had to be careful. He wanted a painting but didn't want to alert any of his colleagues that someone was looking. A good dealer could figure out who was on the hunt and if somehow like Penwell opened his mouth, other than for a dick, that could be all she wrote, no big payday.

The key was to try and get information without letting on he was looking for something important. Ashton came up with a nice little story. Make the art gallery rounds and try to find a painting done during a similar time frame and style as Moran, but worth much less in value.

He would start the conversation, "That's a nice such and such, almost has the look of a Moran, don't you think?" The dealer of course hoping for a sale would enthusiastically agree with Ashton. This would be a big compliment for his shitty second-rate American painting in the style of Moran.

Ashton would then follow up, "Sorry it isn't a Moran. I have always personally loved his work and wanted to get a great example for my own collection, maybe a Grand Canyon."

Since Ashton wasn't really known in the art world, but did seem to hang with very rich men, it was possible he really was one of those rich guys that liked to pretend he was an art dealer but really wasn't. Dealers watch for these so-called art collector/dealers. It's fine if they don't sell much and are really just buyers. Real art dealers don't care if for some odd reason a collector wants to act like a dealer as long as they don't start taking clients and getting the good stuff from their sources. Since Ashton hadn't shown this tendency, he was still considered to be a client not a competitor. Little did they know he really was the ultimate predatory art dealer with no conscience—a dangerous foe and one to avoid at all costs.

If the dealer being questioned hinted at the possibility of an available Moran, next came the most delicate part of the deception.

"Well I might even settle for something in California, if you can't find the Grand Canyon. I do have a place in California so it would be fine until you could come up with something else. I always have been fond of the ocean as that's the view out my back bedroom window in Malibu."

All dealers know Malibu means money and this guy could probably afford whatever he wanted. The seed was planted and hopefully it would grow. Of course, Ashton had no such Malibu bedroom.

Months went by with no luck. There were a couple of mediocre examples that came up at auction. Ashton hated to use an auction because what he paid would become public record. This was a last resort. T.T. had wanted a couple of Morans. Ashton supposed he could fill one order and develop a false sense of security for Tommy as far as his ability to come up with something reasonable. The Moran pieces available however were just too marginal and both were European. One was THE PASS AT GLENCOE, SCOTLAND, which depicted a great ocean and rocks. He thought about erasing the Scotland attribute and just saying, "I believe that rock is near Pebble Beach. I know it has to be somewhere along the coast in central California." But this was too risky for such a small monetary hit. Ashton B. Charmers was not going to blow his first and maybe only big painting sale by representing a Moran of Scotland as if it were of California.

At the end of a year of nothing, he had tried all the main dealers in New York, Santa Fe, San Francisco, and Carmel. He even queried an obscure dealer he had heard about in Tucson, Arizona. Nothing.

Maybe a crooked museum curator could help? Very risky, he knew, as it could fuck him up for good if the word got out, or even worse, lead to jail. Ashton's visit to Picasso Louie had given him a good idea which curators might play ball.

Still, Ashton decided it could be worth the risk, so he started going through all the museum records and catalogs of Moran holdings. His best opportunity would be some small bumpkin museum. He did know of a monumental Green River, Wyoming painting close to where he had grown up, in Bartlesville, Oklahoma. It had two problems. One, it was the wrong subject matter, though an important piece. And two, rural Oklahoma hicks were much too honest.

It's very frustrating for an art dealer to have a huge, hungry fish and no bait for the hook. Even worse, the bait was impossible to locate and the fish only wanted a very specific food, a California Moran. At first, Ashton had thought this search would take him months. Now it looked like it would turn into years.

CHAPTER 37

THE ONE

A 1993 catalog finally revealed the catch. A large 30-by-40-inch oil titled THE LONE CYPRESS, with the words all art dealers love to see, "Private Collection." That decoded in Ashton's mind as, "Available for purchase."

The catalog was from a comprehensive retrospective of Moran's work at the Metropolitan Museum of Art. There were two California cypress/ocean scenes, but one was small and in the Met's permanent collection. He knew to forget that one. The other just said, "Private Collection."

Ashton was in his element when it came to obtaining information. He needed the name of the private collector. To get the information, he would go to one of the lesser curators at the Metropolitan. A male intern would be ideal. To obtain personal information on an important painting requires delicate skill and a little luck.

A new business card was made up: "Head Curator, Penwell Collection." He giggled to himself as he reread his card. The word "head" was certainly true. His plan was to get to an underling with rolodex power and find out the current owner of the piece.

By now it was the late nineties and the painting could be in someone else's collection or worse, donated to some damn museum.

Ashton arrived in NYC for a prearranged meeting to discuss how he might donate a portion of the Penwell collection to the Met. He knew one phone call to anyone who knew Penwell would destroy that ruse, since Penwell was a San Francisco man and his art would stay there. On the off chance of such a call, Ashton made sure he said San Francisco was the likely final ending place, but it never hurt to find out one's options. This last remark guaranteed only a second-class curator would take him seriously. A museum director is not going to waste their time on might's and maybe's.

His meeting was with one Jeffrey Baines II, a recent graduate of Penn State in his first month of work. He was bright, probably gay, and most importantly still green enough to care. Ashton had discussed on the phone with Baines the possibility of a substantial art and monetary gift, indicating he would like to see the holdings of the museum, specifically any Morans. He had explained that Penwell had a very important Moran, GREEN RIVER VALLEY WYOMING, 1872, one of the best, and this particular painting was one that Ashton would like to see in the most important museum setting, the Met.

Ashton played his hand like a true professional. Lots of talk about art and some background history, nothing specific of course. Ashton tried to determine his young host's sexuality as he knew this was a card that worked well for him in many cases. Baines, he decided, was asexual—one of those rare individuals that you can be around for years and not know who or what they are sleeping with. He extended to Baines a transparency of his client's Moran, with all the particulars which he had memorized. Jeffrey was duly impressed and realized from his well-heeled art history training that this was indeed an important work.

"Jeffrey, if we do donate this work we will want to replace it with something else, maybe another Moran you would ultimately end up with as well." The lure was thrown and now to set the hook.

Ashton added, "There is a Moran that would probably work if it is still available. It's in private hands, that's my understanding. It was in your wonderful catalog on Moran. THE LONE CYPRESS."

"Yes, I'm familiar with the image. I don't know anything about who owns it. would you like me to see if I can find out?"

Wham. A strike, and this was a gut hook. No losing this fish.

"Yes if possible, that would be wonderful. I'm on a tight schedule. I was going to see one of the curators at the Whitney today. Penwell will be happy to hear this, I'm sure."

The two went down a side elevator, the kind that required a key and made a thunk when the door closed. It slowly traversed downward, reaching some unknown floor with another thunk and a jerking halt. The air quality in all large older museums is similar to a root cellar in Oklahoma, with a kind of musty aged smell, the type that permeates your clothes. That old grandma scent. It reminded Ashton of home, but not of fond memories.

Computers were still finding their way into the museum world in the late nineties. Most curators still relied on old card catalogs as the Met did.

Baines searched his files, extracting a card. Ashton hovered at his elbow as Baines said, "Let's see here. Yes, here we go. THE LONE CYPRESS, c. 1881, 30-by-40 oil on canvas, original title on reverse and an original Moran frame. Excellent condition. An exceptional painting. We have the owner listed as one Bernard Rashmusen of New York City. Phone is 212-418-1800. Here's the address, too. What I'll do is just check with my boss to make sure it's OK for me to give you this information and then I can get back to you."

Ashton stepped back. "Not necessary, Jeffrey. Penwell I believes summers in the Hamptons with the Rashmusen family. He can see them this summer. If for some reason I do need their information, I'll let you know."

"OK, let me know and I can go through the proper channels," Baines agreed.

The information was already embedded in Ashton's mind. He had memorized every detail of the card. "No need for any channels, my dear," Ashton thought to himself. "What a naïve idiot to let me see the card. A fool. Rashmusen better be willing to deal or he will be in for some trouble. This Moran will be mine, one way or another. Bernard Rashmusen, you just don't know it yet!"

CHAPTER 38

EVA AND WILLY

Despite Aunt June's almost daily help, Eva was finding raising a child by herself to be a challenge. Having one arm added another dimension of isolation. Her main form of relaxation came from drawing and learning human anatomy.

The new career of medical illustration was working out well. She was at the top of her class and almost halfway through the required course. She had used $5,000 of her reserve toward her home's down payment, but still had a few thousand dollars left. She watched every cent, getting back into "poor mode," as she referred to it. She offered to pay Aunt June to watch her boy, but she would have none of that. "Family don't charge family for what you're supposed to do," was Aunt June's retort. Her aunt's babysitting time allowed Eva's drawing to improve rapidly. She pursued drawing as she once had the bass, with a single-minded focus. As her own image of herself changed from musician to artist, it all clicked. Form, color, light, all in harmony. The right-brain neurons simply rearranged themselves as drawing neurons. She became an artist within months.

She decided she would like to draw the human form in motion during some type of sporting event. Eva knew of only one sport in Augusta, golf. Golf seemed perfect. It had a nice, fluid, fairly slow motion that was easy to watch and capture on paper. She decided to go over to one of the local golf courses and see if she could find a model. The golf course she went to was one she had seen on TV that all the locals talked about. It would be a good starting place.

This is how Eva ended up in front of the gates of Augusta National. The gate guard, Henry Jackson, a 60-year-old muscular black man who had worked the same front entrance gate for the last 10 years, smiled widely upon seeing the lovely face of Eva De Plain. Not many young black women graced his presence. He of course knew without even speaking that she had no clue as to what Augusta National was.

"Hi there. I'm looking to sketch one of your golfers for my art class, if that would be all right?" Eva held up her sketch pad and for the first time the guard noticed she had no left arm.

"Unfortunately, Miss, this course is private. No one but members and their guests are allowed on the property. I'm afraid it's impossible to just let you in."

Eva's radiant face never wavered. "Oh I see. Thanks anyway, Mr. Jackson," she replied, reading his name badge. Then she turned to walk away.

"Give me a second now," Jackson said. "Let me call our sister golf course. I know a young man who I bet will help you out. Willy Wilson, one of our local golf legends." Jackson, a veteran police officer who was now on his second career, liked the girl from the git-go and couldn't help but feel empathy for a person struggling with a disability. Besides, she was great looking and he knew he would be doing a solid for young Willy.

"Great, that would just be wonderful," Eva beamed.

Two calls and five minutes later, the imposing Jackson had arranged a meeting at the golf shop over at Augusta Country Club just 10 minutes away.

"Mr. Jackson, what does Mr. Wilson look like so I can recognize him?"

"He'll be the young black man with the big smile greeting you at the front desk." Jackson had known Willy since he was a teenager and lunched most days with his Uncle Ed. Willy was going to like this beautiful young black woman, arm or no arm. He would definitely be smiling.

Sure enough, he was. "Willy Wilson, head pro, and sometimes golf professional at your service."

Eva liked what she saw immediately. The security guard had been right. Willy was beaming, ear to ear, one of those smiles where almost all the teeth could be counted. His front two incisors had a distinctive 5mm gap between them. It made his face and she liked his kind eyes. For the first time in 13 months, she felt movement in her heart. It sped up, catching her off guard, but she didn't fight it.

"Well, you see, Mr. Wilson...."

"Call me Willy."

"Willy, it's nice to meet you. I'm Eva De Plain, a student at the Georgia Medical School in illustration and I want to work from life so I thought that a golfer might be the perfect subject. I'm afraid I don't know a lot about the game other than watching that Tiger fellow, I seem to have forgotten his last name. He's the one that always seems to be on TV when they talk about golf?"

Talk of Tiger stung Willy and his smile lessened just a touch. Now only 28 of his teeth were showing. Ever since Tiger had come on the scene, Willy had been referred to as the other black golfer, not nearly as good as Tiger. After all, there was only one Tiger. Willy could tell by the way Eva referred to him as that "Tiger fellow," not remembering his last name, that she must not know anything about golf. Tiger had long ago gone to one name, but everyone in the golf world knew his last name. Willy thought to himself, "I will never be known as just Willy. Chances are that I will only be an asterisk in some golf magazine or a trivia question about black golfers of the PGA. Like, who was the black man who first invented the golf tee? Answer: George Grant, 1899 patent and the first black man to graduate from Harvard Dental School." Nonetheless, Willy's attention returned to Eva, someone he was very much attracted to. He asked, "Do you know much about the game?" already anticipating the answer.

"No, I really don't. In fact the first time I have ever been to a golf course was this morning at Augusta National, where the nice Mr. Jackson sent me to you."

Ironic, Willy thought. Augusta had also been the first golf course he went to. It was known for its elite white rich status by the outside world, yet she and he had this in common. This had to be more than chance. He would need to thank Jackson personally for his excellent insight. "So, Tiger and I have something in common. We are both professional golfers and also black, if you hadn't noticed."

Eva actually hadn't until he mentioned it. "Yes I guess you are kind of black, in a non-African way," she quipped, taking a little jab at Willy to let him know she had seen blacker. Willy thought of his father who was so proud of his African heritage. Nat would not have been amused, but Willy liked this girl's spirit.

"Eva. I hope you don't mind if I call you Eva?"

"Please do," she encouraged, her voice resonating in Willy's head.

"The golf swing is one of the most beautiful motions you have ever experienced. Once perfected, it is as natural as making love to a beautiful woman." This was as forward as Willy had ever been in his life. It just came out and his face turned crimson.

Eva noticed, immediately deciding to make some fun of the awkward situation. "My current armless condition makes me worried, as I'm sure my golf swing will be poor at best. I hope this won't affect my lovemaking, which I have been told is nearly perfect and hard to compare to any golf swing I can imagine."

Willy's crimson went to a deep tomato red. He gulped, "I have no doubt that anyone who has had the pleasure of knowing your swing, so to speak, would think highly of it. I already do and I haven't even watched you pick up a club yet."

Hearing of Willy's interest in her made Eva's own face blush. The sudden rush of sexual energy took her off guard. She thought that part of her body had died along with her left arm in Mexico City. She surprised herself when she told Willy, "I'd like to see your golf swing very much. I'm here to draw a live golfer and it appears it's going to be you."

CHAPTER 39

LEARNING GOLF

Eva watched Willy, a young man in his mid-20s, swing his golf clubs with abandonment. She was no doubt older than he was, had a child, and only one arm, but the attraction was undeniable. How to handle this situation would be a challenge. By now Eva felt as if she was in her 40s, not pushing 30. She had basically been widowed, disfigured, had a baby, and was starting a new career. She didn't have time for a love life and wasn't looking for one. What she did need was to finish her new training and hopefully leave Augusta. Young men like Willy require a lot of attention and time wasn't a luxury she could afford. Six hours of school per day, then another four of drawing, and then Theo time left little room for a romance, even with someone as compelling as Willy Wilson.

Even with all the reasons why not, Eva still could not resist the excuse to go to the golf course and draw Willy hitting the ball, putting, and giving lessons. The mere sight of Willy intently looking at a putt as the ball headed to the hole and then smiling spontaneously when it went in, aroused her emotionally as well as sexually.

The weeks turned into months and then it happened. That pivotal moment that changes a relationship from one form to another. It's different for all couples, but all have the common thread of a single event that transforms two into one. For most it's a date, a movie, a concert, a weekend getaway, even a museum exhibit. For Eva it was a golf lesson.

Golf is like learning a language. It takes lots of time and intensity. Eva had said the same about music and art. She was sure golf was not her sport. How could it be? She only had one arm, not even a stump to hold the club against.

"Listen to me Eva, you can learn the game. I will teach it to you. One, two, or three arms, it doesn't matter," Willy insisted, pointing out there was a great Australian professional golfer, Jack Newton, who lost his right arm in an airplane propeller accident but was still was able to play and score in the mid-80s afterward.

"Wow he must have been great. In the mid-80s. Of course I don't have a clue what the top score is?" Eva replied.

Willy looked intently into Eva's large green eyes and smiled back. "Lower is better than higher, but what I'm trying to say, my little beginner, is that Newton, who could be great with only one arm, has the same qualities as you. Great hand-eye coordination. I've watched you draw and you definitely have that. It's like watching someone play an instrument, seeing you draw."

His insight sent chills down Eva's spine. She had not shared her former career or life tragedies yet. All she had said with regards to her arm loss was she happened to be in the wrong place and Mother Nature wanted a piece of her, so she gave it.

"Eva, let me try and show you what golf is to me and maybe to you as well." The sincerity in Willy's eyes made Eva believe maybe it was possible for her to learn the game or at least understand its importance to Willy.

"OK, Mr. Golf Instructor, if you want to try to make a one-armed, unbalanced girl learn to hit that little white ball, I'm all ears, just not arms."

"Outstanding. That's the spirit. I want you to stand here, legs slightly apart and knees bent. Make that butt of yours a little more bubble butt-like and then hold this club with whichever hand you like." He chuckled a little into her right ear and snuggled his body up against hers, his legs mirroring her bend at the knees ever so slightly touching them. Slowly taking his large hands, he gently covered her right hand then brought his arm around her body embracing Eva as if she was the golf club.

Eva could feel his groin against the small of her back, his breath in her right ear, and the skin of his left arm touching the outside of her left breast. Her heart raced uncontrollably. She wondered if he could hear it. "You know Willy, you're right. I do like this golf. Is this all there is to it?" she said with a girlish laugh that surprised her.

"No, we are just getting started. I want you to relax your good arm and I'm going to act like your missing arm until you get the feeling of

140

hitting that little white ball. Once you experience what the correct motion is, then you can do it on your own."

Gently, Willy pivoted and swung his body back along with hers, then after reaching the perfect height started to rotate the arm touching Eva's breast at the top of the swing. Their momentum then shifted and the club swung in the other direction. Eva could feel her nipples become erect from the intimate contact. Willy's left cheek gently touched hers as their bodies finished the swing as a unit.

"Now we will try it for real. Take a step forward with the ball in between your feet, and let's go again, this time hitting that little white ball, which is the objective of the game."

Eva and Willy repeated the same motion, but this time there was a clinking noise as the three wood hit the sweet spot of the club and the golf ball flew to the 175-yard marker.

"See that's all there is to golf!" Willy exclaimed.

Eva let go of the club, swiveled into his arms which were still embracing her, and looked directly into his eyes.

"Now I see why everyone likes golf so much. It's quite a high when you hit that little ball, isn't it?" And with that, Eva stood up onto her tip toes to reach the six-foot-two Willy and passionately embraced his lips, hard and long. Breaking away after what seemed to be many minutes, Eva let her intentions be known.

"I'm afraid I may be a slow learner with my arm disability and all, so many lessons just like this may be in order. I hope the cost isn't too much?"

Willy grinned, "It just so happens that for the rest of the year we are starting a special rate for the physically challenged golfers. There's no charge as long as you can put up with the club pro."

"I'm only challenged when it comes to golf. In other areas I'm considered to be quite athletic. I hope that doesn't nullify the deal?"

"I can make an exception in your case." Willy then embraced Eva as he had been hoping to do since seeing her for the first time. They were now a couple, thanks to Augusta National.

CHAPTER 40

MAKING A NEW LIFE

Eva took golf lessons from Willy for three years. During this time she became proficient at hitting a golf ball with one arm. The years of bass playing translated into fine motor control. Her drives were long and straight. When she was on the golf range invariably a crowd would form around her, as they had when she use to play bass on the subway. The sight of this beautiful black woman smashing a golf ball with one arm was inspiring for all those who were frustrated by the game. Often she would sing to herself like a human metronome to get the cadence of her swing in tune with her own circadian rhythm. She was oblivious to the onlookers, lost in her own world. It was great entertainment and Willy was proud of her abilities. Unbeknownst to Eva he would post on his daily events board a note when Eva would be hitting.

Theo at age four had grown into a clone of his mom, curious about the world and musically inclined. He would often accompany his mom to meet Willy after work and have their evening match. It would be Willy, Eva, and Theo for, as they referred to it, "Augusta versus New Orleans Putt-Off." It was their family event, great entertainment and zero cost. Theo would compete for either side depending on his mood that day. Willy the golf pro had to concentrate when he played Eva as she was deadly with her putter. Though usually Eva was not terribly competitive, when it came to these matches she was a shark. Willy had lost on more than one occasion, which little Theo loved, unless he was playing for the Augusta team that night. The act of beating the head golf pro got Eva giggling and her laugh was infectious, even to the loser. Her love for Willy had grown deep and golf cemented the bond. She saw the good in Willy in the way he was around other people, and as she learned the game she realized his enormous talent. The fact that he couldn't be out on the tour where he belonged but was still happy and productive at his job made her love him all the more. Willy, who was extremely competitive, didn't mind when Eva occasionally won. He was truly happy for her. This big-heartedness gave her great confidence that he was a man she could spend her life with. Theo also loved Willy and it was clear the feelings were mutual. It was a forgone conclusion in Eva's and Willy's minds that they were in it for the long haul.

Eva had slowly opened up about the tragedies of her life, including losing her arm in Mexico, Theo's unbelievable birth, and her first deep love, Bernard. She had explained the sudden loss of Theo's grandmother in a car accident, leaving Theo basically alone except for her and his Aunt June. She also shared her training in music in NYC and that at one time she was a serious bassist. She did not, however, feel it was the right time to divulge the story of the Moran. This was not because she was afraid Willy would focus on the money in the painting. She knew in her heart that money was never his main motivator; pride in his job and personal satisfaction motivated Willy. The Moran was something else altogether. It was hers and Bernard's special moment, and someday Theo's inheritance. The early morning talks with Bernard had become fewer since Willy had come into the picture. The morning ritual of drawing her painting continued, but now she sang to herself and sometimes Theo as she completed her drawings. Soon she would be to the point where she felt comfortable sharing her innermost secrets. She was afraid that divulging the importance of the Moran might make Willy feel that he could never compete with Bernard, and of course the painting's back inscription would never go away. The bottom line was that she didn't want to risk damaging the great relationship she was building with Willy, nor the one she had had with Bernard. The fact that a million-dollar masterpiece sat in her forties tinderbox of a home in close proximity to the bad part of Augusta was a worry, but it was her worry and she wanted to keep it that way. Crime was only sporadic and if someone did steal to support a drug habit, it would be for something that could be sold quickly like a television set or jewelry. Any painting in the kitchen was just that; a poor person's form of art, no value there. So Eva kept her secret to herself.

Eva had fallen deeply in love with Willy and it seemed Augusta, Georgia, would be more than a short stopping point in her life. It would be her only stop. It was Willy's home and his affinity for the place was obvious. Eva had finished number one in her class in medical illustration and had numerous contracts with drug companies for illustrations, all of which could be done at home and by mail. This made living in Augusta just fine.

Willy's life was one of coming and going. He traveled six months of the year. Generally he played the Nationwide Tour until his back gave out or his outlay was more than the incoming money. Then he would come back to Augusta Country Club, work as hard as he could while trying to save his back, and earn as much money as possible, giving lessons and working extra shifts. The three years she had been dating him he had never been in town for more than three months in a row.

What Eva could count on was that he would be here for the first full week in April because that was the Masters Tournament in Augusta. This was the only time his employers at the Augusta Country Club would not and could not spare their pro. He needed to be available to schmooze the big-time golfers that came to town. When Augusta National hosted the Masters, all the other golf clubs in the city became important. The courses would double their going rates, sell tons of merchandise with the word Augusta somewhere on it, and fill up their usually empty dining rooms. This was money week in Augusta and whether you knew golf or not, you did golf.

Eva learned from Willy the long history of Augusta National. She remembered how innocent she had been that first day asking to watch the golfers and how dear Mr. Jackson directed her to Willy. Willy Wilson's story was well known around town. Eva even met Billy Bob on several occasions. Their first encounter was at Augusta National's dining room, a place where ties were required. Willy and Billy Bob may have been polar opposites in their life stories, but Eva still liked the man who had befriended Willy, even though he did stare unmercifully at her left side at that first get-together. Billy Bob's eyes locked on Eva's armless dress and finally Willy had to say, "Yep, Billy Bob, she lost that left one, though losing it really does help her keep the ball straight down the middle."

Billy Bob turned red and mustered up an immediate apology in a very Billy Bob way. "Yeah, you would think I'd never seen a one-armed black female golfer here at Augusta National. My apologies for staring. I was just taken by surprise since your boyfriend here never mentioned it." Billy Bob glanced over at Willy. Billy Bob's feelings for Willy had grown over the years as did the way he viewed race. Whether he consciously knew it or not, he was more polite to the black caddies and told endless stories about young Willy Casper

Wilson, his protégée. He thought of Willy sort of as his son and his affection for him was obvious.

The awkward moment was lightened by Eva who tossed in, "Willy says you're one of the reasons he has done so well in life, so no apologies necessary. You'll get used to not seeing it soon enough and forget, like Willy has, that I've lost an arm."

Eva's job during Masters week was to help Willy any way she could, usually with long back massages at night, his favorite meals for dinner, and moral encouragement. It was hard for him to recount his glory days countless times to the visiting golfers: the kid that played Augusta National at 12, specific holes on the course and how he played them, all the people he had met, his best round of 64 at age 19. He understood rehashing all this was part of his job as head pro of the next best thing to Augusta National, but it was depressing. The question he hated the most and received most frequently was, "When are you going to play the Masters? I would think you would kill 'em." His standard answer was, "As soon as I get better on all the other PGA courses, I guess. Then I'll show them how to really play Bobby's course."

Bobby was of course Bobby Jones, the founder of Augusta National and the best amateur golfer ever. Bobby Jones had died just one year after Willy was born, in 1971, and was buried at Atlanta's Oakland Cemetery. Jones was such a hero at the Masters that many visiting the tournament made their first stop at Bobby's grave and left a golf ball or tee to say thanks.

Discussing when he would play Bobby's course often provoked a painful fake laugh from Willy. It bothered Eva immensely to hear this. She knew Willy's deep, rumbling laugh, a sound she loved. This on the other hand was pain masked to sound like what a laugh might be if a piece of food was stuck deep in his esophagus and the smooth muscle tissue was unable to clear it. Eva knew all about human anatomy now and the importance of tissue. It hurt her and she felt for her Willy when he got these questions. Honestly, she hated Masters week except for the fact that he was here at night. Yes, she could count on seeing him, but he was usually exhausted and often depressed.

Willy had to play two 18-hole rounds of golf a day when the VIPs came to town, a requirement of his job. All of the mucky mucks wanted to feel special and Willy was the closest thing Augusta Country Club had to a PGA pro and one who knew Augusta and all its courses. By the end of the week, Willy's back was shot. The pain would often refer down his left leg and cause muscle spasms in his calf muscles. He hated drugs but this week ibuprofen and muscle relaxants were the main courses along with Eva's family recipe for blackened redfish.

Nonetheless, Willy was a trooper during Masters week, working 15-hour days and playing golf. Somehow, he always managed to escape to see the big show, even if it was only for a few holes during a lunch break.

Just like all the others, he listened for a Tiger roar. When Tiger is on the course, the gallery follows his every move. The gallery of fans can be 20 deep. When a great shot is made by Tiger, which invariably occurs, the crowd reacts with one spontaneous yell. It's a phenomenon of golf and golfing crowds that they react as one whole entity when affected by a stimulus. If you are into golf, you know you are bound by this invisible connection. The roar which always seemed loudest around Tiger was something Willy had always dreamed of for himself at the Masters Tournament.

The only thing separating the huge crowds and the professional golfers walking up the fairway was a thin white line of rope on either side of each hole. This flimsy barrier kept the crowds off the course and away from the professionals and those who were supposed to be following the professionals—the cameramen, commentators, and such. The thin white lines excluded the greats from those who only dreamed about being great. That was how Willy Wilson regarded the scenario. He respected the power of the white lines but also despised them. To him it was as if the small white rope had the ability to exclude him from being part of Augusta's history, something he so desperately wanted. When Willy had the opportunity to get close to the white lines, he would press his body against the thin white strip and try to imagine being on the other side, talking to his caddie and the other professional golfers in his group during a practice round. He already knew many of those individuals, but at Masters time he was always looking at them from the outside, longing for their walk of importance into history. Willy wondered if such would ever be his destiny or if he would always just be a club pro looking in.

CHAPTER 41

EVA'S UNEXPECTED SURPRISE

Willy was not around Eva as much as he would like, but the time they had together was always intense. Theo would usually stay with Aunt June, and Eva would come over to Willy's house.

Willy's extended leaves of absence would always make their lovemaking sessions feel like they were starved animals. Deep kisses, passionate fondling of every body part, and he would stroke her long black hair as if it were the finest silk. Eva never tired of rubbing his stout abdominal muscles, which had to contend with the only part of his anatomy that was weak, his back. Her hand would constantly rub up and down the muscles of his taut athletic body like she used to play the bass. The symphony always concluded in sexual satisfaction for both.

They had now been together for almost four years and she had just found out that his last Masters stay also left a special gift. She was pregnant.

Eva worried intensely about her new pregnancy. She prayed that nothing horrible would happen to her or her unborn child. She tried not to dwell on the Mexico City ordeal but it had damaged her. The thoughts kept coming, the deep, dark, painful memories and fear. She didn't want anything to destroy her second child and hoped this time God would give her a husband who would survive the birth, unlike with her last pregnancy. Eva worried even more because no baby names had come to her yet. She was terrified it would take some horrific event for the name to be revealed, like last time. Eva knew this was idiotic. She was only a few months along, yet the worries persisted. She couldn't help thinking about her grandmother's special gifts and wondering if she had these gifts too and something was wrong.

When Willy returned from yet another disappointing golf tournament, Eva finally shared the news. "My love, I have something to tell you," Eva whispered in his ear after lovemaking.

"Yes, love of my life, what is it?"

"Theo is not going to be an only child."

Willy tried to comprehend what she was telling him. "You mean, we're going to have a baby?"

"Yes, I'm two months pregnant. I guess they didn't work you quite as hard as they should have during that last Masters. If you only had been playing in the damn tournament, we wouldn't be in this little mess," Eva joked gently. She knew how Willy so desperately wanted to be in between the white lines and she feared it would never happen. So Eva did what she did best: she recognized his pain and eased it with humor and love.

"Next year, I'll keep that in mind. I'll make sure I make the cut. I would have this year if I had known it would lead to this," Willy retorted.

Together they laughed and discussed their future plans. Willy suggested getting married and making her an honest woman. Eva had warmed to the idea of taking a husband. She would have undoubtedly married Bernard if the earthquake had not stepped in.

This time, no one and nothing would destroy her happiness. It was her turn. Soon she would also share the fact that she was a millionaire, even if only on canvas and she would never sell her treasure. Willy was in for a second surprise: her cheap kitchen art was a famous painting by Thomas Moran.

CHAPTER 42

FINDING T.T.'S MORAN

Ashton now had the phone number for the owner of the Moran, one Bernard Rashmusen. However, he soon found out the number was no longer good. Likewise, the address no longer produced a tenant named Rashmusen. There had been an Upper East Side apartment under Bernard's name, but it had been sold several years ago. No one seemed to know his whereabouts.

A search of the archives of *The New York Times* might turn up more. A man like Bernard Rashmusen who had such an important Moran must be known socially. Ashton decided to start with the arts section during the run of the Met's Moran show back in 1993.

He found Bernard in the style section, under openings and events: a small black-and-white photo of Bernard and Dorothy Rashmusen at some important museum opening. Mother and son looked wealthy.

The search just got a lot easier. He now had a photo and it included mom.

There were no phone listings for Dorothy in New York. The name was unusual so it helped to avoid false leads. Back to the drawing board.

Ashton eventually found something very disturbing but potentially exciting at the same time: the obituary of his prey, Bernard Rashmusen. The article went into detail about Bernard's death in the 1995 Mexico City earthquake, his family, and how his only living relative was one Dorothy Rashmusen. "Time to cross out the photo of Bernard and concentrate only on the old lady," Ashton said to himself as he colored in Bernard's face. After finishing he remarked, "Wonder if I could have been an artist—it's a lot easier to make this shit than steal it."

Another article in the paper discussed how Bernard's girlfriend, Eva De Plain, had survived the ordeal while nine months pregnant. No photos of her were available.

However, another day of research found the next bit of bad news: the death of Dorothy Rashmusen in a hit-and-run car accident. Later issues talked of her generous donation of her artwork to the Historical Society in Long Island. The paper listed a few of the artists donated. It was a who's who of money makers but did not mention Thomas Moran. Ashton crumpled the newspaper photo with the black-faced Bernard and threw it in the toilet then urinated on the dissolving paper. "Shit, this just got harder," he muttered.

Ashton decided to make a little visit to Long Island tomorrow for a discussion about the late Dorothy Rashmusen's generous donation. Penwell might also be making a donation to his boyhood home of Long Island. He had a large Moran to give away, unless they already had one.

It was fairly easy for Ashton to reach the secretary of the curator, a Mrs. White. She sounded ancient. Maybe he could get all the information over the phone. After all, it was a small historical museum. Mrs. White was very much aware of Ms. Rashmusen's wonderful gift of all her artwork. The estate was an unconditional gift. Unconditional meant de-accession was possible. This was great for Ashton because small museums often would get rid of important pieces because they needed money or the curator might get a kickback.

"Do we know if there were any Morans in the collection? I'm a curator myself and we are considering giving a large, important piece if the historical museum doesn't already have one. I thought Ms. Rashmusen may have already given you one?" Ashton inquired.

"No, I'm sure of that. I would have remembered a Moran. We did receive a nice eastern landscape by Bierstadt and a lovely small Turner, but no Moran. We would love to have one since it's a rather glaring omission in our collection," Mrs. White replied chattily.

Ashton wondered to himself, "Where the fuck did it go? She died suddenly, her only son was dead, and she gave this place her entire art collection?" More politely, he queried out loud: "I heard about the untimely death of her son Bernard. What did she do with his collection? I'm surprised it didn't end up at your lovely museum, too."

"Yes, that was tragic. I knew Bernard. He was such a giving man and loved the arts. I think everything was family art, if you know what I mean. If he did have some things, they must have gone back to Dorothy. She died shortly after he did. A horrible hit and run. They never caught the person."

"Sorry to hear that. Those kind of people are the worst, to kill someone and then leave the scene. What kind of animal does that?" Ashton smiled into the receiver as the words came out, for he knew exactly what kind of person that was.

Ashton was at a loss as to what had happened to the million-dollar painting. Could it have been at Bernard's house and someone took it after his death? The paper said that Bernard had a pregnant girlfriend. He muttered, "That's got to be it. The bitch stole it. It was in her boyfriend's house, he died, and she just kept it. Fuck, that's so cool. She's as bad as me. I've figured it out and she will have to sell it if I put the screws to her. This is the big hit I've been waiting for. T.T., get out your check book. I'm looking for $2 million."

CHAPTER 43

MORAN'S FOR ALL

Eva decided to give Willy a special gift, a drawing she had done of THE LONE CYPRESS. She had drawn the image hundreds of times. The repetitive drawing of her Moran had helped Eva better understand shadowing and composition. She was always impressed by the painting's ease in capturing the sublime. Eva had finished this particular rendition last month and knew it was a keeper. It was worthy of special recognition. She had continued to sketch the Moran even after finishing her illustration training. It was a routine she enjoyed. It also helped remind her of Bernard, whose memory was starting to be supplanted by Willy. The drawing would be a natural way to explain her Moran and its extreme value. She decided to splurge and have her image professionally framed, the first time she had ever framed a piece she had made. Eva wrote an inscription in the lower rocks where Moran had signed his piece. Hers read, "To Willy, My Augusta hero. Love, Eva De Plain/Thomas Moran."

Willy was out of town and she wanted everything in place before he got back. Eva hung the rather large drawing in his kitchen positioned to catch the light. She used an extra painting hanger that Dorothy had sent along with the Moran. Eva had no idea if Willy knew who Thomas Moran was, but she thought his natural curiosity would play into her surprise. She left a note under the painting which read, "I have one more surprise, Eva."

Willy was due home in a week, but it might be sooner if he didn't make the cut as his back had been particularly weak of late. She usually rooted for him to win, but honestly this week she was just hoping he would be home soon. She was in the last part of her first trimester and the nausea and weakness made her crave his support. Still no names for the baby.

Ashton B. Charmers found Eva's address in Augusta, Georgia. He had gone to her old New York apartment and talked to the next-door neighbors who remembered Eva fondly. It was tragic about her husband and losing an arm. They liked her a lot and remembered she was moving to Augusta to stay with an aunt. They had received a

153

postcard or two from Eva and still had the last one. "Tell Eva hi and we think of her often," they said. Ashton had no intention of giving Eva the message, but he would be seeing her very shortly. He booked a plane for the next day, the address from the neighbors' postcard memorized.

Ashton decided to offer Eva $50K for the painting. From what he could gather, she was black, one armed, and seemed to have disappeared into a small Georgia town he had barely heard of. How could she refuse that kind of money, especially if she was hiding something, like a stolen painting from the Dorothy Rashmusen collection? He had started to hope Eva was the one who had run down the old lady to steal the piece. This would be something he could relate to, even admire. He could do business with someone who would do such a thing.

The most direct way to get to Augusta required flying into Atlanta and driving 2 1/2 hours to Augusta. If you had a private jet you could fly directly to the city. Ashton vowed to himself, "I will only fly by private jet someday. I am special and deserve private. Commercial is common, like my old name."

Arriving in Augusta was not what Ashton had expected. He knew a big-time golf event was held there every year as many of his clients droned on about how fucking great it was. He could care less about golf or anything about that so-called sport. Augusta confirmed his low opinion of it. The town, as best he could figure, was terribly poor. The interstate made a huge loop around the city. The area he was going to was apparently somewhere on the wrong side of the loop. Abandoned houses dotted the landscape. Their long-ago broken windows and mildewed wood gave a sad appearance next to the great old oak trees. Ashton had grown up in a poor part of Enid, Oklahoma, but comparatively his home was almost middle-class. The thought that a million-dollar painting could possibly be located in this sea of despair seemed nearly impossible. "Brilliant," he said as a light bulb went off in his head. "The bitch is hiding in poverty. No one would ever expect to find a Moran in this shithole. I better be careful. This may be one smart thief and possibly a murderer." Ashton's black eyes grew cold and his knuckles white as he gripped the steering wheel of his rental car, calculating his options for dealing with Eva De Plain.

After a long search through blocks of similarly plain wooden homes, Ashton finally found the two-bedroom nondescript house Eva lived in. No one appeared to be home. He peeked into a side window. Ashton couldn't believe his eyes. Sitting in a breakfast nook was THE LONE CYPRESS. He was thinking about just breaking the window and grabbing the painting when he heard a young boy's voice query, "Where's my pants, Mommy?"

Ashton made a quick exit and went back to his shitty hotel room on Augusta's main commercial strip. It was $65 dollars a night except during the first week in April, when it was $300. He decided if Eva wouldn't play ball, he was leaving with the painting no matter what. "No $2 million painting is going stay in some black chick's pathetic house in Augusta," he muttered. "The painting deserves better." He saw himself as a true art connoisseur now, not just a crooked art dealer.

In case she was unwilling, he devised a course of action to obtain Eva's painting. He couldn't just steal the piece. In the very unlikely scenario it was actually legally hers, it would be too hard to sell for a very long time and T.T. had been waiting years already for his Moran. To get the painting required a foolproof plan and he had one.

That evening Ashton went to Augusta's bad side of town for a steak. He looked for a place ex-cons would hang out. He was scared but it was a necessary chance. The restaurant was Ray's Rib Joint. It had no white customers. Ashton wondered if maybe he was one of the few whites to ever come in. He ordered a steak and then told one of the roughest bus boys he had ever seen, "Sorry to bother you, but I didn't get a steak knife." He pointed at his steaming rib eye.

The obviously irritated black man gave Ashton a look of, "Fuck you, whitey. You got a knife. You probably just dropped it on the floor and want to make me look bad." His left bulging bicep said *LeRoy* intertwined in a spider-web tattoo that enclosed his entire elbow. He roughly tossed Ashton a serrated, black-handled steak knife which bounced twice as it landed on the table. The metal blade made a loud pinging noise as it careened off the old iron table. LeRoy said, "There's your knife, man, enjoy," muttering *motherfucker* under his breath as he walked away.

155

LeRoy's abrupt departure was perfect. Ashton picked up the knife with his napkin and carefully rolled it up, then slid napkin and knife into his coat pocket. From his lap he removed the original steak knife which he had hidden and quietly slid it back onto the plate with the still steaming steak. After eating a few bites of the delicious bloody meat, Ashton quickly exited, living a generous tip as a thank you to his new friend LeRoy.

A mile away, Ashton scored some crack from a 14-year-old kid and put it in the same pocket with the wrapped-up knife and went home, mission accomplished.

Ashton decided to watch Eva for a few days to make sure he knew the family routine and who had access to the house. He noted that three people came and went: an old black lady, the young blackish kid, and Eva the one-armed art thief. Eva looked harmless enough and didn't seem like the murdering kind. She was not what he had expected. The kid looked as much white as black, which probably meant he was the child of the late Bernard Rashmusen. Ashton considered the remote possibility that Bernard actually did give the Moran to Eva, though he still figured Eva's running down the old lady was a better possibility.

Eva's routine was the same for three days. She left the house at 7:30 am with the kid, came back at 8:30 alone, then there was no movement again until 2:30 when she left the house again, returning at 3:30 with the kid. The old lady showed up once at 5 pm. Early morning would be best for his visit. "Time for me to get my Moran tomorrow and I hope she wants to play ball," Ashton said to himself as he conducted surveillance in his rental car.

CHAPTER 44

MY MORAN

Dressed in a black blazer, red polo shirt, black freshly ironed pants, and velvet black shoes, Ashton knocked on Eva's door. His well-dressed appearance seemed completely out of place on the old wooden steps of Eva's house. Ashton had been practicing his introduction as if auditioning for an important movie role. He wanted it to sound just right.

Eva opened the door and was immediately suspicious. White men dressed like this could only mean trouble.

"Yes, how may I help you?" she asked.

"Hello, my name is Joseph Penwell," Ashton commenced, lying through his teeth. "I've come to Augusta to talk to you about a Thomas Moran you have in your possession. May I come in?"

Eva's face flushed. Her instinct was to shut the door and get rid of him. He could only be trouble. But this man didn't look like he would hurt her. He had somehow found out that she had been given Bernard's Moran. Maybe he was just a dutiful curator looking to add it to a show.

"All right. Let's go into the living room," she agreed, leading him into the small, dark living room, where they sat down.

"How can I help you?"

"Well, Eva, is it? If you don't mind me calling you that?"

"Of course, that's fine." Eva's guard was on high alert. He knew her name and about her Moran.

"Yes, Eva, as you know, you have a lovely Moran, one that used to be in Bernard Rashmusen's collection, and I have an interest in the piece."

"What kind of interest?"

"I'm a very serious Moran collector. Obviously since I've tracked you down here in Augusta, you can tell I have great interest in buying the painting."

"It's not for sale. It was a gift to me from Bernard and I have no interest in or intention of ever selling the piece."

It was the way she said "ever" that made up Ashton's mind at that very moment. He knew her "ever" was genuine. As a crook you learn when people say something they mean or just say something they really don't, and Eva's "ever" unfortunately had weight to it.

"I see. No amount of money or quiet arrangement will change your mind?" he asked, already knowing the answer.

"No, I'm afraid not. You see it was a gift to me from Bernard, and money won't change my life as much as having the Moran. I love the piece. So, no. *Never.* "

"I understand. Would you mind if I at least see it once? I have come quite a ways and am such a fan of Moran's."

"All right. It's here in the kitchen." Eva rose, hoping this would conclude matters between them.

Ashton entered the small yet tastefully decorated kitchen. The main wall was salmon colored, outlined with a flower trim of roses and peonies. A large, blue Mexican bowl with a slight chip on the rim sat directly under the magnificent Moran. Ashton took a hard, close look at the piece, making sure it truly was the same piece in the catalog, the real thing. *No reason to kill someone over a fake.*

It was the one. With his body at a slight angle, he slowly inched toward the piece as if to get a very close look. Then Ashton plunged his right hand into his pocket, retrieved the steak knife still wrapped in the white paper napkin, and with a huge lunge, struck out at Eva's chest.

Eva saw his murderous movement coming and leaned back. It was probably her initial hesitance about the man that gave her this small, instinctual head start. She leaned as far back as she could, trying not to fall, grabbing her blue bowl with her hand for balance. The bowl's weight somehow kept her upright just enough so she didn't fall to the ground. Her quick reflexive move saved her from the knife's intended target but the momentum of Ashton's knife continued downward, slicing her right leg from the top of the quadriceps muscle all the way to the patella. She could visualize the individual muscle fibers being destroyed as it happened, her medical illustration background and hundreds of anatomy dissections flowing through her speeding mind.

With her blue bowl firmly grasped in her hand, its force once again trying to save her life, Eva backhanded the bowl at Ashton's face as if swinging her golf club, the little chip on the rim acting as a knife, cutting his left cheek. He stumbled backwards in pain.

"You bitch! I don't like getting cut, especially on my beautiful face," Ashton screamed.

He threw his entire body into Eva, and this time the knife hit its mark, slicing downward on the left side of her neck between her carotid artery and submandibular muscle. Eva knew he had mortally injured her and her unborn child. As she collapsed onto the floor, she could feel her heartbeat pumping blood out onto the linoleum. Both her heart and her child's would stop in less than five minutes. The blue bowl lay next to Eva, still unbroken and once again landing upright. The bowl's underbody was quickly immersed in Eva's bright red oxygen-filled blood. She could see colors of red and blue. Thoughts of Willy, Bernard, Theo, and her unborn son flashed through her mind. The number 418 appeared, easing her pain for some reason. The life quickly ebbed from Eva, her consciousness fading.

Eva's last thoughts were of the painting itself. She could visualize the waves crashing in and it calmed her. With the little amount of energy she still had, Eva used her bloody hand and in the bottom of the blue bowl she weakly reproduced Moran's monogram, an "M." As her life passed away, her arm lay embracing the edge of the bowl, the broken rim chip gently cupping her wrist in a final good bye.

Ashton never looked back at Eva. He had no problem ending her poverty-stricken life. She had been unreasonable, so he had resolved his problem. The steak knife was still stuck in his victim's neck, the last of her lifeblood pulsating around the handle, gently flowing in little rivulets beside the motionless body and damaged blue bowl.

The embedded steak knife still had the unsavory bus boy's fingerprints on it. Reaching into his pocket, Ashton extracted the little bag of crack and sprinkled it on the living room table. He left a small part of the contents in the packet for the police to find. He dipped the near-empty cellophane bag in the pooled blood and tossed just under the couch. He figured the local overworked cops wouldn't do much of a crime investigation on a black woman in Augusta so he needed to make it easy for them to find the perpetrator's bag of crack.

The Moran was now his. He pulled the painting, hook and all, off the wall. As he tugged the art hook and its three titanium nails off, stuffing them into his pants pocket, one of the nails missed and rolled into a puddle of Eva's still bright-red blood. The specially made art nail disappeared immediately, unnoticed by Ashton as he hurried to leave the scene, the Moran carefully secured under his right arm.

He grabbed the shitty little TV as an afterthought and put it under his free arm, then rushed away from the house, never looking back. He figured the knife prints would point to the bus boy with his tattooed spider web who obviously had a prison record. LeRoy's so-called "caught cha tattoo" would hopefully prompt the Augusta police to chalk this event up to drugs and a robbery gone bad. No one would even notice the missing painting. As for Ashton, a little bandage and he would be as good as new. "Now, where to eat lunch," he chuckled as he stuffed the painting into his car's trunk. "Ribs sound good."

CHAPTER 45

LAST TRAIN FROM MEMPHIS

Willy came home the night of Eva's murder. He had missed the cut as Eva had hoped and taken the last train out of Memphis to Augusta. Even though his back was throbbing, all he could think about was getting home to Eva, the love of his life who was expecting their first child. Willy already envisioned teaching their child the game of golf, the next Tiger.

Upon entering his dark house he went to the kitchen for water and saw the drawing Eva had left hanging in a beautiful frame over his kitchen table. Even after turning on the lights he had a hard time seeing what the image was, but the handwriting in the lower right corner was Eva's. "My Augusta hero, Love, Eva" was all he saw. He reached for the phone to call her. It was late but he figured she would want to hear from him.

It was then that he noticed the message light blinking on his answering machine. He pressed for the recording.

"This is Sergeant Brown of the Augusta police. I need to talk to Willy Wilson immediately when you receive this message." The voice rattled off some numbers.

Then a second message: "Willy, it's Aunt June. Something terrible has happened to Eva. You need to call me immediately! It doesn't matter what time."

Willy's eyes filled with tears. He knew it was bad, very bad, and he could hardly dial June's number. She broke the news to Willy that Eva had been murdered in her house in the kitchen. The police weren't saying much but it looked like a burglary. Her TV was gone and some drugs had been found.

"Drugs? What does that mean, drugs? What about Theo?"

June tried to calm the distraught Willy. "Theo is fine. He's at my house and never saw a thing."

June didn't know the details, other than a Sergeant Brown was in charge and Willy was to call him.

Staring at Eva's sweet surprise, tears rolling down his face, Willy turned away and got into his car to race over to her house.

CHAPTER 46

THE INVESTIGATION

Sergeant Joe Brown was in his late 50s but looked older. Years of heavy tobacco use had permanently stained the tips of his fingers a dark mustard yellow and when he spoke his voice was unusually deep and intermittent. His eyes were steel blue with the first stages of cataracts barely visible. It was a white man's face now darkened the color of leather with layers of wrinkles and years of sun damage mixed on top of sleep deprivation. Brown's arms had early little skin cancers everywhere, making an odd appearance as if someone had dumped over a bucket of golf balls and then kicked a portion, leaving an asymmetrical design. The prominent ugly white skin bumps made it hard to focus on Brown's face.

"Sorry for your loss, Mr. Wilson. I understand the deceased was close to you. I just have a few questions for you tonight that might help us. Our best chance of getting this guy is with help from those closest to the deceased. Did Ms. De Plain have any enemies? Someone who would want to see her hurt? Any drug- related problems possible?"

"Listen, I have known Eva intimately for four years and not once have drugs or drug use come up other than her concern that her son Theo never use them. She thought drugs were the scourge of our people and so do I," Willy said, sinking onto the couch. "Do you know Eva was pregnant? This is a double murder. Does that sound like someone who would use drugs? If you found anything related to drugs, it's not hers and was done to cover up something."

Brown wrote all this down in a little book, never looking up to make eye contact with Willy. Willy was afraid Brown had heard this song and dance before and his poor Eva was getting lumped in with the rest of Augusta's drug scum. "Pregnant or drug addicted, either way don't care," Brown was probably thinking.

"Mr. Wilson, was there any money on the premises or other valuable objects that Ms. De Plain owned that could have been a motive for burglary and murder?"

Willy couldn't think of anything she had of value other than her son and that blue bowl from Mexico that she had told him saved her life.

163

"There was a blue bowl Eva cherished, but I don't think it had much monetary value. Was it taken?"

"No, we found the bowl. It was on the floor. It must have fallen during what appears to have been a violent struggle. We've collected it as evidence. Anything else? Jewelry? Cash?"

Willy shook his head. "Nothing I can think of. She was a woman of few possessions and great creativity. An outstanding artist, did you know that?"

"Yes, so I've been told. She worked as a medical illustrator? Self-employed? Did she own any art or was her own work valuable?"

Willy was trying to think clearly. "I don't really remember any art. Maybe a nice poster? Eva didn't have money to purchase art. Her own work I wouldn't think would be very valuable except to me, but art is not something I know a lot about. I should have spent more time talking to her about it. She loved it so." His voice cracked and now the tears started streaming.

"If you would, Mr. Wilson, come down to the Southside station tomorrow and give us some additional details? We did recover the murder weapon. It appears to be a steak knife. Not one from the household."

CHAPTER 47

AFTER EVA

Willy Wilson's life went into a holding pattern. Depression set in. He felt great despair and loss, similar to when he withdrew from the University of Arizona because of valley fever, but this was much more intense. Getting up every morning was a struggle. Golf provoked little interest, and giving lessons even less so. Trying to focus and seem happy was almost impossible. His mind kept replaying Eva's burial. The day had been overcast until the casket had been lowered to its final resting spot, then as if on cue the heavens cleared, leaving a hole in the sky that the sun's rays filled. It was as if Eva was ascending to be with God, which gave him solace. Willy had arranged and paid for the funeral and cemetery plot. It was just west of Augusta National at Westover Memorial Cemetery. Willy had wanted Eva to be as close to him and his beloved Augusta National as possible. He bought two plots, as he would lie with Eva and their unborn child when his time came. The Wilson family had never been laid to rest at such a fine cemetery, but Willy felt it important to always be close to Augusta National, the place that had given him a great life and was instrumental in his falling in love with Eva.

Theo didn't understand what had happened. At four, he didn't have the comprehension. He was staying with Aunt June, his only real relative. Willy kept thinking how Theo would have had a little brother and he would have adopted Theo, but now that seemed like a world away. How one's life can change overnight. Willy even considered suicide as he walked the grounds of Augusta National with his Uncle Ed. Looking at the clubhouse with its great history and seeing the massive oak trees interspersed between the little cabins made him reflect on his life and legacy, if any. He decided there was still something out there for him. Maybe he was meant to have an influence on Theo or maybe he would still make his mark at Augusta National. He would just have to bear the pain. Ultimately he would lay next to Eva in death but for now it was time for the living.

The police had arrested an ex-con, LeRoy Strong, who had been out of prison for only a couple of months. He was ostensibly a drug dealer formerly in prison for assault with a deadly weapon. A full set of prints were on the handle of the murder weapon so it was undeniably his. The knife was from his place of work and he had no alibi. He said he was sleeping when the crime occurred but had no one to corroborate his story. So now LeRoy was in jail, no bail. Eva's TV had been recovered under a box in the alley of the restaurant where LeRoy worked and a bag of marijuana had been found in his home, a parole violation.

Sergeant Brown was sure he had his man. Case closed. Willy couldn't understand how a complete stranger would kill Eva over a television worth 100 bucks and somehow be so absent minded as to leave his crack stash behind under the couch. It didn't jive, but what else would explain such senseless violence? Willy worried that it was too easy a case. No real detective work had been needed. No other evidence relating to the case had been found except a small, very sharp nail that was in a pool of Eva's blood. It was probably so insignificant it was just an outlier. It was easier if that was the case, no more unknowns or surprises in the dark.

Willy worried greatly about Theo, who now had no mother, father or grandparents. He decided to become his Uncle Willy and do everything in his limited power to mentor the boy. Eva would expect this of him and he loved the boy anyway. Living on the road made it hard to be a father or uncle, but he would try. By most standards he was only mediocre at his trade as a professional golfer and that meant sporadic income, with most of his money coming from his pro job at the Augusta Country Club. Still, somehow he hoped he could instill in Theo what golf had given him: lessons of life, truth, honesty, companionship, and the feeling of never being able to master something you truly love. You learn in golf, like life, you only play, you never conquer.

CHAPTER 48

THE BIG DEAL

Ashton dropped off Eva's stolen television behind Ray's Rib Joint on his way out of town. The Moran was safely tucked in his car, just barely fitting. He had been smart and thought ahead, getting a full-size rental. The image of $2 million in a rental car made him get hard. He loved the power of money. He never thought of the girl he had killed. She was just an irritant and that problem was now solved.

A quick stop at a minimart provided an adequate fix for his oozing cheek. The gash was hidden under tape and Neosporin. His only concern was that it might leave a scar. Once home, he might go to a plastic surgeon to keep his face looking pretty, but that was probably too risky. Someone might start asking questions. Ashton smiled in the rear view mirror as he looked at himself, commenting, "Maybe this is better. Battle scar number one, with possibly more to come in the pursuit of great art."

Ashton believed his lack of conscience would make him an exceptionally wealthy art dealer. Art dealers have all degrees of ethics, from the honest and usually unsuccessful ones to the extremely conniving like Ashton, for whom murder was all in a day's work.

He exchanged his rental car at an out-of-the-way location near Cartersville, Georgia, a little town outside Atlanta. The town was really only known for one thing, a wonderful museum of Western art, which was odd to see east of the Mississippi River. "I bet they don't have a Moran like mine," Ashton thought as he drove past the large white building with a huge bucking bronco and cowboy out front. Ashton drove into Atlanta in his new full-size car.

The Westin near Hartsfield-Jackson Atlanta International Airport is a nice, very large hotel, a place Ashton planned to visit more often once he got his $2 million from T.T. For now, he would just stay the night and fly out tomorrow. He debated whether the painting would be safer in his trunk or his hotel room, but was anxious to admire his prize possession. He waited until after dark to bring up the impressive painting. With the massive frame, it was nearly three by four feet. Covering the painting in a large black coat, he carried it up to his room, using the back elevator just at the end of the evening shift.

The Moran was a magnificent piece. The black girl did have great taste in art. Ashton considered keeping his first big score since it had only cost him a cut in his cheek, but he loved money too much to actually keep a spectacular piece of art for himself. The painting was in outstanding condition for an artwork more than a century old. Most of its life it had been in huge homes with temperature-controlled environments. Today it had undergone a more challenging trip in the hot trunks of two rental cars. The cars were worth about as much as the frame. Ashton turned the painting around for the first time to see its official title and old stickers. This is when his grinning face dissolved into an angry frown. There directly under Moran's beautiful script was another hand's inscription: "Eva's Moran, for now and forever. With all my love, Bernard."

"Goddamn that fucking bitch, it was hers! She didn't steal it! It was a gift and her history is now part of the fucking canvas. I so hoped she had run down the old lady to steal the damn thing," he exploded, throwing his velvet shoes across the room. "We will see about this provenance! If I can steal it, I can change it. Just one more added expense. The price is going up half a mil. Sorry about that, T.T., but now I've got to fix this unfortunate attribution."

Feeling less confident now, Ashton decided to find a cheap motel and wait around Atlanta for a week or two to see how the De Plain case unfolded. This would give his cheek time to heal as well. He didn't want a $2.5 million dollar painting in a good hotel room with maids in and out, or people seeing him with his healing wound. At a cheap motel, the help would be less attentive and he'd be more anonymous.

As expected, nothing about the stolen painting was mentioned in the press. The prime subject was an ex-con named LeRoy Strong. "Love that good Georgia detective work," Ashton chuckled. The coast was clear. Two weeks in Atlanta and enough being poor. It was time to cash in.

Changing his mind about flying out of Atlanta, Ashton decided to just load the Moran back into his rental car and drive nonstop to NYC. With his relationship with Penwell so rocky, he'd rented his own place in New York. It was a little apartment in SoHo near Thompson and Spring Streets. A first-floor cracker box, to be honest, but the area was filled with artists. He saw the potential. It just needed 10 more years.

Hanging the painting over his own bed at last, Ashton reveled in its presence. He imagined himself in the painting. He was the lone art dealer, like the tree, willing to do anything to prevail. The waves were all the other lesser dealers, lapping at his feet. He was stronger than them all. Even Mother Nature couldn't harm him.

The inscription by Bernard had to be removed and the only sure way was by lining the painting with another canvas. Relining a piece is a technical process. Art dealers generally don't like to do this to their paintings unless absolutely required, for example, when cracking develops in the paint. If the canvas isn't stabilized, the piece may start to have paint loss from flaking. The relining process requires gluing another canvas to the back and shrinking the painting to the new canvas so the old cracks come together. It's sort of like a face lift for paintings. The cracks disappear and the painting is stabilized. In the case of THE LONE CYPRESS, its canvas was pristine except for that one huge imperfection: the inscription. It was the obstacle that could keep him from selling the piece. No way to explain the attribution if anyone got nosy. They could figure out the piece came from a dead, one-armed black girl. This Moran needed a face lift for sure. It would require covering Moran's original handwriting, which could be photographed and placed on the new back as a record. Some collectors wouldn't buy a relined painting; they only wanted them pristine.

Luckily, Ashton knew T.T. would never understand the implications of a reline job and probably would not know enough to notice. Done correctly, he would never be able to tell. If Tommy or someone with knowledge did ask or examined the painting closely, all Ashton had to say was relining the painting was common for a 120-year-old painting. It protects the piece from deteriorating, like changing the oil in your car.

Ashton bought his own camera to photograph Moran's handwriting of the title. He considered bumping the price up an additional $100K to pay for the $200 camera, but thought he would be generous and just throw it in. All the museum tags would be saved and attached to the old frame. The problem was who should restore the painting? Convincing that person could be tricky. They might need some special motivating. Still, this was a problem that could be solved. *Yes, a new back, no more Bernard, no more Eva, no more problems.*

CHAPTER 49

THE RESTORATION

Finding the right conservator for this job was a must. First, they had to be very good so as not to fuck up the painting. Second, the restorer must be elderly since an old person dying is not that unusual. Third, it had to be someone who was reclusive and didn't get much foot traffic so no dealers would be snooping around. Price was no object since T.T. was paying for it, though he didn't know it yet.

Two weeks of asking around elicited one name repeatedly. Byron Boyd was a conservator of the old school who still used resins similar to those of the old masters. He made everything by hand including his paints. Boyd had been in the conservation business for 50 years. He still had the same little studio in his home on the far East Side near Sotheby's. The prestigious auction houses were even known to occasionally use his services. He was terribly expensive, which was great because it kept almost all dealers away. Boyd's clients were the wealthy who could afford to pay and wait. He was slow, but if enough money was paid in advance, pieces could move to the front of the line. Boyd was very careful not to show pieces in his studio to anyone, which was critical just in case any nosy dealers dropped by. His worst attribute, as far as Ashton was concerned, was that he was supposedly smart. Byron Boyd was going to want to know the reason why Ashton wanted a perfectly good canvas relined. This did not make sense. It decreased value and the only reason would be to hide something. Because this painting had a very unusual inscription, Boyd might figure Ashton was trying to cover it up.

How to handle this? Paying Boyd off probably wouldn't work. He was honorable except when it came to jumping the line and prioritizing a new job. Ashton realized he would have to damage the Moran. Purposefully damaging a multimillion-dollar, 120-year-old painting seemed wrong. Killing Eva was just business. Well, so was this.

Ashton wrapped his hand in a sock and picked the least important area of the painting. The upper left corner was just sky. If it was damaged there and relined, it would be hardly noticeable, especially if expertly done. With a punch like he would do to a kid brother's arm, Ashton hit the painting there with his sock-covered fist. The blow was sufficient enough to cause the paint to crack, leaving an area of circular rings, but not hard enough to go through the canvas or cause paint loss.

"Well, that should do it," he said, looking at his handiwork. "A first, I bet. Damaging a masterpiece so I can sell it for millions. Brilliant!"

Byron Boyd was a man with a great eye for art and no social skills. He smoked three packs of unfiltered Camel cigarettes a day and rarely emerged from his hovel of a studio. He was in his early 70s with wispy gray hair that was usually oily from a lack of showering, which was also apparent by his body odor. He looked up only after he was finished with what he was working on. Usually he was sitting on a high stool, leaning over a painting. Boyd's spine was permanently bent from the years of close restoration work. Only the area of the painting that was being worked on was exposed. Everything else, including the frame, was carefully covered and pinned downed so no snooping eyes could see.

The shop seemed never to have been cleaned. A fine layer of paint dust from the ages covered everything, including Boyd. He had huge painting racks with hundreds of frames and some paintings stacked in between. Boyd had a marvelous collection of antique frames, his only hobby. Many were massive, weighing over a hundred pounds. Boyd had found out early, rich clients often would want a painting cleaned but hated the frame. They would say, "Keep the frame. I'm getting a brand new one," so he would happily take it off their hands. Boyd always found it ironic his job was to make everything look new again yet he loved the antiques. Making old things look new again allowed him to collect old, damaged frames.

The smell in the studio was of cigarettes, turpentine, and a hint of musk from the often moldy paintings Byron restored. One small window at the top of the room let light stream in, and with the light you could see the thick particles of dusk flickering as if the air was from some foreign planet. The paint fumes were overwhelming, the resinous aroma causing an immediate headache for those not yet adapted to their power.

"So, you have a special project? One you would like done quickly? You realize there is a surcharge of 20% for rush jobs," Boyd got to the point.

"I understand you are the best and the extra charge will be fine," agreed Ashton. "It's a very important piece by Thomas Moran. Not a hard restoration job I don't think, but my client has a bit of a compulsive disorder and the recent damage to the piece bothers him tremendously."

"Well let's take a look."

Ashton took the painting out of its carrying case and handed it to the old man, noticing his pupils dilating immediately, a sign of fight, fright, or excitement.

"My, my. One doesn't get to work on one of these beauties every day! I believe I saw this at the Moran show at the Met a few years ago. Tremendous piece." After a quick inspection, Boyd asked, "Is this all you want fixed? This minor circular blow mark here in the sky?"

"Yes, that's it. My client instructed me to have it completely relined."

"As you probably know, I'm quite expensive, but let me save you some money and my time. Just have it strip lined in the corner where the damage is. That will fix it fine. You won't see any of the craquelure and you can save the important writing on the back."

"I already explained to my client about strip lining, but he insists he wants it fully repaired. He feels the extra strength from the new lining will help the piece from any further injury."

"Well that's just not true," objected Boyd, looking up from the painting. "In the old days we did think it helped the whole canvas and so we relined a lot of paintings unnecessarily. It was similar to how orthopedic surgeons used to open the entire knee up for a small problem where today it would just be locally treated through arthroscopy. It's not really a good course of action to do a full lining on such an important work."

"Yes, I'm sure you are right, but it's not mine to say. The owner will get it relined whether it's by you or someone else, and frankly if it's going to be done I would like it to be by the best, not some hack job.

173

After all, it's a magnificent painting. I have already had all the signatures and information preserved photographically. So what do you say, I'm prepared to give you half of what you think it will cost today," Ashton insisted.

Byron Boyd had never had to make this kind of decision before. His ethics said he should decline, but if the client was going to have the painting relined no matter what, it should be accomplished by the best, which he was.

"All right, I will do it, but I will have you sign an affidavit that I recommended strip lining and it was at your request that a full lining be done."

"No problem, I can't blame you a bit. Write it up and I'll sign it. When can I expect it finished?"

"Two weeks. I'll write up a contract and get half the payment today."

"Yes, that's fine. By the way, that huge frame above your head is stunning. It must have been hard to get up there. Must weigh a ton."

"It took two strong men. It's about 200 pounds, I'd guess. I doubt I'll ever see it down from its perch again."

"Oh, you never know. Life is short." Ashton concluded his business.

CHAPTER 50

A NEW PAINTING

Two weeks is a long time to wait for something you really crave. Ashton made use of his time by checking all the papers from Atlanta and Augusta to see if anything more had come of the Eva De Plain murder. It seemed one LeRoy Strong had been charged with first degree murder and was awaiting arraignment. Nothing about the painting. Ashton made the dealer rounds to quietly inquire if anything interesting was going on in the art world, like possible gossip about a stolen artwork. Nothing at all. Ashton had considered waiting a year before selling the piece to T.T., to make sure they convicted LeRoy. But T.T. had already been already been waiting years and Ashton needed the money. The art market was hot now and he could leverage this deal into even more money. That's what he loved about the art racket. Take one stolen piece, make a small fortune, then launder the proceeds into actual art pieces he could sell legitimately. Ashton's twisted yet brilliant mind had come up with a great scheme for getting new clients and he was about to put his plan into action.

Byron finally called Ashton to pick up his Moran and bring the final payment. He wanted to meet him at noon. Ashton told him he was busy all week during the day but could come by in the late evening if possible. Boyd, a man of routines, was not a fan of late night company, but he did want his fat paycheck. He also didn't like having such an important painting in the studio any longer than necessary.

"Fine. How about tonight, say seven?" Boyd proposed.

"Could we make it nine? I know that's kind of late but I'm extremely busy all this week. That's when I will be available."

Boyd thought it strange an art dealer kept such odd late hours all week, but agreed begrudgingly. "Nine will be fine. Bring a check for three thousand."

"Is cash OK? Like the first payment?"

"Fine. Will you need a receipt?"

"Just a hand-written note."

Boyd liked the sound of $3,000 in cash with no real receipt, so to speak. He was old and didn't like giving up his money to the tax man. Besides, with a little extra cash he could add to his frame collection. Too bad the Moran's frame was not available. Anyone dumb enough to line a perfectly good Moran might sell the old frame.

Ashton couldn't be happier. The Moran looked brand new. No more little cracks in the upper left corner. The back had a brown canvas that matched the original canvas's color, but without the writing. All the old tags had been attached professionally to the back of the frame.

"Wow, that's just great! Looks perfect! Can you please put a piece of foam core on the back of the painting before I take it with me?" Ashton liked foam core, a semi-hard cardboard that is put on the back of a painting so nothing can touch or damage the reverse part of the canvas. It also would obscure the back so the new lining would not be visible.

Talking out of the side of his mouth with a half-smoked cigarette hanging from the other side, Boyd replied, "Sure, no problem. For what you paid me, this one's on the house."

A precut foam core that would fit a standard 30 X 40-inch painting was pulled out from a side bin. The Moran lay on the table and Boyd went to work fastening the cardboard protective piece to the frame. One minute later he extracted the Camel cigarette, let out a large puff of smoke, and said, "All done."

These were the last words ever spoken by Byron Boyd. As he tightened the final screw, the end of a 200-pound frame with extra force applied by Ashton came crashing down on Boyd's skull. His cranium cracked like a melon thrown out of a high building. Ashton had one hand on Boyd's death frame and the other on his Moran, which he pulled out from Boyd's table as the frame killed him. The splatter marks of blood fell harmlessly on the white table.

"See, you did get to see your frame once more. Pity it was only for a split second," and with this Ashton started laughing almost uncontrollably. "Now then, let's see how old paint, resins, and dried timber burn. It's kind of chilly tonight. I'm sure everyone would like a nice, warm fire."

Boyd's motionless body was crumpled on the now red table, with a huge frame on top of him. The cigarette was still smoldering in his hand. A few little pieces of fresh paper would keep it going long enough for Ashton to get what he needed.

Ashton found Boyd's rolodex with all his clients' names and numbers, which he confiscated for his own use. He quickly looked at Boyd's files and swiped the current list of paintings in Boyd's inventory for restoration, pulling his own file as well to be disposed of later. It contained Boyd's own photos of the Moran's original inscription to Eva.

Full resin cans were carefully moved to the edge of Boyd's body and then tipped over so the fire started quickly. Remarkably, Ashton didn't have to do anything else. Boyd's lack of cleanliness and years of paint products would take care of the rest. Poof. All gone.

Quietly slipping out the back stairway, Ashton toted his Moran and the mother lode, the rolodex which included clients' names and the paintings they'd had restored over the years. The best was the list of new clients with newly incinerated paintings that would have fat insurance checks to replace their lovely heirlooms so tragically lost.

The Sunday edition of *The New York Times* featured an article in the arts section about the accidental fire and death of well-known art restorer Byron Boyd. A great loss to the art community. The fire had been limited to his floor, with most of the studio and all of the paintings scheduled for restoration destroyed. Apparently a large frame from his collection had fallen on top of him while he was working and his cigarette had set off the fire.

CHAPTER 51

THE PHONE CALL

T.T. was enjoying living in his house next to Cypress Point Club. He could see the famous par three 16th hole of Cypress, a small landing over the ocean that had only managed to give up 10 hole-in-ones since its creation by Alister MacKenzie in 1928, the same architect who designed Augusta National. Usually one would just lay up to the left as it would often take a good accurate drive to get your golf ball to the green with the ever-present strong ocean breezes.

T.T. loved golf, especially at the best courses. He had become one of the owners of Pebble Beach for that very reason. Pebble was one of the best. Having played on the worst golf courses during his adolescence, these special places remained just that, special. He had played Cypress numerous times but the membership was limited to 250 members and being a billionaire didn't mean anything. Most of the members were ancient, their average age in the mid-seventies. It was enough for T.T. to play it occasionally. This kept it fresh and a treat. When you are a billionaire, there are few things that are still unobtainable, and Cypress Point fit that rare category. Besides, he could see Cypress Point from his home and that was good enough. Some days he would sit at his desk and watch the golfers toil at 16. Their angst and joy was apparent even from a distance.

Homes in the Pebble Beach and Cypress Point area varied in size, age, and expense. Generally a large lot with a small house became a large lot with a large house after the original owners died and the kids or grandkids cashed out.

T.T. had one of the few open lots in 1999 and had made sure to take full advantage of its ocean and cypress tree views. The house totaled 10,000 square feet, small by Pebble standards, but all he needed as a single man, age 54. To get to Tommy's house required entering the front gate of 17-Mile Drive, a tourist destination in itself, its winding road leading to the Pebble Beach resorts and golf course and multimillion-dollar estates.

There was still no real art work on the Thompson walls, just blank slates of varying color. His decorator, one of those famous LA persons with two similar sounding names and their own line of

178

furniture, had done the house. T.T. allowed a few decorative paintings in the guest rooms, but his family room and bedroom were waiting for his Morans.

Ashton called Tommy two months to the date after he acquired the great painting. He knew Tommy would purchase the piece so it was just a matter of how much he would get out of him. Knowing you have something a very rich person wants can be very fun for a person like Ashton. He relished power, usually in the sexual form, but "art power" was the ultimate in control.

"I finally found what you were looking for," Ashton proudly declared. "A great Moran. It's called THE LONE CYPRESS. I actually managed to purchase the piece and wanted you to have first look before I offered it to anyone else. I'm sure Mr. Penwell would be interested, but as we both heard him say, you get first right of refusal for any California ocean pieces, whether he really meant it or not."

"Tell me about the piece. Is it big? What does it look like?" T.T. asked.

This was a dead giveaway to Ashton, now 45, that T.T. still didn't know shit about art. His first questions should have been about the painting's time frame, its condition, had it been seen much or was it new to the market, and had it been at auction. Then ask about size and subject matter. Price often comes up rather quickly, but in T.T.'s case it was the last thing, because to him this was the least important.

But T.T. was the client, so Ashton described in great detail the composition of the painting and all the particulars.

"That all sounds good. When can you get it here? And I guess I should know how much?"

"It's $2.5 million, it's ready now, and I will need you to send a plane to New York. That's unless you want me to drive it out there, in which case it will take a few weeks for me to get away." Ashton had already decided Tommy could pay for the plane and he wanted a private jet. After all, he was now an important art dealer and important people needed to be treated as such.

"Sure, I have to go to New York this week anyway to check on some things and get in a little golf. I'll give you a call tomorrow and let you know my schedule. Sounds great. Good work, Ashton. Worth waiting for. Penwell was right. You're good at what you do. I'll see you soon."

A few days later, T.T. sent a car to Ashton's SoHo studio. The sedan took Ashton and his Moran to a private airstrip in Long Island next to a members-only golf course, where T.T. was waiting.

"Sorry to make you come out here, Ashton, but I'm playing golf and have to get right back to California. I love this course. I can keep my jet next door. Great golf out here. Lots of rich and famous New Yorkers belong. Maybe we can get you a couple of VIP names for the old rolodex. If you want to hit a few, I can set you up with one of the club pros."

"I'm always interested in meeting potential art lovers, especially in my new home town of New York, since most of my contacts are still in San Francisco. I'm not much of a golfer yet, so I'll regretfully decline the offer to work with your pro." The truth was, Ashton couldn't tell anything about golf other than he hated it. Rich, arrogant white men all trying to outdo one another in a mindless game. The less he understood about the game of golf, the more superior he felt.

"So let's see that bad baby, Charmers. I need to know if I'm writing a check for $2.5 mil today," T.T. prompted.

Ashton took the Moran out of its new Art Safe carrying case and held it up, letting T.T. admire the painting as the sun brilliantly illuminated the image. Seeing the great painting again in the sunlight made Ashton's mind flash back to Eva's kitchen wall. The thought made him grin.

The back side had a white foam core board over the canvas portion with a few errant blood speckles now apparent in the sunlight to Ashton's keen eye. He had not noticed them before but thought it was cool, like a hunter saving the horns of his kill, a permanent reminder of his triumph.

"She's a beauty! I'll take it. Send me a bill and all the info. I'll go ahead and take it with me in my plane back to Cypress. I'm leaving in an hour or so."

Just like that, no questions about its history or negotiating on the price. Nothing about its condition or resale value, no close examination of the painting looking for the slightest irregularity. Not a word about having a look at the painting under a black light for any clues as to damage or previous restoration. Just, "I'll take it." Ashton loved the super-rich. Maybe he hadn't needed to kill old Boyd after all, but he didn't know if that inscription would come back to haunt him some day. Besides, Boyd's rolodex was going to make him a lot of money. Ashton was surprised at himself. He wasn't worried about letting the Moran leave his possession without being paid for first. He had murdered two innocent people to insure he would get the money, but strangely it felt OK to trust T.T.

"Yes, that would be fine. Take it and I'll fax you over a bill and wiring information. I'll be sending it to my bank in the Cayman Islands. That's OK, I hope?"

"No biggie," T.T. agreed. "Just get me the info and we will take care of it tomorrow. Sorry to make you come out all this way to show it to me, but at least I'm not making you fly back to California to hang it for me. Do you mind if I keep that carrying case of yours?"

Ashton placed the painting back in the case. "It's an Art Safe case. Fire resistant, even. You never know when some unexpected fire might destroy what you love. Also, when you're gone for long periods, you can store the painting in the case. People have been known to kill for a valuable artwork like this."

"Good advice. There are a lot of bad people in the world, though I doubt many of them would kill over a piece of art," T.T. remarked.

"You might be right. Hard to imagine what kind of person would do such a thing, but still, the case will protect the painting. Oh, and just so we are on the same page, T.T., I never showed the piece to Penwell. I know he said he wanted you to have the first opportunity for a seaside Moran, but he can be competitive when it comes to these great paintings. I just thought you might want to know, in case you want to keep your purchase private. Penwell doesn't know and I still would like to find you one more painting. Penwell's generosity might lessen if he knows you have already scored one major painting from his favorite art dealer." Ashton figured the less people who knew about the piece, the better. He hoped by warning T.T. about Penwell, the billionaire would keep his purchase to himself. No blabbing to the world at least for a while—preferably not until LeRoy met his maker.

T.T. nodded affirmatively. "I'll keep that in mind. Now let's get a photo together with my first art purchase. I want to send a copy to my high school art teacher. Come over here." T.T. got his camera and handed it to a caddie.

Ashton hated having his photo taken. He never knew when photos, especially those with a stolen Moran, might come back to haunt him and he sure didn't want any local newspaper showing it in Oklahoma.

"T.T.," Ashton demurred, "it's your day, not mine. Let me take the photo of you with your painting. It's about the art and you, not the art dealer."

"Now, come on, I've just spent $2.5 million with you and I want more than some damn Art Safe case. I would like to remember the moment. Get over here and help me hold up this bad boy. Hell, what kind of business man are you anyway? I'll send you a copy and I guarantee you will put this photo on your wall. It's bound to drum up some more business for you! Someone will recognize me and know you are a very important art dealer."

"OK," Ashton gave in. "I'll hold this end. It's my good side." Ashton had become sensitive to the visible scar on his left cheek and wanted to keep it out of the photo if possible.

"Fuck the good side. Hold that end and say 'cheese.' I've got to get back to Cypress before the sun sets. Got a hot girl waiting for me. Cheese!"

The $2.5 million was wired the next day to Ashton's new Cayman Islands account. He received a confirmation fax. Ashton considered taking the next flight to the Caymans just to make sure he truly was now a multimillionaire. But there would be plenty of time in the near future to check on his money. Maybe on the next big score he would hand deliver the money himself.

His plan was simple: never pay any tax and keep all the profit unless there was absolutely no way around it. How could he claim he sold a Moran for millions and his cost was zero? No records of ever buying the piece, no bill of sale. The Moran sale had determined his path. Pay for everything in cash, then get his payment in cash or a wire transfer to the Cayman Islands. Only as a last resort would he actually claim a sale. Ashton's goal was to work hard for the next 10 years. A new century was coming, the year 2000. Using his knowledge of buying and selling, his career was now hitting its peak in his mid-40s. He could legitimately make money and still rip off the occasional old lady of her heirloom. Try and put away a million a year, then disappear. Ten million dollars was a reasonable goal, he thought, especially if he wasn't paying taxes. It would take the IRS that long to catch on. Live reasonably, pay cash for everything. Move to some Central American country, maybe Costa Rica. It was supposed to be safe. Get a hot, young Latin boy to spend his days with. He would be the Joseph Penwell of Latin America. Deal in Pre-Columbian art, maybe.

His first order of business was to upgrade the digs in SoHo. Keep the overhead low, but make it look like a well-heeled art dealer's studio. Put in good lights for art and start buying a limited inventory in cash. Ashton never wanted more than half a dozen pieces at any given time. He could get paintings from other dealers on consignment once he started spending money with them. Brokering was safer. Find out what a client is looking for and then go to a dealer and get the painting. Hammer the dealer on the price, mark it up even more than the original retail, and voila, he would have just made more than the art dealer with the expensive art gallery on Madison Avenue.

All Boyd's clients from decades in business were now in Ashton's possession. Each name had little references to the paintings they owned. He also had names of those individuals who would all be getting large insurance checks shortly and they would be looking to replace their lost loves with new ones by the same artists.

All Ashton had to do was start finding the paintings and filling the orders. He would send out a newsletter to Boyd's client list with brokered paintings that just happened to be by some of the same artists whose works were destroyed in the unfortunate fire. They would call him and explain how a check would be coming shortly. Ashton would then say, "No problem. I'll hold it for you," then immediately go back to the dealer who owned the painting and hammer some more on the price, pay cash which often would get him another discount, and own the piece outright by the time the client got their check. Thompson's Moran money gave Ashton the ability to buy important paintings and negotiate great deals from unsuspecting art dealers. Ashton considered just going around the country killing off other restorers and using their client lists, but it wasn't necessary.

His plan worked. His next few years were the most outstanding of his entire career. Having a built-in clientele, he already knew their wish list in advance of any other dealer. Within two years, he'd made $4 million in sales, almost doubling Tommy's money. He paid more in taxes than he wanted since it was hard to get real clients to pay in cash; that was much easier with art dealers. So his overall take was less than he'd hoped, but way ahead of schedule. When he hit $10 million in profit it would be *hasta luego*. His Spanish lessons were coming along nicely. Ashton was still looking for another Moran for Thompson, but finding one-armed black chicks that have a painting stashed away in a crappy house was tougher the second go-around.

CHAPTER 52

THE TRIAL

The first few years after Eva's death were the hardest for Willy. He spent as much time with Theo as possible. His appetite to compete in golf was diminished to nearly nothing. It was the early 2000s, he was in his 30s, and he was chronically depressed.

The trial of LeRoy Strong finally arrived. It was a roller-coaster ride of emotion. Willy attended every day and couldn't wait to be called to the stand to testify about Eva's feelings about drugs.

The public defender, who had more cases than he could handle, made a weak defense, insisting LeRoy only dealt marijuana. He tried to confirm his position by deposing a variety of ex-cons who testified that LeRoy was only a doper, no heavy drugs.

The prosecution then asked each one of the cons had they ever done hard drugs. All confirmed they had. LeRoy was guilty by association.

All the public defender could really come up with was that the crack they found wasn't LeRoy's because other cons had testified LeRoy didn't use crack cocaine and Eva was not a drug user and she was pregnant, so it must be a plant. Yes, the steak knife was from the restaurant he worked at and yes it had his fingerprints on it, but it was also a plant. He had no idea how it got there and yes LeRoy did have some enemies and maybe one of them had stolen the knife. It was LeRoy's job to clean up dishes so he was always touching the silverware.

The defense never saw the images of the "M" in the bottom of the Mexican blue bowl. Photos had been taken, but Sergeant Brown didn't notice there was writing in Eva's own blood on the inside of the bowl. The overworked public defender had only glanced at the blue bowl photographs; if he would have taken the time to study them or better yet look at the actual bowl he would have seen the blood-inscribed clue, the proverbial smoking gun. The only photo submitted into evidence during the trial was the one of Eva's hand lying on the bowl as she was sprawled out on the kitchen floor in a pool of blood. Eva's blue bowl sat unnoticed in the evidence room, still waiting to save another person, this time LeRoy. If anyone had bothered to look at the photos or done a blood sample on the chipped edge, where a small amount of Ashton's left cheek skin still lay embedded, they would have come to a very different conclusion.

Likewise, the little nail found in the victim's blood was only mentioned as one more piece of evidence that could mean someone else could have been there. No explanation for its origin or how it got into Eva's blood pool. That it was an extremely expensive art nail used by art professionals was never discovered. If it had been, the three corresponding holes in Eva's kitchen wall might have been discovered.

When LeRoy got on the stand, Willy expected to hate the man and was at that point sure he had killed Eva and their unborn son. Yet LeRoy completely denied any wrongdoing and was extremely convincing. So convincing it seemed hard to believe he had committed this horrible crime. Maybe LeRoy was so high during the crime he really didn't remember his heinous act. Willy wanted to believe this was Eva's killer and finally put the pain behind him, but somehow it wasn't jiving with his inner voice.

Great golfers have a defined inner voice they listen to constantly. This voice is what allows them to make the pressure putts when it is noisy and distracting on the course. The voice develops at an early age. You hear this voice as clearly as you hear anyone talking to you. The voice guides you in all aspects of the game. It filters information, then steers you in the right direction with the given information. The voice may say, *Yes, that is the break*, then you make the putt and you win. You always, always listen to the voice when it speaks. It allows you to make the right decisions. Golf teaches you to be true to the voice and Willy's voice was telling him LeRoy's testimony was truthful.

Willy was called to the stand by the prosecution as their closing witness. He told of the love he had for Eva and how they were both anticipating the birth of their child. He described in detail Eva's ordeal in Mexico City, and that she had made a new life since surviving that travail. Willy's testimony, which was all true, helped convict LeRoy Strong of the first-degree murder of Eva De Plain and her unborn son. LeRoy was given the death penalty. Willy felt sick to his stomach when he heard the verdict. His inner voice was saying, *Doesn't fit. Something's wrong. That's the wrong break in the green*.

CHAPTER 53

STALE FRY GREASE

Theo De Plain wondered how he had ended up in such a shithole as he stared at a vat of revolting chicken grease, its stale odor making him nauseous with every stir of his large wooden spatula. A boiling chicken wing surfaced every so often as if it were a dead corpse floating to the top. Theo's mind kept drifting from what was to what could have been. His life had become another body floating in a vat of unsuccessful humanity.

The taco/chicken dive that Theo worked at was a cheap man's Taco Bell/KFC. The restaurant's name summed it up: Kenny's Taco Bron & Fryer House. Cheap name, bad food, and an establishment you would never want to visit more than once.

The so-called restaurant was in an old, abandoned KFC with a colonial-style exterior and red roof. The roof, which had not been painted in over a decade, was more of a salmon color now, long ago losing its hot red color that connoted, *Come in.* Now it said, *Come in at your own risk and you must be damn poor.* The interior was even worse. Half the roof panels were missing and the ones that had been replaced were a yellow color, making the whole roof look like one of Aunt June's crazy quilts. Intermixed with the colors of yellow and off-white were flashes of shimmering tinsel that still remained from some Christmas past. They were too hard to remove without real effort and no one at Kenny's wanted to work that hard. The fact that the roof had ever been decorated was a mystery to Theo. The floor was always sticky no matter how often it was mopped. Years of neglect had given the linoleum tiles a taffy-like texture. It was easy to trip if one shuffled. An odd high-step walk was the custom at Kenny's, since no one wanted to tackle the floor problem either. Like everything in the restaurant, it was all about just getting by.

The health department was so taxed in Augusta, Georgia, in 2009, that it didn't have time to check on the Kenny's of the world. Their main concern was policing eating establishments that tourists might visit, especially during the Masters Golf Tournament in April when no one seemed to care about the city's poorer, darker inhabitants. When a miracle did occur and a health inspector did show up, they got treated as a VIP with free food and drinks, and somehow Kenny's

187

always slipped by. No one ever seemed to notice the dripping refrigerator, animal droppings, or mouse tracks in the bits of biscuit mix that somehow always dropped onto the sticky floor. *Nope, a little fried chicken does the trick*, Theo thought as he drew images with his foot into the fallen biscuit mix he had been observing for the last two days. *The man will always look the other way if you give him food. I'll remember that*, Theo thought as a grease bubble popped on his arm, awakening him from his after-school job from hell. The authorities likewise ignored Georgia's laws about minors under the age of 16 being prohibited from working more than three hours on a school day or after 7 pm. Theo was 14 and tall for his age. Besides, this was Kenny's and all the money was in cash and everything Theo earned he got to keep. That was the deal Theo had made with his Aunt June, who had forced him to take the job.

Theo was low man on the totem pole at Kenny's, whose staff included an ex-convict and a supposedly clean drug addict. Theo wondered why life was so unfair, but he'd known it was since he was born. Theo's specific job was to make sure there was always enough chicken in the warming beds. If he accomplished this simple task, work was bearable. The chore should have been easy except for J.J., Kenny's night manager. J.J. didn't want any food waste. It made him look bad. Nobody made J.J. look like he couldn't manage the place. Theo had never met J.J.'s superior, Kenny, but he was pretty sure it wasn't Kenny Rogers, just some older black dude one small step up from J.J.

Theo's job was to make sure the ratio of chicken cooked to chicken eaten cancelled out at the end of the night, otherwise it would be Theo's ass. There was nothing worse than J.J. making him feel lower than a 14-year-old already does. Theo reminded himself that he was saving to buy a new guitar, and after that he would tell J.J. to fuck himself, and then he would lose his shitty job. "Sorry, Aunt June." So he planned.

His daily challenge was to determine when the big chicken-eating crowds would cycle through the restaurant. There was the 5 to 6 pm rush of parents getting their little darlings a meal after school. These were, of course, not wealthy parents because if they were, they would have stayed out of this shitty part of town and gone somewhere clean like a real KFC. After the kiddy rush came the 7 to

8 pm dinner crowd, usually hard-working single moms getting ready to go to work or just getting off. They opted for small orders, usually legs and thighs, not a lot of white-meat eaters among them.

In the bad neighborhoods of Augusta, white meat was not a popular food or people color. Theo wished his skin was darker than the light black shade God had burdened him with, along with his reddish brown hair and green eyes. Even Barack Obama was darker than he was. Never knowing much about his father bothered Theo greatly. The fact that his father was white was even worse. Working in Augusta's blackest neighborhood meant black was beautiful and white might get the shit kicked out of you if you looked the wrong way. Theo felt he had to overtly make up for this even though he really didn't feel black or white, just lonely with skin whose only real distinguishing characteristics were the various healing scabs caused by the stale fryer grease. Not black, not white, just damaged.

The 11 pm to 2 am shift was always a tossup. Theo only worked this shift on Friday and Saturday nights. You had to be a magician to predict the amount of food then, although it was a given that drunks and party goers would be in just before close so those tended to be extra chicken nights.

It was a good weekend when J.J. took off early and let the crew manage on its own. J.J. was tall and lanky. His limbs reminded Theo of a daddy-longlegs. J.J was in his mid-thirties and looked seven feet tall when his afro was completely combed out. J.J. would eat at least a bucket of chicken every shift, but still only weighed 160 pounds fully clothed, gold chains and all. He resembled a tall, undernourished cornstalk with a full black tassel. His ineptness when it came to ordering supplies was legendary. If they didn't run out of food by the end of the week, it was a miracle.

Theo recalled one week when J.J. and his girlfriend Latisha were fighting. By Saturday, the offerings looked like a concentration camp meal. No buns, no ground meat, no ice cream, no hot sauce, no thighs, no legs, and no biscuits. This amazing lack of food for even a shitty restaurant was beyond belief. Theo considered letting J.J. get his due and not covering his ass. Let Kenny find out what a douche bag of a manager he was. But Theo did semi-like J.J., an Augusta Junior College dropout, too thin to make it as a basketball player even in JUCO. What he respected about J.J. is he knew what it meant to be a

189

black man; no white blood in those veins, pure African heritage, black as space itself. Theo's Uncle Willy, though he wasn't a blood relative, had Kenyan heritage. Theo respected and loved Willy but rarely let him know how he really felt. He appreciated that sense of self that both J.J. and Willy possessed, even if J.J. was a fuck-up in every other respect. He still knew who he was and embraced it.

Theo's first memory was of his mother's voice, a melodic sound he still struggled to recall. The timbre was low, sweet, and calm, so very calming. He could never remember anger or angst in her voice. He hadn't seen her for 10 years now. In Theo's mind, all he had was bad luck. His Uncle Willy, who he knew loved him, had turned into a failure, or at least when it came to money he had. *He should have been rich, not some hack golf pro in Augusta, Georgia. Why does it have to be so hard? Why couldn't my mom still be with me?* As with most 14-year-olds, life sucked for Theo. Anger for Theo came easily. Happiness, on the other hand, was harder to bear.

On this particular Saturday afternoon, Theo ran out of food due to another J.J. ordering fiasco. Bartering became the name of the game, a Southern style "Deal or No Deal." "How about two of our famous pickles instead of a biscuit? We can make that a chicken taco, it costs more than ground beef. I'll throw in three breasts since we are out of thighs. Deal or no deal?"

There's no doubt that Kenny got fucked that Saturday as Theo had to give away drinks and lots of food in order to fend off the pissed-off, so-called clients. J.J. never knew how close he got to getting canned, but Theo did. It was one of the few things in Theo's life he felt positive about. At least he could help out a real brother. He always wished he could have a real little brother but life can be cruel, as he had already found out.

CHAPTER 54

TIME FLIES

Ten years plus a few months had passed since Eva's death and it still seemed like yesterday. They say time has a way of healing all, but for Willy and Theo, it must be a different kind of time. Willy was 39 as 2010 began. Theo was approaching 15 and in his freshman year of high school.

The teen years sucked for Theo. He lived with Aunt June when Willy was on the road playing golf, and with Willy the rest of the time. Theo's and Willy's relationship had turned into one of moments. Theo referred to the only real father figure he had ever known as "Willy" or the "Old Man," or if he was mad he would call him "Billy Casper," a little jab at the namesake Willy had never been able to live up to.

Aunt June's mind was deteriorating and Willy thought Theo would soon have to live with him full time. He had talked to June about adopting Theo. Because Willy had played in the PGA, he ultimately would get some retirement funds that he wanted to bequeath to Theo. When June remembered the conversations she would agree with him: "Damn good idea, Willy. Theo's heading down the wrong path, going to end up like that killer LeRoy if we ain't careful."

Theo's only real interest was music. He was a natural like his mother and could play the guitar like a pro. He loved heavy metal, particularly the screamo bands. His long, straight hair covered most of his face and made Willy wonder how he could be so different from himself at that age. Granted Willy wasn't blood, but he had given Theo all the building blocks for success in a very difficult world. He had tried to teach him golf, but Theo had no interest. "Theo, you know your mother could hit the ball 180 yards with one arm and she also liked music. Come and play golf with me. You will be a natural at that, too," Willy tried to persuade him. Even if Willy couldn't get Theo onto the course, Willy still tried to instill the ethics of golf in Theo. You call penalties on yourself when you make a mistake, you don't cheat, you work hard and practice harder, and you listen to your inner voice as far as what's right and wrong since it doesn't lie. It knows the truth. This final lesson still bothered Willy since he suspected LeRoy might be innocent and Eva's killer still at large.

191

LeRoy was scheduled to be executed May 18, 2010, only a few months away.

Theo hated golf mainly because it took Willy away from him and seemed to make him very sad at times, especially when he missed a cut. Theo also hated how Willy put everything in life into golf terms:

"Theo, you are double-bogeying all your grades. You need to get at least pars, and a birdie or two would be nice."

"Theo, you are heading into the deep rough. If you don't change, you will end up out of bounds and lost forever."

Theo might not like playing golf, but he did understand every rule and knew all the players. He would follow the different tournaments, but never gave Willy the satisfaction of knowing that.

Once in a hormonal tirade, Theo told Willy, "I hate you. Why couldn't my dad have been Tiger? Tiger knows how to win at Augusta National and always makes the cut. I wouldn't be so damn poor and have to work in some shitty chicken shack if I had a real dad who was any good at golf. I would have money and be safe, not dealing with hungry crackheads eating chicken wings. You don't give a shit about me. You just feel sorry for me 'cause my mother was murdered."

It's amazing how teenagers can cut you to the quick, knowing just where to put salt in your wounds, Willy thought, after the devastating outburst. All Willy said to Theo was, "I'm not your father, I'm no Tiger Woods, and I'll see if we can't get you a job that isn't so dangerous. I love you, Theo, and I loved your mother."

Theo's response: "Whatever."

Willy talked to the deceased Eva regularly. She had become sort of his second inner voice. He would visit Eva's grave and have a conversation about her son and how they were progressing in life. It was during one of these cemetery sessions that Willy decided to change his swing. Willy said to himself and Eva, "What do you think about my changing up the swing? Furyk is still out there and winning, and that's a pretty funky swing."

He reasoned, "It will be one last attempt at being a great golfer, or at least one that makes a living. I'll see if my back improves so I can start winning again." He still had the same hunger he'd possessed at age 12, playing Billy Bob for the first time. Aunt June was fading fast and he was going to need more money to get Theo through college. He needed a swing that would allow him to play with less pain so he could have a chance at making the tour cuts.

Besides discussing golf with Eva, Willy also talked of the drawing she'd given him of the lone tree on the hill against the crashing waves. Willy thought Eva somehow knew of her death and wanted Willy to have something to calm him and help him through his troubled times. It was funny how art had come into his life this way. Art to Willy had always been an afterthought, never the primary thought. His time with Eva and this detailed drawing had changed him. It had given him an appreciation for looking at the world from an artist's perspective. Art could change you in a positive way if you let it grab hold.

When going through Eva's personal things after her death, Willy had found two additional drawings of the tree. He had them both professionally framed and placed one of them in Theo's bedroom and the other in the kitchen at Eva's old home that Aunt June had moved into. Willy liked the drawing in Eva's old kitchen. The light seemed to hit it just right. Aunt June had told Willy at one time she thought Eva had one of her drawings or a painting in the same place, and she remembered her sitting looking at a picture on that very wall. Willy vaguely remembered something in the kitchen but when Eva was alive they mainly stayed at Willy's house to give Theo his own sense of belonging at home with his mom. Nonetheless, Willy's inner voice recognized that painting on the kitchen wall and said, "Yes, that's the place. It's like I've seen it there before. See how the light envelopes the piece? Eva would like it here."

Willy suggested that Theo do his homework in the kitchen so his mother's force would be with him. He told Theo, "Your mother always is looking out for you. The only reason she survived that horrible earthquake, she told me, was she wanted you to grow up to be a strong, good man and change the world in a positive way. Your spirit helped her live when all others perished. I truly believe she is watching you and me through these drawings she left us. They are here when we need help. So do your homework in front of your mother's drawing. It will help you."

Theo would shrug, "I should have just died in Mexico. It would be easier for everyone. I hope she's watching me because she can see I hate my life."

After Theo's last big tirade about Tiger and hating his job, Willy had gotten Theo a job at Augusta Country Club. He was cleaning clubs, getting water bottles, and doing general go-fer work. Willy was mad at himself for allowing Aunt June to let Theo work at Kenny's to begin with. Aunt June had insisted, "He need to see what lazy, drug-dealing black folks look like so he don't become one."

At that point she was still his legal guardian and Willy had to respect her wishes, but he finally convinced her it was too dangerous at Kenny's. On the golf course he could watch Theo to make sure he didn't get into trouble and the pay was better. She finally relented when Willy told her, "Theo's new job will build character. Plus, I got him a job working Augusta National during this year's Masters and he will be on the litter patrol."

The litter patrol was a choice job given to Augusta high-school kids. They dress in yellow jumpsuits with Augusta National yellow hats embossed in green letters saying "Litter." The kids get to keep the hats after the tournament is over and generally one or two of the pros will sign their hats, which they can then sell for big money. They're forbidden to sell their caps during the tournament and if they do, it is grounds for an immediate firing, which Augusta golf marshals have ordered in the past. The officials at Augusta take these sorts of things quite seriously. Willy figured with his connections he could get the hat signed and Theo could sell it for a thousand bucks. Some rich guy would want something he couldn't purchase during the tournament. Litter hats were never sold at Augusta National, only given to those who earned them working the litter patrol. Aunt June thought trash duty would be good for the boy. Teach Theo an honorable job was a good one. Just look at Willy's own dad: he had worked for the sanitation department his whole life and look how well Willy turned out.

CHAPTER 55

PEBBLE BEACH

Willy Wilson had been grinding out the years on the Nationwide Tour, making it into the PGA for two memorable years. But when he fell out of the top 150 golfers two years ago, he figured his pro career was over. To get back into the PGA now, he would probably have to go back to qualifying school, or Q school as it was known, like a rookie. That was a hard pill to swallow once you have already played in the PGA. If you don't make it in Q school, then it's back to the Nationwide, assuming you make that cut. The money on the Nationwide tour was marginal except for at the top. It was a hard way to make a living. You got $90K for a first place finish, and barely $1,500 for last. Paying for hotels, caddies, travel, food—it was a breakeven proposition most weeks and a loss on others. The two landmark years he had been in the PGA and played for the big bucks, Willy's performance had been disappointing. Best finish: 45. He still had made 10 times the money during those two years than he had all the years on the Nationwide tour where a last-place finish, if he made the two-day cut, was worth around $15K.

At this point, Willy had pretty much decided it was his lot in life to be a pro at the *other* private course in Augusta, Augusta Country Club.

Then Willy received an unexpected invitation from Tommy Thompson to play in the 2010 Pebble Beach National Pro-Am. Incredibly, it was one more chance. It came out of the blue. Willy hadn't communicated with T.T. in over a year.

Willy had first met T.T. at Augusta National as a teenager in the eighties when Billy Bob had sponsored them both. As rich as Tommy was, it didn't mean he could just show up and play Augusta National. He had to come with a member. He couldn't even get onto the property until the member arrived and he couldn't stay on the grounds after the member had left. Strict rules, no exceptions, not even for billionaires.

At the time, Billy Bob, who had made his fortune in the rental storage business, was very familiar with the Dynamite Steel Company and was more than happy to sponsor Thompson as this would allow him time to ask his advice on world economics. He was thinking about selling his company and it never hurt to bounce such an idea off a man like Tommy Thompson. After all, you don't get four hours with a billionaire every day. Billy Bob asked Tommy if he would mind if a couple of his friends joined them. Tommy replied, "You know I wouldn't mind at all. I heard about this young black kid you play with. How about if he joins us?" Billy Bob, though he cared a great deal for his little Willy Casper, really wanted to bring one of his close business relations to show off. Instead T.T. wanted his golf protégée Willy? Not much choice. Billy Bob thought momentarily about just saying no, he couldn't make it happen, and inviting his crony instead, but lying didn't sit well with his Southern roots. So Willy, age 15, had ended up playing golf with Tommy Thompson, and upon T.T.'s request even rode in his golf cart!

It had been 25 years since that first meeting and amazingly Willy and T.T. had kept in touch. Nothing much, just a card or two early on and now emails. Willy still remembered the day he got a long handwritten letter from T.T. who had heard about his valley fever and how it had hurt the career of the young man from Georgia and he'd sent words of encouragement. Willy had kept that letter and reread it from time to time. The last lines read: "Golf is only 18 holes, five hours at most, but ultimately it's still a great game. You've learned the lessons of golf and the real secret to success. You don't always have to win to be a winner." He remembered these lines and his mind wandered back to the day in Augusta when Tommy and he played for the first time. Tommy sure wanted to win, but even when Willy thrashed him, he was still smiling and giving him career advice. A man who understood the real meaning of golf indeed. Even when Willy was 15 he realized life was bigger than winning and losing.

Flying into Pebble Beach today at age 39 was a treat for Willy. It had been a while since Willy had played in California. Descending into Monterey, the ocean was visible along with what appeared to be a fire raging in the mountains of Carmel Valley. Huge plumes of brown smoke curled into the crystal blue sky, "An omen," Willy thought.

Tommy's driver picked Willy up at the Monterey Airport. The drive into Pebble was 30 minutes and it seemed like a different world. Willy had been to California before, playing in the Pac-10 for Arizona. Even though it was years ago, he still remembered its lushness with smells of the ocean and exotic plants. The memories came flooding back. Willy stuck his head out the sedan's window like some hound dog on a ride to the vet's. He didn't care what anyone thought. He soaked it all in. This might be his last chance to play in an important professional golf tournament, and with a billionaire at that.

T.T. was one of many owners at Pebble Beach and had managed to get a special exemption for Willy Wilson to play in the Pro-Am. Tommy truly believed Willy had the qualifications to be there.

Willy had heard himself referred to as *the other black golfer* many times. They said he was good at putting like the best-known black golfer, but he just never made it. Today, Willy figured, *the other black golfer might be good for business since the best in the world doesn't like to play the bumpy greens at Pebble and would pass on this tournament.* Willy loved bumpy greens. Really, he didn't give a shit what the greens were as long as it meant a possible payday for himself and Theo. They could use the money. This was a professional event and he was still a professional, even if he wasn't really considered anything more than a footnote to the world's best.

So Willy sucked in the California coastal air, his eyes shut and his head outside the window. If it was his last hurrah as a professional, at least it would be at a great venue, Pebble Beach. T.T. was covering all the expenses and had even arranged for Willy to have a posh hotel room at the Pebble Beach Lodge.

Pebble Beach Golf Course is one of the pantheons of golf. The course sits above the city of Carmel and is carved out of the cliffs that overlook the Pacific Ocean. The course is a public course with over 60,000 rounds played annually. It is public, but the public who play the course are rich. You have to have a room at the lodge if you are playing Pebble. Rooms start at around $900 a night. A round of golf is $500, regardless of the course's condition. This does not count caddies, who really are needed if you want to score. The course can be unforgiving, especially in February, when this tournament is played. You can be assured at least one of the days will be for shit, with rain and winds sweeping in off the Pacific, which laps directly onto the course's ocean-facing holes.

Pebble Beach was a wonder, right up there with Augusta National, and Willy couldn't wait to have at it. He knew it would be a challenge and he was ready for it. He couldn't help thinking of his Uncle Ed and himself at 12. He had the same kind of childish exuberance in the pit of his stomach now, wanting to play and play well.

CHAPTER 56

THE LODGE

"Welcome Mr. Wilson, we have been expecting you," said the distinguished-looking doorman, who was almost as tall as Willy's six-foot-two. Willy knew this man had seen them all, the wealthy, famous, and everyone in between. The doorman probably assumed, since he was associated with T.T., who was an owner, that Willy was some bigwig, not just a second-rate pro from Augusta, Georgia. Willy enjoyed the moment and a smile crept onto his face.

The front desk was hopping. All the important people of the world were attending the Pro-Am, not just celebrities. Rich amateur golfers played alongside PGA professionals. Willy was the professional with a special exemption, and Tommy the rich amateur. Willy hoped that T.T.'s game had improved since the last time they played although he doubted it. Since T.T.'s wealth had tripled to multibillionaire status, his game had probably suffered due to excess work. Willy tried to keep his expectations realistic for the tournament. He had no local knowledge, had never played the course, and hadn't played in a PGA event in two years. On the plus side, he had been practicing religiously.

When you're a pro at a country club, there is often down time and Willy had been reworking his swing during that time. If he wasn't going to play in the PGA anymore, what did it really matter if he changed it up? And if he did get the chance to play in the PGA again, it might help him survive the rigor. Willy's lower back was the one part of his body that kept him from being a spectacular golfer. If he played golf frequently, invariably the pain would return to the L5/S1 region in his lower back, the bones never having filled in properly. Willy thought if he changed his backswing and followed through to a slightly different angle it might take the pressure off and he perhaps could play without constant pain. It's funny how Tucson had given him valley fever, but it had also given him Jim Furyk with his peculiar swing. Willy knew from Jim, if he could always reproduce the swing it didn't matter how odd-looking it was. He could score, maybe without pain. So Willy had a new swing and he damn well could reproduce it. He had never tried it in competition to see how well it would hold up but he was about to.

His room at the lodge was on the top floor. Its balcony was just above the magnificent old oak trees, allowing a great view of the ocean and the course. A group of crows had set up residence in the oak trees' top canopy. Their constant chatter reminded him of home where a murder of crows at Augusta Country Club were his constant companions, the social birds always seeming to recognize him and follow him around during his daily activities. It was if they too had flown west for this event, and their banter eased Willy's nerves. Just like the golf groupies, the crows had shown up to watch their favorite golfers.

Pebble Beach is a money-making enterprise generating over $80 million a year. There are shops all around the lodge with clothes, jewelry, art, and golf memorabilia. When the PGA comes to town, everything picks up in the retail establishments. Money arrives and is spent with abandonment. The "talent," as they are called—referring to the golf groupies who follow the PGA golf tournaments around—appear magically for the week. The seriously rich are here with their entourages. Willy was part of that scene. He was the hired gun to have fun with one of the captains of industry, Tommy Thompson. He knew it, but didn't care.

The vacation homes lining the edge of the golf course are a who's who of innovation in the business world, with rich oil barons from Texas and a class-action lawyer or two in the mix. Homes on the course, if you can find one to buy, start at around $20 million. To Willy, who lived in a two-bedroom, one-bath circa 1940s home not far from the bad side of Augusta, the wealth seemed unimaginable. He didn't envy his lack of such a home as much as he just didn't understand why one would spend money on such a luxury when so many lacked so much. But growing up the son of a garbage man has a way of putting money into perspective that most people don't have.

The top PGA players made the type of endorsement money that afforded them homes like these. Tiger Woods made easily over $100 million and was head honcho of the golf industry and could have a couple of such homes. When Willy was on the PGA tour he made nearly $200,000 in endorsements in two years and $100,000 in winnings before his back gave out. The money now seemed unbelievably huge. He wished he could go back and save all that dough that he had just frittered away. First-class air flights. An imported luxury car. Expensive hotel rooms. At least he did pay off his house, which was very smart. It seemed back then that he was going to make it to the top. His mantra had since become: *No back, no dough, no life.*

Willy had missed the PGA at Pebble Beach both times he was eligible to play. He had played very well during the January PGA tournaments, then right on schedule, his back went out and he had to rest most of February. The last time was two years ago, a lifetime in golf. But now, "A new swing. Who knows, anything could happen," Willy told himself. His new mantra became: *New swing, new back, new life.*

From Willy's hotel windows, he could admire Point Lobos in the distance as well as the number-six green with its lone cypress tree. Number 18, a par five, was barely visible, just a sliver of the fairway. Every so often, a golf ball would bounce up on the sliver and he knew those belonged to the professionals. To get to the sliver, you had to fly the ball over the ocean then onto the fairway's small landing area. Most of the pros would just lay up and then have a very long shot to the green, or play it safe and get to the putting green which overlooked the hotel's grand lobby, in three. The risk takers, who knew their game and had great control, would take it over the crashing ocean waves to the sliver of fairway. Willy's goal was to be one of the greats, fearless, and fly his ball over the ocean. He might even look up from the 18th fairway sliver and find the balcony of his room, his aiming point. There would be no layups this weekend. He would either miss the cut badly or score aggressively to win. When you realize it's your last opportunity, there is no laying up, ever. He hoped T.T. would understand. Whether Tommy did or not, it would become obvious very quickly that Willy would be going for it on nearly every hole, à la John Daly style.

Willy thought, "I'm going to have fun, get a couple of Pebble shirts, hats, and of course, new balls, and enjoy myself." Somehow it still was special when Willy picked up a new sleeve of golf balls. You don't forget the value of something you once couldn't afford, even when you now get them for free. Free balls were fun.

He felt great about the week. He understood this was more than likely his last dance at the big leagues so he would enjoy it like Jack Nicklaus did at St. Andrews during the 2005 British Open when he was 65 years old. Everyone knew who Jack Nicklaus was, of course, while nobody but trivia buffs knew Willy Wilson. Getting onto the senior tour for golfers 50 and over would be harder than the PGA, but that would be 10 years away for Willy. Jack had won the Masters at 46, but Willy was no Jack. The two did have one thing in common. Both had played Augusta almost as many times. Not bad for a black kid from the south side of Augusta. Willy needed this Pebble trip. His mind had been so preoccupied back in Augusta, where thoughts of death row had been haunting him. He tried not to think about the man who was scheduled to be executed. He needed to focus on golf now. Just golf.

CHAPTER 57

THE PGA TOURNAMENT

The weather was rainy and cold the day before the opening round, which was not unusual for February. Willy and T.T.'s practice round would have been miserable, except Willy's attitude was so upbeat they both enjoyed the day. For Willy, it was as if he were a kid again having fun hitting the driver with the new swing and his back felt fine. The drives were long, even into the 25 mile-an-hour wind. He finished with a nice little draw and no pain. Tommy, who had an aversion to wet, cold weather, had hoped to call it in early, but Willy would have none of that. He told T.T., "I know you're paying for all this, so you're welcome to stop, but I'm going to get our money's worth. After all, I came all the way from Georgia." They both finished 18 holes, then Willy went back and played hole 18 over again. He aimed for the fairway each time, oblivious to the ocean's influence. Each time he hit the sliver but barely. It was clear if the winds or the golfing gods were not on his side, then going for the green in two could be his undoing.

The thought of making the cut solidified in Willy's mind during the practice rounds. Hitting the fairway on 18 gave him confidence in his new swing and new outlook on golf. To make the cut would be a triumph. No one ever expects a pro they haven't seen in two years to be competitive, much less one with a new weird swing. All the golf analysts had taken him off the active list and were surprised to see Willy at Pebble at all. The golf gurus didn't even bother to mention Willy's name other than as an oddity. The buzz within the PGA was that his appearance here was simply a pity play, a special exemption given to a rich Pebble owner, nothing else. Almost a joke, since every spot should go to someone who at least has a chance to win. They thought Willy had no chance. "Willy the Back," he had heard himself called by one of his so-called colleagues. "A childhood wonder turned adult wash-up. Nice guy. Could have been great, but golf's a cruel game."

Willy's first day on the tournament was brilliant. He had four birdies and no bogeys. He led after 18 holes. T.T. played fairly well, but more importantly, he stayed out of the way and made Willy feel comfortable. The best thing T.T. brought to the game was his personal caddie, Brad, an athletic six-foot-two-inch 30-year-old who had caddied Pebble for 10 years and two years at Cypress Point. He knew every nuance of the greens and understood Pebble's weather. The story at this year's tournament was about the elements. If you didn't know how to gauge the ocean's continuous winds, you were toast. This was especially the case for the benign-looking hole number seven, a short 106-yard par three, a troublesome hole if you don't have an excellent understanding of the wind. The green is very small. Sand traps surround the hole on all sides and the ocean guards the right and back of the hole. If you go long or right, you're shark bait. The hole can play 60 to 225 yards, depending on the wind. The caddie's analysis is critical. The golfer picks the club with respect to wind, not actually distance to the pin. Brad gauged the wind speed and direction perfectly every time. Willy listened and scored. Uncle Ed had taught him long ago to listen to the caddie. He repeatedly told Willy, "Don't let your pride get in your way, boy. Especially if you don't know the damn course." Willy didn't know this damn course other than watching it on TV so he listened to Brad. Willy was one of five that birdied the hole that first day. It played 185 to 225.

His first day's final score was 68. Now everyone wanted to interview the pro from Augusta Country Club. The forgotten black pro with an unusual new swing suddenly made great news, but Willy knew one day does not a tournament make. The golf analysts were scrambling to get current background info about Willy Wilson, asking, "Where the hell has he been?" and, "What's with the Furyk-like swing?"

Day two was a repeat of day one. Cold, wet, and very windy. The course was unforgiving. Willy had no birdies, but no bogeys. He scored a 72, even par. Four under for the tournament. Willy achieved his goal: he made the cut and did it in style. He was number one going into moving day. Of the 144 pro golfers that started the tournament, 70 made the cut for the last two days of play. Making the cut assures that the pro wins money. Willy heard comparisons to the other black golfer, Tiger, now. There were no more jokes about "Willy the Back."

Willy was not used to the accolades, much less the pressure. The thought entered his mind that maybe he could win some real cash. A paycheck would be great. The money was bigger now. Making the cut assured a minimum of $15K for last place and he wasn't likely to finish last. There would be no blowing his winnings this time. Theo needed college money and Willy needed a new roof. He knew if he played it safe he would never forgive himself. He needed to win.

Day three, also known as moving day, was when the big boys made their push and those unfamiliar with the territory faded away. It was also the first day the sun made an appearance. The wind was strong but manageable. Listening to Brad had made the difference the first two days. Now Willy needed to be the difference. He knew the weather was no longer as much of a factor and the cream would rise to the top.

Willy hunkered down and took some chances. Hole six was a monster par five. Hitting a huge drive was critical to get on the green in two. His first shot made it to the base of the hill in a 325-yard blast, followed with a seven iron pin high. Willy's eagle incited a mini Tiger roar, his first roar ever. The seventh hole was a short par three that he had birdied on day one and he birdied it again. When he followed up with a birdie on the eighth, a hole that had ruined many, he got a real Tiger roar: his first shot was a 200-yard layup, then he hit 185 over a huge canyon with ocean below. Eagle, birdie, birdie in three consecutive holes. The crowd was following Willy now. For the first time in his professional career he felt like a real pro golfer. It was ironic, considering his business card had read for over a dozen years: "Head Pro, Augusta Country Club." He went into the clubhouse in a tie for first.

Day four brought a peaceful dawn. Willy had slept well and was ready for the final round. He got up early to see the morning's sunrise as it glistened off the broken clouds. Eva had shown Willy the beauty of early morning bliss. The weather was ideal and it would be a great day for February. He visualized hitting his final ball off hole 18 and watching it hit the little sliver of grass he could see from his room. This was his day and he wanted it more than anything. The only thing he wished was that Eva was with him to see it.

That final day, Willy went for it just like he had the last three. No layups, no safe golf, no trying to keep the lead. It was golf with no regrets. Play aggressively and let the rest of the pack have the challenge of beating him. His back still felt great, like it had at age 18. No pain. The swing had held. If he could win today, he would get to play The Masters—his dream. He had never gotten to play his own home course and the hope of being a part of Masters history became as important as any money or resuscitating any ruined career. A chance at the green jacket was only two months away.

Willy started to feel the pressure coming into the home stretch. He missed two important putts, one on hole 16 and then lipping out on hole 17. Going into 18, he was in a tie for first, a tying score having already been posted in the clubhouse. It was sliver time. There would be no playoff. He would either win with a birdie or blow up. That was his game plan and he was not about to change. His final thought as he hit his drive was of Eva's face. The ball left the club head at the perfect angle and gently bounced up to the place he had seen at sunrise. With a twirl of his club and a wink to T.T., he started walking to his destiny. When he got to his mammoth drive, Willy looked toward the lodge and saw the red handkerchief flapping that he had attached to one of the oak trees outside the lodge's balcony. As he looked at his distant red marker, a group of vocal crows flew overhead. A large smile crept onto Willy's face, a personal joke between him and the crows. The announcers were going ballistic: the pro from Augusta was one calm cucumber, smiling for the camera as if he had already won the tournament.

The second shot into the green released as perfectly as the drive and stopped next to the hole for a tap-in birdie. Willy Wilson, age 39, head pro at Augusta Country Club, was the PGA Pebble Beach champion! The take: $1.2 million for the week, roughly equivalent to six hours of bank interest for his host, Tommy Thompson. The prize winnings would be a life changer for Willy and Theo.

CHAPTER 58

T.T.'S PARTY

Winning the Pro-Am brought Willy acclaim like he'd never experienced. His back had never felt so good, as if he could still keep playing. His local caddy, Brad, probably had been the difference but the golf commentators never really mention the caddies. They attributed it all to Willy's new golf swing. The comparisons to Tiger began, everyone anticipating April's Augusta National showdown. The story of Willy Wilson, the Billy Casper namesake, was an old one that everyone recycled now as if it were new. That Willy had played Augusta National more times than Tiger and now they were going to have a matchup there had a made-for-TV-movie feeling to it. Some were saying that since Willy had won at Pebble without ever playing the course, he was a shoo-in to win this year's Masters.

It's funny how everything Willy had experienced—his struggle with his back, dropping out of college, achieving very little for the last 20 years, his girlfriend's murder—didn't seem to matter to the press. He was today's success story and would be tomorrow's trash. Willy understood this was an opportunity primarily for Theo and himself, and he would try and make the most of the highly unusual circumstances.

Willy was the guest of honor at T.T.'s 16TH Ranch the night after winning the Pebble Beach PGA Pro-Am. T.T. was thrilled not only for Willy but for his own insight in arranging for the exemption to play the course in the first place. The guest list was small, consisting of a couple of other owners, a few close friends, and of course Willy Wilson, the newest Pebble Beach champion.

Tommy's driver picked up Willy at the lodge and drove him up 17-Mile Drive to the secluded, gated entrance of T.T.'s home. Willy had never seen anything as grand in his life. The cypress trees were like the ones in his drawing back at Augusta, the branches at odd angles due to years of wind and water pressure. The thought of Eva and her gift brought a tear to Willy's eyes. "Eva if you could see where I am now. It should be the both of us at this party," he murmured.

Walking up the perfectly manicured yard with monstrous sago palms lining the path and huge numbers of flowers in every color layered in between, made Willy think of April's azaleas and dogwoods in bloom at Augusta National. *I'll be inside the white lines this year*, Willy thought, entering T.T.'s house.

"Willy, you are the man, the golfer of the year, I would predict!" boasted a tall Oklahoman.

Next to him, T.T. bellowed, "Willy, this here is Cody Preston, one of my oldest friends, I've known him since grade school. Bad golfer, good liar!"

"Nice to meet you, Mr. Preston," Willy replied. "I hope you're not lying about golfer of the year."

"Call me Cody. No, that's no lie. I watched you from the main dining room on 18. One of the gutsiest moves I've seen, going over the water like that. Could have blown the whole thing. Looked like something Tiger would have done."

More Tiger references. Willy had to toughen up. His name and Tiger's were being mentioned in the same breath even more now. Not that this was a bad thing, it's just hard to be black and follow the greatest golfer ever who also happens to be black.

"Yes, Tiger would have gone for it too, I'm sure. He is the ultimate competitor. I hope I get to meet him head-on someday soon," Willy said, with a smile.

T.T. grabbed Willy's arm and pulled him away from the drunk Oklahoma oil man. "Willy, let me show you what a great product like Dynamite Steel and a lot of oil can buy."

The house tour went through numerous rooms, hallways, and guest wings. The art was nothing special. Willy found himself noticing things like art now, because of Eva. Then T.T. took him into his master bedroom, a 2,000-square-foot room overlooking Cypress 16 and the entire ocean, all of which could be seen through a giant window. What Willy saw next paralyzed him momentarily.

By the large picture window was a huge white wall and directly in the center was a painting that was identical to Eva's drawing. Identical.

"What's that painting, T.T.?" Willy asked, his voice slightly quivering.

"Good eye, Willy. I had the room built around where I would place this piece. I don't let many in here as it's my special room, although probably a few too many women have seen it, if you know what I mean," T.T. grinned. "The painting is called THE LONE CYPRESS. It was done by Thomas Moran in 1881. Quite an exquisite work, wouldn't you say?"

"Moran, Moran," Willy said it twice, letting the words sink in. All Willy could hear was his inner voice saying, "There is a connection. This is too much of a coincidence. Things like this don't just happen. Eva is talking to you."

Willy's identical drawing had the word *Moran* on it, and it was truly identical—the shading, the tree, the water. All the same except that Eva's name was also on his piece.

"Come on over here, Willy," T.T. motioned closer to the painting. "See, this is Moran's monogram, a little 'M' with arrows."

"T.T., thanks for the tour. I'm feeling a bit out of sorts tonight. Probably all the stress of winning and all. You think I could go back to the main room and maybe call it an early evening?"

Tommy understood. Willy did look pale and shaky. "Not a problem, the Pebble Beach champion needs to keep his health up. My driver will take you home."

"By the way, T.T., if you don't mind me asking, where does one come by a Moran like that?"

"These cypress tree pieces are very rare. The ironic thing is it didn't come out of California. The painting's history that accompanied the piece said it came out of a private collection in Atlanta, your neck of the woods. Who knows, you may have seen it in the original owner's house. It probably belonged to one of those Augusta National members. They all have money."

"Sorry again, but do you remember when you purchased the piece?"

"Sure I do, it was just over 10 years ago. Come here. See this photo? This was taken the day I bought the painting. That's the dealer I purchased the piece from standing next to me and my plane. I did the deal in the airport parking lot, $2.5 million, if you can believe that. I overpaid at the time, I know that now, but time has caught up and now it's worth close to $5 million. After the photo was taken, I flew the Moran home in that jet and it's hung where you see it ever since. I look at the painting every day. I haven't heard from the art dealer, a guy named Charmers, in a couple of years. I understand he's still dealing in the dead guys—that's the term art dealers use for deceased artists—and doing well."

Willy examined the photo of Ashton and T.T., Ashton's dark eyes staring into space and a prominent scar on his left cheek. Willy's mind was racing: "Atlanta. I wonder if that painting was ever in Augusta. Eva gave me her Moran drawing for a reason. She had seen this very painting, I'm sure of it. Her drawing was identical. She couldn't have made it without sitting in front of T.T.'s painting. Eva told me to get it just right, you have to do it from life. Your subject needs to be in front of you."

Then, as if a lighting bolt hit, Willy realized, "Just over 10 years ago, that's when Eva was killed!" His legs buckled and he collapsed onto T.T.'s bed. There was some horrible connection between Tommy's painting and Eva, he knew it.

"What's wrong, Willy? What's this muttering about Eva? I don't understand. Should I call a doctor?"

Willy, still sitting on the bed and now a pasty color like old golf balls, began telling the story of Eva De Plain, starting in Mexico City, then their love affair, and finally the horrible murder. As he related Eva's life story, his voice cracked at particularly sad parts.

T.T.'s face lost its golden California hue as the blood drained out. He plopped down on his bed next to Willy, feeling sick to his stomach.

He told Willy how he knew of Eva. "It was my company's steel girder that she talked about to all the press. The Dynamite beam and her bass saved her life. I even had my PR department contact her to see if she would want to do commercials to promote the company. I remember thinking it was kind of a ghoulish way to advertise, but my business department thought it would sell steel and they wanted to make sure the story was the steel beam, not the bass. And we figured she could use the money." Tommy told Willy how he was surprised and happy the girl didn't want to profit on her story.

"I remember thinking she must be a very strong and exceptional person. I regret never meeting her. I wanted to. Ironically, my Dynamite Steel business took off after Eva's survival story broke worldwide, especially internationally in those areas that have seismic activity. The stories were all about the miracle baby saved by a super steel beam."

Willy explained how he had the same exact cypress tree image in his house, and it was drawn by Eva. "Eva put Moran's name on the drawing, and left a note about a surprise for me. She was killed before I found out what her surprise was. I think the painting being from Atlanta, Georgia, is too close to home. Eva created at least three drawings of this painting and this took time and access. She worked and had a child. There was no time for travel to Atlanta. All Eva's free time was spent with me. The painting must have been somewhere in Augusta where she could sit for hours drawing."

T.T. realized that his obtaining the painting shortly after Eva's death was a very scary coincidence or worse. It could be directly related. He would find out. "Don't worry, Willy. I'll get to the bottom of this. When a man of my wealth tells you that, you can take it to the bank. Now let's get you home. You've had a hard day."

That night, as his guests partied downstairs, Tommy Thompson made numerous phone calls. Two hours later he had one Priscilla Counihan on the line.

"Ms. Counihan, sorry to call you so late, but I'm a man that has been advised you are the best in the field of authenticating paintings. I only want the best. Is this true?"

Priscilla Counihan, who was a night owl and still wide awake past midnight, replied, "Yes, I am. I don't leave any stone unturned until I find out the truth or what is known about a painting. I've been hired for many high-profile cases including Holocaust reparation cases, which are some of the hardest. Since you have me on the line, you already know my reputation. I will find out what there is to know."

"That's what I wanted to hear. I'm going to ask you to make this your top priority. Tomorrow I'll send you by private jet a Thomas Moran painting I have some serious questions about, and I need to know everything you can tell me. Tell me the truth, no matter where it may go. I will also send the package of papers that came with it 10 years ago. It will be there by afternoon. I'll have my driver Nelson hand deliver it to your office."

"Who did you purchase the painting from and for how much?"

"$2.5 million from an art dealer, Ashton B. Charmers. I believe he has an office where you live, New York City. Do you know him?"

"I've never met him but I know of him. Not flattering things, sorry to say."

"Shit! I was afraid of that. Find out everything and give me updates. I'll send my contact info with the painting. I will include a $25,000 retainer, if that seems appropriate to start."

"More than enough to get started," Priscilla agreed.

"Great, I'll talk to you tomorrow. And please call me T.T."

"Fine T.T., tomorrow."

CHAPTER 59

COMING HOME

Willy's return trip to Augusta in T.T.'s private plane should have been filled with thoughts of the Masters Tournament in April and his new millionaire status. He was flying for the first time in a private jet, a mode of transportation he could only have fantasized about a week ago. Instead, his mind was filled with thoughts of Tommy's painting, currently sitting on the front seat of the plane inside a black art case, going somewhere in New York City for evaluation after he was dropped off in Augusta. Apparently worth $5 million, the painting had a definite connection to Eva. Willy felt an intense closeness to Eva that he hadn't sensed in years. She had a connection to this piece and so did Willy. The years of gazing at its image had permanently affected Willy's consciousness. His mind was now consumed with the painting, Eva, and her life, as he flew back to Augusta. No looking out the window this time.

Willy's best guess about Eva's surprise previously was that somehow it was pregnancy related, or maybe she wanted a quickie marriage. Now he was sure her surprise was something entirely else. It related to the Moran and the drawing she had left for him. Could it involve LeRoy Strong, soon to be Georgia's latest execution? What about that little nail they had found in Eva's blood? Golf was the last thing on Willy's mind as he flew home. Tomorrow he would try to make arrangements to visit LeRoy Strong on death row.

CHAPTER 60

TRYING TO SAVE LEROY

Warden Malcolm T. Blackstone didn't brook with thieves, liars, or cheaters, which comprised most of the Georgia State Prison population. His heart went cold for those that took another life. A religious man, he took God's words literally and "thou shalt not kill" was at the top of the list. Break the rules and life inside the prison walls became very difficult, to say the least. "An eye for an eye," was another of Blackstone's favorite sayings.

When the warden got a call from Augusta's newest golf star wanting to visit the soon-to-be-executed prisoner LeRoy Strong, he was surprised.

"Why, with the Masters just around the corner I figured you would be practicing every chance you could. I know that you and Ms. De Plain were quite close. Are you looking for some closure from that bastard Strong? Nothing wrong with a little personal retribution."

"Honestly, warden, I don't know. What I do know is that I need to look Strong in the eye and ask some hard questions. So yes, in a way, I guess closure. And you're also correct that I should be practicing my new golf swing right now."

"Son, I'm more than happy to let you talk to him, and if you want I can put you on the list to watch him meet his maker, as well."

"Thank you, Warden Blackstone. I believe a visit is all I can think about now, especially with the Masters around the corner. You think I could see him soon?"

"Willy, I love the Masters and we are rooting for one of our hometown boys to finally bring home that green jacket. Can you get over here today, say 4 pm?"

"I'll be there. Is it also possible I could talk to Sergeant Brown? He was the man in charge of the case 10 years ago," Willy inquired.

"Little out of my jurisdiction, but I'll see what I can find out. He's a local Augusta cop, as I remember."

"That would be fantastic, thanks."

"No problem," the warden replied. "By the way, you think I could get a couple of tickets for this year's Masters? I'd love to come watch you play."

"Absolutely."

Death row is one of the most intimidating places on earth. Willy had heard about the horror of the place but feeling it first hand was terribly upsetting. He could only imagine what LeRoy must feel.

Death and fear filled the air. The desperation was palatable the instant Willy walked into the compound. In the last months before any execution, the prisoner is usually isolated from visitors. Very few personal items are allowed except a bible, which Warden Blackstone insisted all inmates have. The state of Georgia wants to insure that they are the executioners, with no surprise suicides from slit wrists or strangulations.

LeRoy Strong was brought out to the small waiting room in arm and leg manacles. He looked much older and fatter than Willy remembered. His black, curly hair was now completely gray. The stress had definitely aged LeRoy. Willy wondered if he looked as much older to LeRoy. It was basically Willy's statement that got him the chair, Willy's talk of the love of his life and their unborn child. The years on death row had definitely taken their toll on LeRoy.

Willy took a polite tack. "LeRoy, thank you for seeing me. I just needed to ask you a couple of questions, if you don't mind."

"Listen, I know you think I killed your girlfriend and your baby, but as God as my witness, I am an innocent man. I have done some very bad things in my life which I must ultimately pay for, but never have I killed anyone. I feel sorry for your loss, as I feel for my own, but I'm innocent," LeRoy insisted.

Willy watched the way he said *innocent* and his inner voice told him it was true: LeRoy was innocent and was going to die for a murder he didn't commit. "LeRoy, I believe you."

215

Leroy's face muscles relaxed, then he began to sob uncontrollably. To see a man so tough and hard cry like a baby in a public setting was very disturbing. Willy gave him a moment to collect himself.

"Thank you, God. You see I'm not the guy! I was set up. No one will believe me and they are going to kill me in less than three months. I've done 10 years locked up and soon I'm going to be dead. Can you help me? If you would ask the judge to review the case maybe it would have some impact. Maybe some new evidence? Or they could use this DNA shit they can do now? I did not kill her. Someone else did and they are probably still out there."

Strong's statement resonated with Willy. Eva's killer was free and maybe close by. "I'm going to do everything I can, LeRoy. I'm going to talk to the detective that handled the case, Sergeant Brown, and review the evidence."

"That fucker Brown is dead. Cigarettes got him. Someone named Goldblatt is in charge, a girl cop. You got to work fast. My time is running out! And by the way, congrats on winning that tournament. Golf's not my thing but if you come from Augusta, you still watch it no matter what color you are."

"I'll do everything I can," Willy assured. "I'll start by telling Warden Blackstone I think you're innocent and I'm going to try to reopen the case. He will hate that, but I'm going to get him Masters tickets so he'll get over it. Tell me, LeRoy, about the couple of days before the murder. Did anything odd happen to you?"

"I've had 10 years to play it over and over in my head. Nothing unusual. The one kind of odd thing was a white dude came in the restaurant the night before your girl got killed. I remember he asked me for something or about something. He seemed odd, not from our parts, for sure. And why does a white gay guy want to eat at Ray's Rib Joint, not in Augusta's finer neighborhoods? The thing I remember the most is he gave me the biggest tip of my life. For what, I asked myself. I couldn't remember what I had done for him. Honestly, I was high that night and don't remember anything but the money. I told that to Brown, but he never even looked up from his notes, just kept on saying that I'd confessed to being high, so maybe I was insane at the time, not responsible for my actions, and that I should admit I killed her and he'd keep me from getting the chair."

"LeRoy, I'll give the information to the new detective in charge of the case. Tell me more about the good tipper. Well-dressed?"

"Yep, looked rich to me and left $10 on the table. A lot of money for a busboy."

"Any idea what that nail was that they found at the crime scene?"

"I've thought about that, too. You search for needles in haystacks when you're facing death row, but shit, I don't have a clue what it could be. Not a regular nail, used for something unusual, they said. It was short, sharp, and some weird kind of metal. Your girl was an artist. Maybe something she would use in her work?"

"Maybe," Willy pondered. "OK, I'll look into the case and talk with Goldblatt as soon as I can. Hopefully she's smarter than Brown was."

"Keep me updated and I wish you luck. I know I'm overdue for some myself," LeRoy sighed. "God sent you to me."

"God and Eva sent me, and I'll take all the luck I can get." With that Willy went to have a chat with the soon-to-be-pissed-off warden. Good thing he was a Masters fan.

CHAPTER 61

SERGEANT GOLDBLATT

Sergeant Goldblatt was a small, stout woman in her early forties with a hard Eastern accent, probably from Brooklyn. How she ended up in Augusta was anyone's guess.

She was all business. "I've quickly reviewed the file and we still have all the evidence the late Sergeant Brown cataloged with regards to the De Plain case, including the bowl Ms. De Plain was found lying near. Photographs, hair, blood samples, the whole kit and caboodle. Everything stays in place until the Strong execution, and then if you want I can retrieve the bowl and any personal items. Why do you think the man that murdered your girlfriend is innocent?"

"I know this sounds strange, but I believe LeRoy. I always have. I found Mr. Brown to be single-minded in his pursuit to convict LeRoy Strong and he may have missed something important." Willy didn't want to go into the Moran painting coincidence as it sounded farfetched even to him. How would he explain the note and seeing the painting in a billionaire's house in California and how it was somehow all related?

"OK, let me get up to speed on the case and review everything and then let you know what I find. This is a capital murder we're talking about and we don't want the wrong guy to fry."

"Sergeant Goldblatt," Willy said, "LeRoy told me about a white guy that came into his restaurant and talked with him the night before Eva was killed. LeRoy said the character was very out of place, well dressed with money. He told Brown about it, but Brown seemed to blow this guy off, according to LeRoy. Ray's Rib Joint is not the type of eating establishment rich, white guys visit. Also, do you know if any DNA samples were ever taken? Maybe some evidence would show someone was there other than LeRoy. One other thing never explained was that unusual nail found at the crime scene. Maybe someone could look at it again? It was apparently a special type of nail, maybe related to the art field?"

"I'll check into the nail. As far as DNA analysis, 10 years ago they didn't routinely run DNA samples so this should be looked into, might be a reason to reopen the case, especially with your recommendation," she agreed.

Willy thought maybe he could grease the wheels a bit, Augusta style, and get Goldblatt to make this a priority. "By the way, I'm going to be playing at the Masters this year and if you can use some tickets I'm sure I can get you a couple?"

"Thanks, but don't know anything about golf, other than it's big here, so don't waste 'em on me."

Definitely not from here, I was right, Willy thought. Too bad.

Willy talked to LeRoy every week and gave him updates but most of them were along the lines of, "I spoke with Goldblatt twice this week, nothing yet. I'm sorry, still waiting...."

It was mid-March 2010, the Masters less than a month away and Leroy's death date two months away, when Goldblatt finally called with more promising information. "I've gone through the file and just found something very interesting and disturbing that was missed in the first trial completely. It's good enough to have a judge take a look, maybe even for a new trial. The bowl which has been in the evidence room, the one your girlfriend was found lying next to? It had handwriting on the bottom. The writing is still present and appears to be in her blood. Does the letter "M" mean anything to you?"

Willy dropped the phone. It bounced off the linoleum tile. "Are you there? Willy? What happened?" Goldblatt kept asking.

Picking up the phone, his hands trembling, Willy said, "Sergeant, you need to come to my house right away. I think we may have the connection between Eva's death and why she was killed. The 'M' stands for Moran, and I have the smoking gun hanging on my wall."

"I'll be right over."

CHAPTER 62

PRISCILLA THE FERRET

The Moran painting was delivered as promised to Priscilla Counihan by Tommy's driver, Nelson. Priscilla put on her rubber gloves and gently removed the Moran from the Art Safe. The most important aspect of finding clues is simply through inspection. Pricilla's ability to let the artwork tell the story of its past was legendary in the art world. Critical clues were found by careful inspection. A frame might have nail holes at odd angles, telling Priscilla the frame was not original to the painting and possessed a different life. The frame's patina, whether original or modified, the wire the painting hung from, or the wooden keys in the corners to keep the canvas taut, could all reveal essential information.

Tommy's painting had two museum tags which looked as if they been taken off the original canvas and professionally replaced onto the back of the frame. The frame itself appeared to be original and consistent with the painting. The wood had a nice aged patina. Only where the foam core had been attached were there any signs of recent changes. The frame had a couple of areas of breaks in opposite corners and some loss to the guild, but it was a wonderful vintage frame.

Removal of the foam core backing revealed a fairly recent relining. This seemed very odd as the painting looked to be in near perfect condition excluding what appeared to be a small concussion mark in the upper left corner of the piece. "Nothing bad enough for a complete relining on such an important piece," Pricilla commented to herself.

Using an ultraviolet light, Pricilla slowly passed the light up and down the surface of the canvas, looking for any signs of restoration.

She found what she was looking for in the upper left corner of the painting in the sky where there had been well-done restoration of some small, concentric rings. What she didn't find was any additional injury to the canvas. The U.V. evaluation confirmed her initial cursory examination of the canvas. There had been nothing significant enough to require relining the multimillion-dollar painting.

She had been in the art world since she was a child. Her father was an important museum curator and had taught her the ins and outs of the art world at an early age. He had told her two things. Number one, become an expert in any field but not an art dealer. That's a cutthroat business and an old boys club. Two, don't depend on a man for support. Be your own boss and in charge. The latter advice was more prophetic than her father would ever know. Priscilla cared not for men, not her cup of tea. She had a partner now going on 20 years. Each had their own lives in different cities. Both were content with their relationship. They were partners for life, just geographical misfits.

Priscilla had considered an academic lifestyle as a professor at some large university teaching art history, but that purer road was not paved in gold. She liked money and loved a good crime book. So she had decided early on to specialize in authenticating artwork, using her art history degree with an entrepreneurial spirit. Art experts in the field of law are rare, in demand, and very well paid. Lawyers suing, those being sued, and insurance companies seeking to authenticate were among those who sought her out. All roads led to Priscilla Counihan when it came to ferreting out misdeeds in the art world. She was a master of detection and when it came to big-ticket artworks, she was the best.

She recognized who had done the relining job immediately. It was the late Byron Boyd's handiwork. He was a perfectionist with his pieces. She could tell how he had meticulously joined the two canvases at the edge leaving a nearly unperceivable joint line. "Yes this is Byron's work. He must have done the back and I would expect he put on the foam core covering as well," she mused to herself. Priscilla could have complete conversations with herself, answering questions she posed.

Her African Grey Parrot, who had a huge vocabulary and shared her office, would often repeat what Priscilla had just said as if she had been talking to him. "Put on the foam core," the bird squawked. Bird and owner had been together so long that each just expected the other to talk.

As she reexamined the foam core backing she had so carefully taken off, she kept her hands covered with sterile surgical gloves. She never wanted to destroy critical evidence. Priscilla wore a head lamp and magnifying glasses as she methodically examined the backing, starting at the top and working her way down. In the lower corner of the white board were a couple of very small, darkish red splatter marks. Not paint, but something else. "I bet this is from Byron's studio," she said as she took a sample for analysis. She had known Byron very well. He had died 10 years ago in what was described in the paper as a fluke accident. A large painting frame had fallen from its overhead bin, crushing Byron's skull. His smoldering cigarette had caused a subsequent fire that had destroyed millions of dollars in paintings. She remembered at the time thinking the whole scenario sounded odd and anything classified as a fluke probably wasn't. He was old, a serious smoker, and it was in the realm of possibility, yet if the insurance companies had hired her to investigate maybe she would have found something other than a huge frame slipping out of its bin. Boyd was a seasoned professional and restorers make sure their pieces are securely stored.

The puzzling thing was why the lining on an expensive and obviously healthy canvas? "Byron must have been paid a lot of money," she said. Why? "To hide something on the back, possibly. That must be it." Her African Grey shrieked, "Hide something on the back!"

Priscilla called T.T. that night to give him an update. She had already found some serious inconsistencies and she was going to track down the museum-show tags that had come with the painting. She had ordered an analysis of a sample of some odd-looking splatter marks found on the painting's foam core backing. The analysis and the museum work might take a few weeks. Once she had something more definitive, she would call him. She did plan to call Ashton Charmers, but wanted all her ducks in a row first.

T.T. warned, "Be careful, Priscilla. There is a possibility that someone may have been murdered with regards to this painting and I don't want you to take any unnecessary chances. You have the certificate of authenticity and provenance I got from Ashton when I purchased the painting. Maybe something's there?"

Tommy also went over his conversation with Willy, including all the details of Eva's life and her relationship with Willy, the existence of an exact copy of the painting in Willy's home, and the fact that the painting T.T. had purchased had surfaced around the time Eva was murdered.

"Is this by chance Willy Wilson the golfer who just won the Pebble Beach Pro-Am?"

"Yes, that's him."

"I have one weakness," Priscilla confessed. "I love golf, both playing it and the players. I've watched Willy's career and always hoped he would make it big someday. He's an Augusta native, the wonder kid of Augusta National. I will work as hard as I can on this case. My goal is to have made significant progress, with hopefully some answers, by the Masters. I already have my Masters tickets but I would love to meet Willy Wilson in person."

"Not a problem. I'm going myself. We will get together for lunch at the clubhouse and I'll see if Willy has time to join us."

Priscilla eyeballed her golf bag in the corner of her studio, longing to be in Augusta in the frenzy of the Masters. "It's a date, T.T.!" She blushed at the absurd thought of having a date with a man, even if he was a billionaire.

The museum tags were easy enough to track down as was the curatorial history. The Moran had been in two shows: one in England in the 1920s and then the large Metropolitan Museum of Art 1993 retrospective. The Met had recently changed directors and the new director was a stickler for privacy regarding its lenders. Strict protocol was required to get any privileged information. This included letters of reference, a letter notarized to document the reason for the information, and a list of those who would be privy to that information. The donors had to be contacted and they had to agree to give out the information. Priscilla filled out the paperwork as she had done numerous times in the past and then just had to wait. She asked her usual informants but none had heard about the painting ever being on the market. Those in the know had thought it might be out of some old New York collection.

Eva De Plain was easier to find. There were articles about her bass playing, her Manhattan School of Music graduation, the ordeal in Mexico, and ultimately her murder. Pricilla read about Eva's relationship with Bernard Rashmusen. That was a name she recognized. She had met Dorothy Rashmusen, and heard about the generous donation to the Long Island Historical Society, with the new Rashmusen wing of American art.

"No Moran's currently in the Rashmusen collection, but maybe they did have one, THE LONE CYPRESS. A little more detective work and I won't need the Met's info," she mused. Picasso, her African Grey, screeched from his cage, "Moran, Moran."

The lab work came in on the splatter marks: human blood type A negative, a very rare type. "How did blood get onto the back of that painting? Could it be that Boyd was murdered while this painting was in his studio? The murderer, possibly Ashton, was there and took the piece? I know Byron's handiwork on the back of that painting was done to hide something." Picasso's echo machine chimed in behind her, "Murdered! Boyd murdered."

Priscilla called Tommy with the findings so far. She was waiting to find out Byron Boyd's blood type. She thought the new lining should be removed from the back of the Moran as all roads were leading that way. It was an expensive and labor-intensive task and wasn't without risk. She didn't think it had to be done quite yet, but ultimately it probably would. She explained a radiographic evaluation could show something but the definitive answer would be found upon removal of the lining.

She didn't want to talk to Charmers yet. Nothing incriminating enough, but it was coming and soon. Priscilla had heard only unflattering things about Ashton B. Charmers. The best thing said about him was that he was a great salesman. The art world is small, even in New York City, and dealers talk. The rap on Ashton was he would take advantage of any situation and had been caught in lies, including skimming money off the top of deals. His knowledge of art was only so-so, and he seemed to have no real background. His eye was good enough, but it was always about the money, not the art. He had done very well for himself, especially when he first came to town, but always wanted to be paid in cash which bothered other art dealers. No one thought he was a sociopath, but then again the most dangerous sociopaths are the ones that seem normal.

The Metropolitan Museum of Art called with the information Priscilla had been waiting for. The owner was the late Bernard

Rashmusen. No current contacts known for the whereabouts of the painting.

Priscilla's skin turned clammy and her heart started to race upon hearing the Rashmusen name. Bernard was Eva's late boyfriend, and then she had been murdered. No mention of a Moran being stolen at the time and the supposed murderer was scheduled for execution. As Priscilla pondered the implications she got her second call, Byron Boyd's blood type: A negative.

CHAPTER 63

THE MEETING

It was early April 2010. Priscilla's flight to Augusta for her annual Masters getaway was in 12 hours. She would be meeting T.T. for lunch at the clubhouse tomorrow. The Masters seemed like an inappropriate time to fill him in on all the news, most of which looked bad, but better to do it in person. He could make up his mind about the next step, removing the lining. There was something suspicious behind the relining, she was sure. The police were the step after that. This painting had an exceptionally shaky record of ownership and was associated with two murders.

Priscilla drew up a document that stated Thompson would give his full permission to have the painting's back canvas lining removed professionally. The release stated he was aware and had full disclosure of the possibility of canvas damage during the process. The chance of damage was minimal since it was really a very expensive procedure which he could easily afford. But if something did happen, her insurance wouldn't cover a $5 million dollar painting.

Priscilla had been to Augusta National and the Masters many times, five to be exact. The excitement of eating in the clubhouse was making her lose almost as much sleep as the Moran debacle. To pass through the white ropes that segregated the haves from the have-nots had always been something Priscilla secretly dreamed of. It was odd that this was such a big deal to Priscilla. After all, in her world she was important and dealt with very rich and sometimes famous, but Augusta was different. If she hadn't been such a fan of the game it wouldn't have been such a thrill. But for real golfers, being able to be in close proximity to the best of the game is like movie buffs attending the Oscars. Priscilla had always had general tickets, which in themselves were extremely hard to score. To get through the white lines of Augusta and have access to the clubhouse and locker rooms, you must have the right color badge. The badges represent the royalty of golf admired by those without. The flimsy general tickets that blew in the wind around most of the necks of Augusta spectators looked common next to the pin-on Augusta badge with its color coding and stated member/guest.

The timing was tight, but if she were to give a complete report to Tommy she needed first to meet in person with Ashton B. Charmers and see what kind of story he had regarding the Moran transaction. She knew something was wrong with the provenance and the back had been tampered with. Ashton was involved in some way, she was sure. Probably he had bought the painting from someone who had somehow gotten it out of Eva's possession. Maybe it was hers or maybe not. Maybe she was involved as well, though not in Bernard's death, that seemed certain. You can stage a fire and painting coming down on someone's head, but not the destruction of a city. Boyd's death was after Eva's so whoever killed Boyd probably killed her. That also meant Ashton probably knew the killer so she better be very careful. Priscilla knew Ashton had managed to meet and sell a billionaire a multimillion-dollar painting, so he must have some good people skills in addition to salesmanship. Many art dealers looked at lying as an art form. She figured he must be one. Well, time was running out so she'd better call him.

She launched in by introducing herself and soft-pedaling her mission: "I was hoping I might be able to have a little of your time. I am working for Tommy Thompson and we are just getting a little background information about a wonderful Moran he purchased from you 10 years ago. He's going to loan it to a museum for a show and the museum people just need some additional history for the catalog."

She didn't expect to get much information from him over the phone but didn't want him to clam up, or worse, disappear. She knew Ashton would have to give her something to keep the museum from starting to call around further. A close friend of Priscilla's was the director of a small, prominent museum that would cover for her in case Ashton decided to verify the story.

Ashton was taken off guard. It had been over a decade since he had sold Tommy Thompson Eva's Moran. The deal was one of many, even if it had been his very best hit. The original $2.5 million was still in his overseas account and doing quite well. A nosy inquiry, much less a museum show, was not good, to say the least. Ashton had to think fast. *I'll meet her at my place, see what it's all about, tie up some loose ends.*

"OK, Priscilla," he responded. "How about my studio tonight around seven?"

"Sorry that won't work. I'm leaving town tonight. Can you manage a quick lunch, somewhere near your studio? It's at Spring and Thompson, correct? How about Louise's? It's close by for me as well. My treat."

"That's fine. I'll see you in two hours at Louise's. How will I recognize you?"

"I'll be wearing a large yellow sun hat. And you?"

"Oh, I'm just very ordinary looking. I'll find you, just have the hat on." Ashton quickly hung up.

Priscilla began having second thoughts about the meeting. He never asked what the title of the exhibit was or its venue. Even more disturbing was the reality that she had not been able to find a picture of Ashton on the Internet, which was surprising. Most dealers go out of their way to toot their own horns. They are the brand and you always promote yourself. Priscilla figured even if Ashton was a true sociopath, she would be leaving in 12 hours and she could talk with the police upon her return and then deal with him. Luckily, the meeting with Ashton was in a very public place and she would be on high alert. After that, Augusta was waiting and she would have a complete report when she had lunch at the clubhouse tomorrow. The thought of the Augusta clubhouse made Priscilla smile.

CHAPTER 64

AN EXPENSIVE LUNCH

Ashton Charmers started to pace as soon as he got off the phone. He had heard of Priscilla. Her nickname was the ferret. You didn't want her on your scent if you had something to hide. She sounded friendly enough on the phone, probably just doing some fact checking for a wealthy man showing off his Moran to the world, but if she was on to something she was going to be in deep shit.

Ashton had given T.T. a fairly accurate history of the painting. He had listed the two museum shows it had been featured in. For collection provenance he had written the history in chronological order:

Thomas Moran, THE LONE CYPRESS.

Purchased directly from the artist by a Scottish gentleman.

Descended through the family in a private collection, New York City.

Private collection, Atlanta, Georgia.

Collection of Charmers Fine Art, New York City.

All was true except the Atlanta part should have read: "Stolen, Augusta, Georgia." Ashton at the time pondered whether to include the provenance of Atlanta, but he figured if it ever came out that the Moran was Eva De Plain's painting he could say he bought it for cash at an antiques store and produce some generic receipt for $2,000. He could always claim the poor black girl may have pawned the piece or sold it for drugs and he was just in the right place at the right time. He was in Atlanta at the time considering relocating there. It was such an interesting and vibrant community. He had explored Atlanta for a couple of weeks to check the art scene out, got lucky when he hit the antiques store, and found a great Moran. In retrospect he now knew he had fucked up. He should have just left Atlanta/Augusta off. Ashton knew better now but he was still very green 10 years ago with respect to what to list when doing a painting's provenance. He hadn't thought long-term about the consequences. At the time he just wanted to get the deal done and make sure the painting stuck.

If the ferret got sniffing around, she might be able to put the puzzle pieces together. Ashton decided ferret season was now open.

Priscilla showed up 20 minutes early. She wanted to make sure she got a table that was very public just in case Ashton went ballistic. She had decided she was only going to feel him out about the restoration and the Atlanta provenance and leave it at that. She hoped she could gauge his reaction to her questions. Maybe he would shed some light on the whole mess if he really was innocent.

After 40 minutes waiting at Louise's, Ashton was a no show. She went to the lobby and called his number.

Ashton answered the phone. "So sorry, something unexpected came up and I couldn't make it. I tried your phone but you must have left early. Again, please except my apologies. I will be happy to meet with you when you get back in town, just call me."

"Fine, I'll call you next week. I need to get a little information. The museum writer is trying to finish up the catalog. I'd rather not tell T.T. I don't have the information they need, so you can understand me wanting to talk soon."

"Yes, Tommy is a man I wouldn't want angry at me."

"You're right, powerful men can be dangerous."

As Priscilla hung up, Ashton, who had been talking to her from his forwarded home phone to his cell just a hundred yards away, said to himself in a low, menacing voice, "Yes, powerful men like me are dangerous."

Ashton followed the yellow hat back to Priscilla's home, staying close. She never suspected a thing. He planned his pace behind her perfectly and pushed himself through Priscilla's door just as she opened it.

"What you are doing? Help! Help!" Priscilla yelled, out of breath, pupils dilated.

"You asked to meet me. It turns out I am available, Ms. Counihan," Ashton responded, shoving Priscilla into the apartment and slamming her door shut. He looked around. "I see you got my Art Safe. I love those things, don't you?'

Priscilla jumped behind the huge cage that housed Picasso, her yellow hat crushed against the cage. "Help me!" she howled. Picasso started screaming, "Murder, murdered Boyd, aaahhh."

"Nice fucking bird. Seems we have been talking to him? Impressive vocabulary." Ashton extracted a long knife from his pocket. He noticed a set of golf clubs by the door.

"Golfer, are we? I hate that fucking game and I see we have some Masters tickets. Going to visit, are you? Isn't that in Augusta? I was there once. Not very memorable except for the art." He switched the knife to his left hand and picked up a three iron. "One of my boring clients told me it's almost impossible to hit with one of these things. I'd like to find out for myself."

With that, Ashton lunged at the bird cage, flailing the knife at Priscilla with his left hand, the right arm cocked with the iron. Picasso's giant cage tipped over, crashing to the ground. The old bird escaped and began flying around the room screeching, "Murder, murder, Boyd murder! Hide something, Moran, Moran!" Agitated and confused, Picasso knocked things over as he swooped around the room.

Ashton stabbed at Priscilla and as she fell backwards to avoid the knife, the three iron in his other hand made solid contact with her right temporal area and jaw. The breaking of the bones was audible. She crumpled to the ground, blood oozing out the side of her face.

"My God, golf is fun!" Ashton was elated after making such solid contact with Priscilla's now badly damaged face.

Ashton bent over and was about to stab her in the heart when the large parrot swooped down, his long talons grabbing the back of Ashton's neck. Picasso then released Ashton and hovered around the room shrieking, "Moran, murder, Priscilla." Then Picasso screamed, "Help me!"

Hearing people coming up the steps, Ashton quickly grabbed his Art Safe, some paperwork with T.T.'s name, the Masters tickets, and made an exit out the fire escape. Ashton was breaking rule one of thievery: never hit the same place twice. Stealing a Moran twice was the same thing but he muttered, "Rules are made to be broken," as he scrambled down the fire escape.

One of Pricilla's neighbors barreled through the door to find the bleeding, unconscious Priscilla with Picasso sitting on her shoulder screaming, "Moran, murder."

CHAPTER 65

THE EXIT

Ashton had not made sure Priscilla The Ferret was dead. The pain from the bird's sharp talons and the intrusive neighbors had distracted him from doing his usually thorough job. Hopefully the golf club had found its mark and if not, at least caused a severe brain injury. Either way it was not his usual clean kill and he knew it. Time to start speaking Spanish. He would arrange an escape to Central America and start a new life. He had a little over $8 million in Cayman banks, not as much as he had hoped for especially after such a good start. But the art business was hard. It seemed you needed to kill people to make the big bucks.

It was obvious T.T. was about to find out about the hidden inscription. Ashton had Priscilla's release in his hand along with her Masters tickets and a note from T.T. saying he was looking forward to seeing her in Augusta. Priscilla's vicious bird had screamed "Boyd" and "murder," so it was likely Priscilla knew too much. Thompson might know as well. It looked like Ashton had some unfinished business in Augusta. He was hitting his clubs so well right now, it seemed a good time to visit his old friend Tommy. "I need to thank him in person for giving me back my Moran and Art Safe!" Ashton laughed. Like Priscilla's bird, Ashton repeated, "Thank him in person," as he slipped down a back alley to his SoHo studio.

Safely back in his studio, it was time for Ashton to make his long-awaited escape. The Masters began tomorrow and ran through the weekend—and he had tickets. It wouldn't be long before the police would be involved with Priscilla. Ashton didn't want a pissed-off billionaire on his tail, so he might need to kill T.T. before he caused too much commotion. Tommy was single and there would be lawyers after his remains, no doubt, along with CEOs trying to grab for power. Nobody would care or find out about the Moran for a while. They would have bigger fish to fry.

"Wonder how the steak is these days at Ray's." The words made Ashton laugh. "I'll miss LeRoy this time, hope he's got a brother working there." The laughter was now unstoppable.

Ashton hired a private jet, a luxury he had always yearned for and this was his opportunity. Then he cleaned out the paperwork in his studio, which he always kept to a minimum anyway so that there was nothing around for anyone to find. He had all his Cayman bank papers tucked into a safety deposit box under an alias, the bank numbers memorized.

There were only a couple of paintings in inventory at the moment. Nothing that great, so he decided it wasn't worth his precious time worrying about them. Besides, if anyone came looking for him, it would appear that he was still around. What art dealer would leave valuable paintings behind?

"Not like me to leave $30 grand on the table, but sometimes you got to know when to fold, and I've got an evening plane to catch. Sure nice of Tommy to give me my Art Safe back. They are so strong you can put a $5 million dollar painting in the baggage hold and not worry about a thing!"

As he packed his bags, Ashton planned his future. "Time to stop being common. First stop, Augusta, to take in the Masters. Next stop, the Cayman Islands for a little banking. Then another jet to parts unknown. Hope I can get the plane parked right next to Tommy's, how nice would that be." The boyish giggling gurgled up as Ashton thought of the irony: T.T.'s painting arriving in Augusta in the jet next to his.

CHAPTER 66

SAVING LEROY AND THE MASTERS

Sergeant Goldblatt brought the evidence that had been so poorly overlooked in the first trial to one of Augusta's finest but most conservative judges, Judge Eagerly.

Eagerly had a reputation as a fair but stern judge. He was appalled to see poor Eva's death message had been unnoticed. A complete investigation was ordered and he immediately moved LeRoy off death row. Willy provided a sworn oath about Eva's drawing of the Moran, and the multibillionaire Tommy Thompson added that the Atlanta provenance of the Moran painting was being investigated.

The patient blue bowl that had been sequestered in the evidence room for 10 years finally revealed skin tissue on the edge of the chip and it was not LeRoy's. It was tissue of Caucasian descent. Though the sample was extremely desiccated, it was obvious it must have been acquired from a significant scrape, probably with the real murderer.

Willy proposed LeRoy's release on bail, guaranteeing the money himself thanks to his recent PGA winnings. Judge Eagerly responded that he would take it under advisement, explaining, "We need to be sure before I release an ex-con on death row out on the street, especially during Masters week. I would think you would understand that, Mr. Wilson."

Willy took Eagerly's words to mean, "No black ex-con murderers set free during the festivities. Don't want to upset any of that Masters money. We only want happy headlines about the tournament in the paper."

The Augusta local paper published only minimal back-page coverage with regard to LeRoy's case. The paper was almost completely devoted to the upcoming Masters from the front page onward, as usual.

The Masters was bearing down on Willy. His first two days of practice were already behind him. He was not sufficiently focused. He had practiced every day and made use of his course access that the other pros could only dream of, but the truth was his game was off. His inner voice was only talking about Eva, insisting, "The killer is still out there." It wasn't saying, "Stay focused, this is the Masters. You've waited for this your whole life." It was a bad sign for this week's tournament.

Theo had gotten his yellow litter suit and worked the course for three days already in preparation for the tournament. The first day was about learning what was expected of the litter patrol. The young men, all from Augusta high schools, worked in teams in certain areas every day. With the hundreds of thousands of visitors, there actually was surprisingly little trash. Masters fans so revere the entire event that they generally make sure the trash they discard goes into trash cans. The litter patrol members often busy themselves picking up tree litter, pine cones, and leaves, talking to each other in hushed tones, and staring at all the rich people. Occasionally they get an autograph on their yellow litter hats from one of the pros during practice rounds.

Willy did enjoy the nine hole par three contest that occurred the last day before the big show. Players were encouraged to bring their kids to caddie, so he arranged for Theo to be excused from litter patrol for the nine hole tournament. Willy halfway expected to win, since no winner of the par three had ever won the Masters. Tiger usually skipped this event as he felt it was a distraction. For Willy it was a big deal to compete with Theo at his side, a chance to act like father and son.

He didn't win, but still he took pleasure from sharing the competition with Theo and having a chance to secure a green jacket at the Masters.

The first day of the Masters Tournament, Willy had Uncle Ed on his bag. Ed, in his decades of caddie service, had never gotten to caddie for a professional at Augusta National's Masters until this week. He had retired from caddying but came back out and had been in training ever since Willy's unlikely Pebble Beach win. Ed had to be there for Willy's moment no matter how stiff his joints were. Now that the big event was finally underway, Willy figured with his own poor concentration it would only be a two-day deal for him and Ed, as he probably was going to miss the cut, a huge disappointment for Augusta's natives. It doesn't matter how many times you have played Augusta or how good you are, if you aren't focused completely you will never win, and Willy Wilson understood this.

Day one went as Willy had expected: not great. It was apparent from his opening drive on the first tee that the day was going to be a grind, when he hit the ball directly into the big bunker on the right. Willy had played two years as a teenager before he had ever fallen into that trap on number one.

Ed gave him as much encouragement as possible, trying to keep him loose like he had years ago on his first outing with Billy Bob. "Listen, my little Willy, we are going to have fun today whether you like it or not, remember?"

Willy remembered this same advice from the first day he ever played Augusta National. "OK, Uncle Ed, I get the picture. Relax my swing like I'm trying to out-drive old Billy Bob."

"Yes sir, that's the little Willy I know!"

The day proceeded with no exceptional play, but Willy had done a lot worse under easier conditions. The course never plays as hard as it does for the Masters Tournament. Willy had always tried to play the course the first week after the Masters to experience those extreme conditions. He remembered saying to himself, "Don't ever forget these speeds, greens of glass...."

Willy tried to concentrate on the task at hand. Every so often he would get completely in the moment and be in the zone, then one of the yellow litter boys would catch his eye and he would remember Eva's killer was still loose. "Maybe on this very course," he thought. He knew it was terribly defeating to allow this kind of self-talk, but it was beyond his conscious control.

Hole 18 was his favorite. Willy could almost always count on at least paring the hole depending on his drive. If it was straight and long, it was an easy pitch and putt for a birdie or par. Unfortunately, Willy often ended up right next to the trap and under the big tree. For some reason his eye always seemed to see the hole this way and invariably he would find himself in this position. Today was no exception, under the tree. Willy had played the hole so many times from this position it felt normal. He didn't get as many birdies, but he rarely bogeyed either. Usually the shot was a pitch and run with his five iron. He could occasionally do a flop shot depending on where the pin was or if he had driven it far enough past the large oak tree's wing span. Today's position was the usual, missed to the right and the five iron. Willy was amazed how the people gathered around his somewhat errant shot, the white lines jutting in at the point closest to his ball. The crowds were larger than he expected, undoubtedly due to his local favorite status. Willy saw T.T. with his big smile. The billionaire had worked his way down from the green once he saw where Willy's ball had landed and figured he would watch the approach shot then try and run back up with the masses to the green to see Willy putt.

A perfect pitch and par. T.T. greeted Willy and Ed as they walked off the green. "I'll see you in the clubhouse for a bite after you get cleaned up."

Ed, by now exhausted, his cigarettes and age finally catching up with him, declined T.T.'s offer. He simply said, "Willy, tomorrow we make the cut and I've got to get my rest if I plan on seeing it."

Tommy, with his Member Guest badge, quickly slipped into the sanctuary of exclusivity behind the white ropes and waited for Willy to join him for supper.

CHAPTER 67

THE MASTERS DINNER

Willy met T.T. for an early dinner overlooking the first tee box and the practice green. The dining facilities were in two separate areas: one was indoors in a very formal dining room, requiring coat and tie in old Southern style. The other was the outside patio that is set up in front of the dining room just opposite the players' lockers and a large, magnificent oak tree where all the players are interviewed for the golf channels.

That was where T.T. awaited Willy. It was an amazing spectacle, an operatic theater of golf, as the big names flowed in—Jack, Tiger, Arnie, Phil. The excitement crescendoed with frenetic reporting by news and radio hosts, all of them trying to get the inside scoop from the greats. The tide of reporters came in with the VIP golfers. People like T.T. and Willy entered the theater, and the tide went out, a couple of local news channels showing interest but nothing national and definitely nothing international. People like Tommy could actually come and stand next to the golfers and the news reporters as they gave their interviews. The special ones, that was how Willy heard them described. An elderly pale man with an old Augusta Masters hat gave T.T. a little elbow. "Those guys around the reporters, they are the special ones!"

As Willy stepped up to give his 10 minutes worth of interviews rehashing day one of the tournament, he looked back across the ropes at the hordes of the watchers, now observing him, special for the moment.

Then Willy and T.T. went over to the bar to wait for their table.

Willy said, "T.T., I asked Eva De Plain's son Theo to come join us after he gets through working the litter patrol. I have always considered him my son even though it's not official."

"That's wonderful, I can't wait to meet Eva's child. He had a very special mother and her courage helped my steel company more than I will ever know," T.T. replied. "Now before Theo gets here, I know it's a shitty time to bring this up, with the Masters pressure and all, but I wanted to update you on the painting investigation. Today, I was supposed to meet Priscilla Counihan for lunch so she could tell me what she uncovered about the painting. She didn't show and I knew this was not like her. She is one of those type triple A personalities that's never late, and the kicker was she's a huge Masters fan. The idea of getting through the ropes back to the VIP area was a very big deal. She was hoping to meet you."

T.T. sighed. "When she didn't show, I called the police in New York and pulled a few strings to find out what was going on. Turns out, she'd been found unconscious in her studio, viciously attacked with what they think was a golf club out of her own bag."

Willy interrupted, his appetite now gone. "What are you saying? Was she killed?"

"She's in a medically induced coma in ICU. They drugged her up to lessen the pressure on the brain, so we don't really know how bad it is. The doctor told me he's hoping the majority of damage was done to her jaw and not the head, though she did have a significant skull fracture."

T.T. took a sip of his cocktail to fortify himself. "Here's the part I wish I didn't have to tell you. When they found her pet parrot, it was on top of her unconscious body. He probably saved her life. The bird was screaming, "Murder, murder, Moran." The forensic experts found fresh human skin under the talons of the parrot and it wasn't Priscilla's. I gave the police's top investigator a sizable donation to the pizza fund to run an immediate DNA test. Turns out the tissue matches that on Eva's blue Mexican bowl. A perfect match. It's the killer."

Willy tried to absorb this. "Eva's killer just tried to kill Priscilla? Priscilla found out something about the painting and the killer got wind of it?"

T.T. nodded. "That's the gist of it. One more thing: the Moran is gone. Priscilla had it and now it has vanished, along with her Masters tickets. Also, the art dealer Ashton Charmers, who sold me the Moran, has disappeared. Priscilla told me she planned on talking with him before her flight down here. I sent a private eye over to his studio, one that knows his way around a sticky door knob. He reported everything looked normal, nothing off the walls, nothing unusual, the bed was made and all the clothes still in place. I'm sure Ashton Charmers is involved somehow, but I don't know how. Maybe he's our man or maybe the killer is just cleaning up loose ends and he was next in line."

T.T. slid a photo across the bar. "Here's a copy of the photo of me with the painting and Ashton, so you remember Ashton's face in case he shows up."

Willy picked up the photo. "Wow. Unbelievable! It puts my marginal day out here on the links in perspective."

Then from a distance, Willy heard his name, "Uncle Willy!" as a teenager leaned as far over the white ropes as he could without falling in or being scolded by the Augusta guards. It was Theo in his bright yellow suit, still wearing his litter hat although now backwards, a full blast of straight, reddish-brown hair spilling out from underneath.

"How about some food, Uncle Willy? I'm starving. You think you worked hard, try picking up litter all day."

Willy and T.T. walked over to the ropes, the special ones on the inside.

"Theo, I want you to meet Mr. Thompson. He's the one who got me into the Pebble tournament, the man I told you about. He's why I'm getting to play Augusta. No Pebble win, no Masters."

"Hi, Mr. Thompson." Theo extended his hand across the rope line as the guards peered at the odd pair. "So what's it like to be so rich? I bet you never had to wear a yellow suit and pick up leaves when you were a kid."

T.T. shook Theo's hand. "Actually, I vividly remember working in the petroleum fields in my oil-soaked overalls during hot, humid Oklahoma summers. What I learned was I'd rather own the oil fields than work in them. So I got the best education I could and now I'm on this side of the ropes, if you get what I mean."

"Sweet," Theo nodded. "Speaking of the ropes, how about somebody giving me a VIP badge so I can escape average land?"

Willy pointed, "Follow me down to the end just past the locker rooms where they sell the merchandise for the pros and VIPs. I'll get you through the ropes there. There's a white door with no label on it. That's the restroom for the caddies. You can change out of your suit."

Then Willy walked on his side of the ropes, terrain that was open with a few VIPs and professionals talking, unlike Theo's side, where the kid had to push through the crowds to keep up with Willy who looked like he was taking an evening stroll. Theo, after dozens of, "Excuse me, coming through" requests as he shouldered his way into the crowd, finally reached Willy just outside the pro shop. Willy showed the guard his badge and Theo slipped in with the specials, no more jostling.

Theo found the unmarked white bathroom door where Uncle Ed had changed for decades. As Willy stood waiting for Theo to emerge, he noticed for the first time the huge billboard that read in green letters, "The Masters." All the players' names, the city they were from, and their daily scores were listed in alphabetical order. Directly above Tiger with his 68 score was one Willy Wilson from Augusta, Georgia, 74. If Willy could repeat his score, he would probably make the cut, but all he could think about as he looked at his name was, "The killer is out there and still trying to kill. At least they have the Moran, maybe they'll run."

The three finally settled in for dinner in front of the clubhouse. There was small talk about Willy and the tournament, about his chances of making the cut, and about Theo's job and the people he'd met. A couple of white dudes from Minnesota had tried to buy his hat for $200 dollars. He'd told them he would consider it, but knew he would get fired and Willy would be disappointed. With that Theo pulled out his hat from his back pocket.

"Uncle Willy, how about signing your name on my litter hat? I'm going to sell it on eBay after this is over. If you could somehow get me Tiger's name after the tournament, I really could get some money." Theo blushed when he realized he had just dissed the person closest to him in the world and hastily added, "Of course after you win this thing, yours will be more valuable, especially here in Augusta, Georgia."

Willy slung his arm around Theo's shoulder and gently said, "I'll try and get Tiger's autograph before he gives me the green jacket, so I will wait to sign your litter hat when all the cameras are rolling. That way you can attach the video clip to your eBay listing and get bigger bucks, how's that?"

Theo, T.T., and Willy all laughed. It was the first feeling of relief for Willy all day.

CHAPTER 68

THE KILLING ZONE, AUGUSTA STYLE

Ashton B. Charmers arrived in time for the first day of the tournament. He spent the day scouting out his prey, a hunter looking for the big game, in this case a multibillionaire. He searched for six straight hours through the tens of thousands of crazed golf fans. Ashton's frustrating pursuit reminded him of trying to find Penwell in San Francisco at his first art opening in a sea of gay men. All the men at Augusta looked like Tommy: same golf cap, same golf shirt, same white face. Just as the course was shutting down and the have-nots were being escorted out, he sighted Willy, Theo, and his target, Tommy Thompson, sitting and having a nice evening meal.

Ashton was already pissed. The Masters tickets he had stolen from Counihan were the cheap general admission type. On the open market they would bring a thousand dollars or more, but they were common to Ashton. "You would think Tommy would have gotten the bitch VIP tickets, where I don't have to wait in line to pee. But now I've got the big VIP asshole Thompson in my sights. I know just where to find him. Tomorrow he's mine."

He needed a plan, and it irritated him to watch T.T. enjoying his meal while he, Ashton, was hungry and tired. "Why the fuck couldn't you have left the Moran on your wall to show to your rich friends?" he lamented. "No, you wanted to show the Moran on some worldwide trouble-making museum tour. You had to be Mr. Big Shot Art Collector, even though you don't know shit about art, and it's going to cost you your life, you stupid dick. Only thing returning in your jet will be your body!"

Ashton knew nothing about golf except the names of a few high- end golf courses that his clients obsessed about, especially Augusta. They all talked of the great Masters. It bored the hell out of Ashton. The grounds were nice, but the little cabins and the clubhouse looked out of date. The course itself was the only attractive sight for miles, the rest of the city consisting of cheap shopping malls and waffle houses. "Low roofs, wooden buildings, and shitty art. What's the big deal? I'll make it a big deal when I kill a billionaire and slip away, then it will be special," Ashton muttered.

That night Ashton pulled out the most important thing he'd brought with him besides money and the Art Safe with the Moran painting: a black umbrella with an engraved silver handle. This umbrella was unique. Its handle had a special hidden button and when pushed it would release an eight-inch long silver stiletto blade. The Augusta front-gate guards would never suspect a thing. The weather forecast was for intermittent rain all week, so there would be thousands of umbrellas. Ashton's umbrella was made for an English gentleman in the late 1800s. "Who knows, it may have been Thomas Moran's personal piece," he smiled wickedly at the perverse thought. "Killed by Moran's knife over one of his paintings, charming."

Ashton slept well. He was readying for tomorrow. No evening dinners on the veranda for him, just a quick escape on a jet to the Caymans.

In contrast, Willy Wilson's sleep was troubled, a night of intermittent terror. He kept thinking of Eva and her bloody "M." As his dreams progressed, Eva kept warning him, "Be careful, remember the number."

Usually at a major golf tournament the pros don't sleep well as the next day's match is all-encompassing. Tonight Willy never dreamed of golf, but of a woman getting beaten with a golf club and the assailant next turning it on him. Eva screamed, "Find my killer! He killed our son!"

CHAPTER 69

MAKING THE CUT

Ashton woke up around nine. He spent the morning sharpening his blade and making sure he had a car waiting to get him out of Dodge once he had filleted Mr. Big Shot. The plan was to get to the Masters around noon, hang out, inch as close as he could to the clubhouse, and wait for Tommy Thompson. He figured T.T. would show up around noon also, get a bite, talk to the other billionaire types, and then go down to watch a little golf. When Ashton had him in the right place where Tommy couldn't escape, he would find the right moment and impale him in the back, right through his heart with a fatal twist. It would be so fast that T.T. wouldn't know what happened and with all the excitement of the game, timed during a nice big roar of the crowds, no one would even notice. Tommy would hit the deck, another overweight white guy succumbing to heart disease. By the time help arrived, Ashton would already be out the gate to the waiting sedan. "Cayman Islands, here I come."

The best place would be around hole 18. It was the closest hole to the outside world and his car. Ashton figured all the bigwigs like T.T. don't like to walk far. "See a little golf on 18, then drinks with the pros, right next to 18's green." Ashton was ready and excited at the thought of killing in broad daylight during a huge golf event, murdering a multibillionaire while stealing his multimillion-dollar painting. After Priscilla Counihan, Ashton embraced the power of being God and taking a life. He knew killing at such a high-profile event would be the most thrilling accomplishment in his life, much better than stealing.

Who would have imagined that Franklin Hare, the petty criminal from Enid, Oklahoma, would end up an important art dealer with the power of life and death over one of America's richest men?

―――――――――――――――――――

Willy had basically eaten nothing since Tommy's news. He tried to down a biscuit and milk for breakfast, and skip the coffee. Coffee would only exacerbate Willy's already frayed nerves and he didn't want to miss a two-foot putt because he had helped himself to a morning pick-me-up. His horrific night had done him no favors. His eyes were swollen, his back stiff, and he felt exhausted. Something was bothering him. It was the small nail. It was a clue related to the murder, not from LeRoy but from the real killer. As he sat in his dim kitchen re-evaluating whether he should brew some coffee, his eyes rested on Eva's drawing.

"What was it? Was that little nail related to your death?" Then it hit him. He took down the drawing that Eva had so carefully hung on his wall 10 years ago, and found three small nail heads and a professional-looking art hook. He pulled out one of the nails... exactly the same as the one found in Eva's blood.

So, she had used these nails to hang his painting. Somehow one was left at her place. The sun would be up in 10 minutes and he had to be checked in at the Masters in less than two hours or he, as well as those in his group, would be disqualified. Willy took a chance and ran to his car. No coffee needed now. He had to go to Eva's old home.

He arrived at her house, now Aunt June's, as the sun's rays hit one of Eva's drawings that Willy had hung up for Theo. Aunt June and Theo were already gone, as the litter patrol started at 5 am. As he approached the kitchen, the sunlight streamed onto the kitchen wall and the Moran drawing by Eva. He took Eva's drawing off the wall and laid it carefully on the floor. Ten inches to the right of where the painting hung, he saw what he was looking for. Three small little holes in the plaster. Removing from his shirt pocket the art hook and nails he had taken from his own kitchen, those that Eva had hung her gift to him on, he carefully tried them in the three holes. An exact fit! Now he remembered! *There had been a painting on the wall here before! It used the same art hook as his, with the same spacing. Could it have been the real Moran? Was Eva killed over the painting? Was this the surprise she had left the note about? Was it possible a multimillion-dollar painting hung on Eva's kitchen wall all along and she was killed for it?*

Willy knew he had found the missing link. It had to be. But what to do now? He still had a chance of making the cut and that money was needed. He had to concentrate, to do what he did best, play golf, and then let Tommy, Sergeant Goldblatt, and the warden know he had their smoking gun.

At last night's dinner, he had told Tommy to meet him on 18 as he finished his round today. Chances were he would miss the fairway as always on 18, and if T.T. situated himself where he was the day before he would get to see the final big shot. Willy always missed to the right so he told Tommy to stand near the big tree where the white lines jut out. He also told Theo to pick up trash on the 18th fairway so he could follow Willy and get a VIP pass before he went to the clubhouse. "Look for Mr. Thompson. He'll be near the big oak tree on the right side of the 18th fairway," Willy had told Theo.

Chances were very good now with all this distraction that he wouldn't make the cut, so after the round he would let all of them know what he had discovered. Maybe finally the local newspaper would have a story about the Augusta National that the locals would be interested in: the release of a wronged man, LeRoy Strong, and a warrant for art dealer Ashton Charmers.

The second day of the tournament was much more difficult. A golfer has to think he is going to win, not hope to make the cut, or worse, say to himself, "Oh well I tried." Ed was the only thing keeping Willy in the game. He was upbeat and helping him make the right club selections. On the tricky 170-yard par three number 16, also known as Redbud for the trees lining the hole, the golfer must hit over a water hazard. The hole's pin position was in its usual far right corner. Willy totally misread the wind and was getting ready to fly over the green into the back bunkers and trees when Ed actually took the club from his hands as he was preparing a practice swing. "Mr. Wilson," Ed said forcefully, "I believe this eight iron is the one I would choose for you. Mighty strong wind to our backs, don't you think?"

Willy snapped out of his trance. "Yes, don't know what I was thinking. That was a club I used to use when I was 13, think I'm a bit stronger now." He birdied the hole.

Seventeen holes of golf and he was somehow only two over par. If he could par 18 he would most likely make the cut. The hole was his favorite and his confidence returned for the first time all day.

His drive off the tee shot was OK, not long, but arriving at its usual landing place next to what he referred to as Wilson's Oak. As he walked up to the ball, he reminded himself, "Make this final shot to the green be the best one you can. Concentrate on this one. Think golf."

Willy then saw T.T. and Theo in his yellow suit along with a crowd of others waiting for him at his ball as he approached for the next and most important shot of his life. Willy knew he should only be looking at the ball and the green. T.T. and Theo were beaming at him as were hundreds of spectators watching to see if their native son would make the cut, all intently staring at him, with the exception of one.

Watching golf from inside the white lines you can observe certain repetitive behaviors from the crowd. When a golfer approaches and hits his ball, all eyes watch him and then switch to eyeball the shot. They don't watch the golfer after the shot, they watch the shot.

One spectator stood out to Willy now, one who was not intently watching him but someone else in the crowd. A short man with a scar on his left cheek, an umbrella in one hand and what appeared to be a small stick in the other, was looking fixedly at T.T and Theo. It was Ashton B. Charmers and it was not a stick, it was a *knife!* Willy recognized Ashton's face and the scar from Tommy's photo.

Willy already had his club selection in his hand, the same one he always used, a Titleist five iron. There was no time for hesitation, he had to act fast. He addressed his golf ball and then squarely aimed it at the imposing crowd and yelled with all his might, "FORE!" Those who follow the game or have ever played golf understand the meaning of *fore*: a ball is headed in your direction and you should immediately duck and cover.

The entire gallery, except the one non-golfer, Ashton Charmers, hit the ground en masse, including Tommy and Theo.

Ashton did the exact opposite of the crowd when he heard *fore* coming from the 18th fairway. He stood straight up and turned to look where the scream had originated. Charmers almost instantaneously felt the searing pain from Willy's golf ball, which careened directly into his sternum, breaking the hard bone cleanly in two pieces. Willy had taken dead aim with all the concentration and

249

strength he could muster from 30-plus years of golf experience and smashed the ball with complete precision into Ashton B. Charmer's chest. His final thought as he took the swing was of Nat Wilson, his father and coach, who always said, "Only hit the ball if you know where it is going to go." After he had followed through completely with his swing, Willy heard Eva's voice, "*418.*"

Ashton crumpled with the knife still in his hand, a white golf ball with the number #18 bouncing down next to him. The only thing holding the gasping Ashton from hitting the ground was a small white rope.

CHAPTER 70

THE AFTERMATH

The unbelievable display of Willy's five-iron shot at Augusta National led to utter turmoil as the special undercover forces sprang into action. The crowd parted where Ashton fell, as if to give Willy room to play his next shot.

Willy dropped his five iron and ran over to embrace Theo as a father would a long-lost son, then he hugged T.T. The live television feed kept going back and forth from the white ball marked #18 and Willy's long hugs with Theo and T.T., as if unsure which was the real story. After Willy concluded that Theo and T.T. were unharmed, he picked up his golf ball still lying next to the incapacitated and gasping Ashton, put his arm protectively around Theo in his yellow litter suit, and headed directly toward the clubhouse, the crowd parting and becoming their own white line showing Willy the way home.

Ashton was taken in critical condition under armed guard to the local hospital, which was crawling with reporters. Diagnosis: a broken sternum with bruised lungs and heart. He would survive his life-threatening injuries to end up in the same prison in which LeRoy Strong had spent the last 10 years.

One month later, Ashton B. Charmers cut his last deal as an art dealer. He negotiated himself out of the death penalty and into a life sentence without parole, a good deal, he thought, considering his options. To do so he had to give a full confession to the two murders and one attempted murder, including explaining how he set up LeRoy Strong. He also had to disclose the bank accounts where his $8 million dollars resided.

What Charmers didn't know was that Warden Blackstone had made a sizable bet that Willy Wilson would make the cut that year at the Masters, and the warden was not happy with Ashton's interrupting the play and costing him a significant chunk of change. The other problem for Ashton came in the form of one Albert Strong, LeRoy's first cousin who had just been incarcerated for a 10-year sentence for distribution of marijuana. Warden Blackstone thought Albert would make a great long-term roommate for Ashton, seeing as how Ashton was already acquainted with the family. Nobody screws with the Masters.

CHAPTER 71

A BLUE BOWL FINDS A HOME

Tommy Thompson's plane picked up Willy Wilson, Theo Bernard De Plain Wilson, and a large package at Augusta's private airport. Willy and Theo had both recently had birthdays: Willy was now 40, Theo, 15. And Willy had officially adopted Theo.

They were delivered four hours and a sedan ride later to Tommy's hillside home recently renamed from Cypress 16TH Ranch to Cypress 18TH Ranch, in honor of Willy saving Tommy's life on the 18th green at Augusta. Willy's heroic act cost him the cut but saved a life and he forever would be known as the one who made the greatest golf shot ever at Augusta National, better than the Nike logo ball shot on 16 by someone named Tiger. Willy Casper Wilson's legacy at Augusta National was forever insured.

Tommy and Willy had a surprise for Theo, an unveiling of sorts. In Tommy's bedroom where the Thomas Moran once hung was a large easel with a white sheet draped over it.

"Theo," said Tommy, "your new dad and I wanted you to see something very special your mom wanted you to have." Tommy pulled the sheet off the painting, exposing the back of the canvas, which read, "Eva's Moran, for now and forever. With all my love, Bernard."

The teary-eyed T.T. explained, "This painting was your father Bernard's, and he gave it to your mother, and now I'm giving it to you. It's a very special painting, one that will help you in life like it did your mother and father. A friend of mine, Priscilla Counihan, almost died making sure this painting was saved. The painting is yours now, Theo. I've arranged for it to be exhibited on loan to the Metropolitan Museum of Art just as your late father did. In three years when you turn 18, you can decide what you would like to do with the piece. Until then, it will be safe and enjoyed by many at the Met."

T.T. added, "Also, a friend of mine, Joseph Penwell III, and I have set up a foundation in your late father's and mother's names. We have both donated $2.5 million to endow the scholarship. The $5 million trust will be open to any under-privileged residents of Augusta, Georgia, to attend a four-year college anywhere they like, fully paid. The potential candidates must write an essay about how they have overcome obstacles in life and how they can leave the world a better place. The first two selectees will not have to write this essay as they have already proven themselves: Theo Bernard De Plain Wilson and LeRoy Strong."

Willy then gently moved the easel to the side, and approached the empty painting hook that the Thomas Moran had once hung on in T.T.'s bedroom. In its stead, Willy hung another painting, a surprise that Theo and Willy had transported from Augusta for T.T. It was a very rare piece by a gifted artist who had died far too young. Willy hung up one of Eva De Plain's remarkable drawings of Thomas Moran's THE LONE CYPRESS.

"Tommy, we had an extra Moran drawing now that Theo lives with me full time. This was the drawing that hung in Eva's old kitchen. I think she would have wanted you to have it," Willy said.

─────────────

Two months later, T.T. flew to Augusta on his jet and picked up Willy and Theo to take them to the Metropolitan Museum of Art to see Theo's Moran. There they met Priscilla Counihan, fortunately almost recovered from her near-death experience, her jaw having taken the brunt of the hit. Priscilla had arranged for a personal tour of the enormous museum.

Theo and Willy brought Priscilla a small thank-you gift, a green and yellow Augusta litter hat signed by all the golfers of that year's Masters Tournament. Prominently appearing on the brim was the note: "To Priscilla, Sorry we missed you this year, hope to see you next!—Willy & Tiger."

As Willy, Theo, T.T., and Priscilla entered the great hall of American paintings they saw a single museum settee across from a large painting of a lone tree perched on a rocky outcropping surrounded by a wild ocean. The painting had been carefully positioned next to the settee so individuals could rest and reflect on nature's raw beauty. Under the painting, a simple wooden table had been placed, on top of which sat a slightly chipped blue Mexican bowl. Directly below the painting and above the bowl, two bronze museum tags were inscribed. The first read: "THE LONE CYPRESS, Thomas Moran, Private Collection." The second tag simply said: "20th Century Mexican Ceramic, Estate of Eva De Plain."

THE END